<u>Praise</u>

"Mayhem and more."—*Kirkus Reviews*

"[Scarantino] is skilled with complex plotting and has a talent for expository dialogue...Though she is fictional, Aragon, who sports a crewcut and a baby face, is an intelligent, hard-boiled heroine of whom Santa Fe can be proud."—*Santa Fe New Mexican*

<u>Praise for *The Drum Within*</u>

"*The Drum Within* is a superb novel, and this is a hearty welcome to an insanely talented newcomer, Jim Scarantino."—Lisa Scottoline, *New York Times* bestselling author

"*The Drum Within* is a gritty police procedural that will make you rethink everything you know about justice. A tour de force of good guys and bad guys. A masterpiece. I loved it."—Robert Dugoni, #1 Amazon and *New York Times* bestselling author of *My Sister's Grave*

"*The Drum Within* keeps many ducks in a row through a maze of gritty encounters, bitter confrontations, and some very clever red herrings."—*Santa Fe New Mexican*

"A thrilling police story."—*Suspense Magazine*

THE
PRICE
OF
VENGEANCE

JAMES R. SCARANTINO

A DENISE ARAGON MYSTERY

MIDNIGHT INK
WOODBURY, MINNESOTA

FIRST EDITION
First Printing, 2018

Book format by Bob Gaul
Cover design by Shira Atakpu

Midnight Ink, an imprint of Llewellyn Worldwide Ltd.

Library of Congress Cataloging-in-Publication Data
Names: Scarantino, James R., 1956– author.
Title: The price of vengeance / James R. Scarantino.
Description: First Edition. | Woodbury, Minnesota: Midnight Ink, [2018] |
    Series: A Denise Aragon mystery; #3 |
Identifiers: LCCN 2017038794 (print) | LCCN 2017042167 (ebook) | ISBN
    9780738753898 () | ISBN 9780738750675 (alk. paper)
Subjects: LCSH: Women detectives—Fiction. | Terrorism—Prevention—Fiction.
    | GSAFD: Mystery fiction. | Suspense fiction.
Classification: LCC PS3619.C268 (ebook) | LCC PS3619.C268 P75 2018 (print) |
    DDC 813/.6—dc23
LC record available at https://lccn.loc.gov/2017038794

Midnight Ink
Llewellyn Worldwide Ltd.
2143 Wooddale Drive
Woodbury, MN 55125-2989
www.midnightinkbooks.com

Printed in the United States of America

To those who pay the price.

ONE

"WE'VE GOT THE GREAT combo plate caper," Detective Rick Lewis said. "Hubby makes dinner for the wife who kept a .38 in the drawer with the hot pads and coffee filters. Things got crazy, then ugly. But was it the tacos, the enchilada, or the burrito that made her go from hungry to bloodthirsty?"

"The chile was too hot," Detective Denise Aragon said, watching the dry hills on Santa Fe's east side coming closer, able now to see people on wrap-around balconies on the big houses hanging off the slopes. "He laughed at her scraping her tongue on paper towels. He wouldn't stop so she made him. She drank milk and ordered the dinner she really wanted before dialing 911." Aragon put on a singsong accent and raised her voice an octave. "*My husband, the father of my children, who never got tired of laughing at me, he's face down in his beans and rice. Yes, I'll stay here. My pizza's at the door. What happened? I shot the big joker, that's what happened. He set me on fire and thought it was funny. No, not that kind of fire. Hold on. I need to find my purse to pay the guy.*"

1

Back in her own voice, Aragon said, "The pizza delivery kid was calling 911 at the same time, reporting the dead man he saw through the window. The news can't stop playing the tapes. *I shot the big joker, that's what happened.*"

"But Sarge says forget the dead husband with the hole in his cheek. Do a welfare check. Since when do Santa Fe's two superstar homicide detectives, the unbeatable team, the standard by which all others are measured and fail, do welfare checks?" Lewis was driving, the windows down on both sides of the car, a hint of cool air washing their faces. Now they were on gravel, now on packed clay. He sprayed washer on the windshield, making mud before the view returned through a brown smear. "Funny," he said, "how millionaires will live on dirt roads as long as those roads have Santa Fe addresses. Think about it. It's the same lowly dust on old pickups and rattletraps in trailer parks as on that Mercedes and Land Rover over there."

"Your deep, heavy thought for the day." Aragon shielded her eyes from the sun above the cone of Monte Sol, pinyon and juniper dotting its dry slopes, a perfect sky above the line of higher mountains in the background. New Mexico's true colors: dusty brown and pure blue. Sometimes a little green when it rained. Sometimes white when it snowed but that never lasted. The dusty brown and pure blue were always there.

Great view from the top of the hill. Aragon had run it many times, passing slower walkers getting out of the way for the short brown woman with the buzz cut, doubling back before they had crested. Up there you had all of Santa Fe at your feet, the green curve of the Rio Grande in the distance, the smudge of Albuquerque's haze to the south beyond empty desert, only the black line of the interstate breaking up the landscape. Here on the shoulders of Monte Sol you looked down on everything without having to go higher. Lewis's lowly dust cost a whole lot more in this neighborhood than any-where else in the state.

"Sarge gave it to us 'cause we're closest." She checked the text from Sergeant Perez for the house number. They were almost there. Tall stone columns supported mechanized gates at the ends of driveways leading to four-car garages and hangars for RVs. Handmade goat fencing, crude sticks standing upright and bound together by steel wire or twisted hemp, wound through the trees with no goats anywhere in sight. Poor families built these fences because they couldn't afford chain link or lumber. The people in these houses paid to have them custom built.

A brown roostertail rose behind them even though Lewis was rolling slowly along the packed dirt.

"I believe she watched her husband die before calling," Lewis said. "While drinking her milk."

"She was on the phone to Pizza Hut, ordering personal size, dinner for one, extra cheese and absolutely no damn chile." Aragon rolled up her window and Lewis followed. The millionaires' dust was getting in the car. "The place is just around the corner. The address sounds familiar, you know?" She googled it on her phone, first getting hits for places other than Santa Fe, then narrowing it down. There.

"It's Senator Sam's house," she said.

The house was a brown adobe, single-story, with wings added over centuries since conquistadors had laid its foundation. It sat on an acre lot, kept company by larger mansions behind pinyon and juniper. As they approached down the drive between columns of red cut stone the angle let them see that the house had a courtyard in the middle, accessible only from inside. Construction waste blocked them from getting closer: plywood scraps, busted drywall, a pallet of cinder blocks, lumber butts, bags of mortar spilling onto a blacktop driveway that made no sense at the end of the long dirt road. The windows were boarded up and new fiberglass replacements leaned against the stucco exterior.

Beyond the construction waste was a pile of uprooted trees and brush. The area around the house had been cleared of vegetation. Fresh stumps poked above dusty soil.

Lewis pointed to a much larger house covering a nearby ridge. "Isn't that owned by the King of Jordan? He can walk over with a six pack. United States Senator Sam Valles and a king in his turban and robes, grilling brats, tossing back cold ones, watching the sun set over the mountains and solving the world's problems."

"This is one of the real old ones. A fortress." Aragon nodded at the house before them. "Look at those walls. At least two feet thick. And the roof, there's a yard of dirt on top of tree trunks. It stopped Indians from breaking through. Those walls would never burn."

"Looks like nobody's home."

"So we press the bell and leave a card," Aragon said. "And ask Pop why he wasted our time." Pop being what uniforms and detectives called Sergeant Perez, retired from Albuquerque PD and the Bernalillo County Sheriff's Office, now pulling a Santa Fe paycheck on top of two pensions. An old guy with beads on the seat of his car, liver spots on his small hands on the wheel, slow and careful in traffic and making cops always in a hurry go nuts.

The walk to the front door was a long one, with solar footlights along flagstones, a ceramic statue here and there, Indian things for grinding corn on smooth rocks, cracked Mexican planters with dead flowers. Weeds connected the stones in the walkway, not much attention paid to upkeep while what looked like a major remodel was underway. Aspens that should never have been planted on the south side rattled in the breeze. Dead branches scraped coarse stucco walls.

They heard the bell ringing inside, a complex pealing of chimes each time Aragon pressed the button. Nothing after two tries. Pounding a fist on a weathered oak door, Spanish colonial style held together with metal bands and huge cast iron nails, got the same response.

She slipped a card from her wallet and fit it into the frame just above a handle of twisted wrought iron. Very Spanish colonial, like the knocker with some sort of coat of arms.

"Denise. Don't move."

Lewis was staring at the side of her face, his size blocking the sun and putting her in shadow.

"What do you mean, don't move? We're done here."

"There's a laser sight on your cheek."

Her hand went to her face before she realized how stupid that was. "No closer than the street from now on."

A voice. Coming from where? From inside the house to their left.

"The laser went out," Lewis said. "It didn't move. It just went out."

"That was a warning. Now get out of here." Slight Hispanic accent. Male, not young, not old. "Tell Valles it's his life for his family. Let's see what kind of man he is."

Lewis stepped off the doorstep. With him out of the way Aragon saw that a square of plywood in one of the boarded windows had been cut out, the tip of a gun barrel barely visible inside and pointed at her. Then the hatch closed and she couldn't tell where the gun port had been, the shutter fit that tightly.

Lewis was ahead of her, backing away, his Glock nine out of its holster, directed skyward with nothing to aim at. Now he was on the far side of their car, beyond the piles of waste, squatting, putting the engine block between him and the house, waiting for her.

The voice and its words kept her with one foot on the doorstep.

"Jesus Christ, Denise." Lewis close to shouting, waving at her. "Get the hell out of there."

She hoped Lewis was too far away to hear her whisper, "Pete? Is that you?"

TWO

THE HOUSE DIDN'T ANSWER.

Behind the car with Lewis, she telephoned Perez, not wanting anyone with a scanner hearing this.

"That welfare check you asked for," Aragon told her sergeant, "at Senator Valles's house. Get SWAT rolling." And then she reported. But the question hanging in her mind—*was that Pete Cervantes in there?*—she kept to herself.

"The senator's life for his family," Perez said, and then revealed why he'd texted them about the welfare check and not put it on the radio for the closest patrol car. "That was the message they got in DC, and they asked us to check the house. Senator Valles is in Europe. His wife's not answering his calls. She's supposed to be in town overseeing work on their house."

He ordered them to hold their position and not approach the house again. They squatted behind the car, without shade, eyes across the hood and trunk on the front door and boarded windows.

The piles of construction and landscaping waste now looked like barricades, blocking any vehicle from getting close to the house.

Aragon's head burned. She'd had her buzz cut trimmed the day before and nothing kept the sun off her scalp. Time she bought a hat. A Stetson with a snap brim, she'd been saying for years. Give herself an image, a trademark. Coming out of the car with a swagger to match the hat. Maybe it would make her seem taller. People would look for the hat instead of the shortest cop in the state.

Nope. She couldn't even manage not to lose baseball caps. She'd forget the Stetson on the back seat and it would be crushed when they shoved someone in there, or a drunk would use it to catch his puke.

"Expect the crazy-hot defense," she said to Lewis, then answered the puzzled look coming across his face. "Our combo plate killer. The crazy-hot-chile-made-me-crazy plea. She's got Marcy Thornton, the same lawyer who ran the human brewery defense."

"Fermenting tortillas," Lewis said.

"My client wasn't drinking, Your Honor. He'd been eating at his mother's house. A rare genetic condition prevents his stomach from properly digesting carbohydrates. Instead they ferment. The empty cans of Coors rolling around his Lincoln was litter he'd picked up from the street. It had nothing to do with his blood alcohol. May it please the court, it's the brewery in his gut that is responsible here."

"Thornton lost that case. Her client is eating the State Pen's tortillas and somehow managing to stay sober."

"Thornton gets to roll the dice. Look for some whore expert telling a wide-eyed jury about runaway endorphins triggered by high levels of whatever it is that makes chile burn. Charts, lab tests, computer simulations. Lab monkeys going loco when their banana is laced with habañeros. New Mexico's spin on the Twinkie defense.

The jury's going to hear it. You watch. Thornton's raised money for every judge on the District Court."

The Santa Fe Police Department's SWAT unit arrived first and set up a perimeter, men scattered in the trees at the edge of the property, some climbing Monte Sol and looking down on the courtyard and radioing back that a tarp had been erected in there, they couldn't see into the open space. They were reinforced immediately with a State Police tactical unit. Aragon and Lewis got out of the way and found shade under a thirsty elm.

She caught a glimpse of some of the FBI's Critical Incident Response Group arriving. Broad backs stretching lettered black T-shirts. High-tech sniper rifles she didn't recognize. Lots of gear inside hard plastic cases and electronics Santa Fe PD would never own. And then men and women with briefcases, binders, and binoculars, smaller bodies but still strong. One crew would go in heavy if it came to that; the others were the talkers, the negotiators, who would try to make the shooters unnecessary.

She stepped away from Lewis and dialed a number that didn't answer, Pete Cervantes's voice saying, "Talk to me and speak clearly. Don't forget to say your name. If you're selling something, I don't want it. Now, go."

Then they were called into the sun next to a dark panel truck and debriefed by two of the negotiators, a man and woman who looked like fit college professors with .40 caliber semi-autos on their hips. With the thick glasses, these two were definitely not snipers. The woman for sure didn't look dangerous. She had cat hairs on her rumpled shirt and when she leaned forward you could see past the black eyeglass frames to a single black brow above darker eyes. Narrow shoulders, no chest. Strong arms and large hands that didn't go with the rest of her body. A dark fuzz on her lip moved as she talked.

Magnano was her name. She pronounced it like "mañana" with an "o" at the end.

The man who acted like her boss, the chief FBI negotiator, gave his name as Helmick. A senior professor type who might spend weekends outdoors to get that tan. But sneezing, snorting, blowing his nose, wiping snot off his lip. He was having problems in this air. He studied Aragon with red, puffy eyes and she had a hard time seeing him as the steady rock in hostage negotiations.

She and Lewis told him everything that happened, with Aragon again holding back her guess as to who might be inside the house. Magnano took notes while Helmick fired questions when his face emerged from his handkerchief.

They were finally released and instructed to join up with SFPD officers establishing an outer perimeter across the dirt roads leading uphill to the Valles house. Instead, Aragon drove Lewis to a house on the edge of a tall hill a half mile away. It had a *For Sale* sign at the end of the drive. She hadn't been expecting that. She noted the realtor to call later.

The Valles residence was below, sitting in a gash where the trees had been cleared away. Further down the hill, houses were framed by cottonwoods where the streets were paved and there was a water table to make things green. At the end of the drive to the Valles house, they spotted the panel truck from which the FBI negotiators were operating and saw HRT rifle teams behind volcanic rocks on the far side of the Valles property. More people had climbed to the top of Monte Sol, men in black shirts lugging heavy packs and long guns, someone setting up a spotting scope on a tripod.

"You said you wanted to see something," Lewis said. "The panoramic view?"

"This house," Aragon answered and jutted a thumb. It was an adobe as old as the Valles residence but half the size, dug into the slope of the hill, with a huge, modern concrete patio that doubled as a retaining wall holding back a level space for an irrigated lawn.

"This is Peter Cervantes's place," Lewis said and followed her to the door. "We came here with the bad news about his son and daughter-in-law. He was pouring the patio and stepped backward into wet cement when it hit him."

"That voice telling us to back off." Aragon reached the door and pressed the buzzer. The drive had given her time to grow certain that the voice was more than familiar. "I could swear it was Pete."

"You know it that well?" Lewis stood behind her for the second time as she pressed a doorbell. "That case was two years ago."

"We get together when he's depressed. Or when the anger boils up again. Sometimes he calls at night and we'll meet. I'll have a beer or two, but he doesn't drink and he never seems to get tired. Sometimes it's enough for him to talk on the telephone, if it's not a bad night. I'm doing the victim assistance the DA's office forgot. It's been a month, maybe two, but I know his voice."

Aragon leaned on the buzzer and rose to her toes to peer through a window. Mail was scattered on shadowed Saltillo tiles where it had skidded from the mail slot. No lights inside. No sounds. She pulled out her phone and dialed Cervantes's office and got a receptionist who said, "Cervantes and Sons Construction. We build dreams."

She asked for Pete Cervantes and learned he had sold the business. Another surprise to go with the realtor's sign. Aragon asked if the receptionist might know how to reach him. She said he still came around to help the new owners but was taking a vacation and would be gone a couple weeks. Scouting elk in the Pecos. He couldn't be reached until he returned.

Aragon ended the call and felt sick.

"I don't get it," Lewis said. "Why would you even guess it was Cervantes inside Senator Valles's house, putting a laser sight on your face?"

Aragon looked again through the window into the dark house, then faced Lewis. "It was the words. 'Let's see what kind of man he is.' He said that about Valles last time we had a therapy session over chips and salsa. I was drinking, he was talking. Some shit the senator said got Pete riled, cost him sleep." She faced down the slope toward the Valles house, SFPD patrol cars blocking streets, more black vans arriving, a helicopter approaching from the west. "If it is Pete Cervantes down there, he's not the only one in deep shit."

"Who else is?"

"That would be me."

THREE

"We were at Tito's Cantina. I'd never seen him so furious, then sad, collapsed and old, then furious again. He stabbed his food, like he was trying to kill it. I had to tell him to drop his weapon and explain what was going on. He left his fork sticking straight up in a tamale. He'd read about a speech Valles gave against stripping federal law enforcement funds from cities that ignore immigration laws. The sanctuary city thing. He heard it on the radio, then pulled it up on the Internet, read the whole thing, he couldn't believe it. That family murdered by an illegal up in Seattle, the one that got the sanctuary city thing in the headlines again. Different year, different dead Americans, same Congress doing nothing. Valles pretty much said their deaths didn't matter in the bigger scheme of things."

"Undocumented guest, Denise," Lewis said. "You got the memo from upstairs. There's no such thing as an illegal alien in Santa Fe. And we're not a sanctuary city. We're a 'welcoming city for immigrants and refugees.'"

They'd driven to the river running through the center of the city, a trickle of water from a weak monsoon season and sparse snow in the mountains. Aragon parked in the shade of Siberian elms and was quiet for a minute while she thought how to explain what had happened next.

"They were slaughtered, the family," she said, "waiting in line for the Space Needle, by a guy who should have been deported. The Seattle police didn't report him to ICE when they picked him up for being drunk and taking a leak in that marketplace they have up there, all the tourists watching men throwing fish around and this guy wetting the floor. They ignored the federal detainer in the system that would have sent him back to Central America. That guy had agg assaults, armed robbery busts going back years. Deported twice long ago, but he was back." She rolled down her window and loved the cool air against her face. Even the tiny stream made a difference if you got close enough. "Everybody using the case to attack sanctuary cities, go after illegals—undocumented migrants … "

"Undocumented guests."

"Excuse me—undocumented guests as the cause of everything wrong in the country. Valles said the family's murder was 'an unfortunate bump in the road' on the way to a 'lasting, just solution for the nation as a whole.' Pete had the words written down. 'A better future always comes at a price. That is the story of this nation. In the end, we're all better but getting there is never pain free. There is always a price to pay for progress.' Some crap like that. It set Cervantes off."

"I can see why. His son and daughter-in-law, killed in the robbery at his business."

"By, you guessed it, an undocumented guest in the catch-and-release program of Santa Fe courts, an MS-13 thug who should have been exported back to El Salvador. But he chose a sanctuary city to have his fun."

"Valles was the star of City Council when they put that through." Lewis pulled protein bars from the door sash and offered one to Aragon. She waved him off. "He always was the grand visionary," she went on. "I remember him telling people losing their homes when a development was going in, them standing at the mic during public comments, that you have to break eggs to make an omelet, don't you know? They didn't appreciate being the eggs."

Sante Fe Baldy, a mile higher than the city, wore a dusting of snow. Aragon had smelled cedar smoke driving to work before dawn. The cool air was coming from up higher, not from the inch of water in the river. This was the heart of elk season. If you wanted to hike the Pecos Wilderness now, you wore lots of international orange and didn't expect solitude. The mountains were crawling with armed men who drank a lot.

Hunting was how she'd met Cervantes, long before she worked his son's case. She'd been tending camp for her brother Javier's outfitting company to use comp time before it was wiped off the books. Rousing the men at 3 a.m., saddling the mules, boiling coffee over embers, and taking her own cow elk when the work was done. Cervantes and his sons had been clients, a last trip before the eldest son went off to Iraq. An Army corporal. He didn't come back from Fallujah. Fifteen, seventeen years that was before the last son was killed without having to leave home.

The Cervantes men had bought muzzleloader hunts. Pete shot a six-by-six bull she helped field dress. Another time she was with him when he dropped a bull while it was running at over two hundred yards. That hunt he'd been using the finest rifle she'd ever seen, a CZ-USA in a monster caliber.

Pete didn't flash his money, but it showed in his guns. The muzzleloaders he and his sons used were works of art.

"His last call was one of the times he wanted to meet at night," she said. "Pete needed to be with someone, talking on the telephone wouldn't work. We met at a restaurant he liked. We were holding up closing, the only customers while waiters put chairs on tables, last call had come and gone but I probably didn't need any more beer. I made the mistake of telling him I knew Valles from college days. That was when Sam Valles had a ponytail and believed women and gays should faint when he walked in the door. He had a little business I'll tell you about some time you want a laugh. That guy on the Armed Services and Intelligence Committees, making life or death decisions for millions of people, you won't believe how he picked up walking-around money."

"Valles with a ponytail? Our senator with the chin and steely look?"

"Hair down to his ass. Anyway, Pete asked what Valles was like and we talked. And talked. He'd met Patricia, Valles's wife. Patricia, I knew her from college, too. She'd hired Cervantes & Sons to remodel the house. He'd done it for the prior owner and knew all the problems with the old adobe. He didn't know if he liked Patricia. You're not quite sure who's talking to you. The smiling, friendly face, a little girl voice, nice enough. But you get the feeling there's someone else behind the eyes. As for Sam Valles, we agreed he's a waste of skin. I was the one who said somebody should take him out."

"Take him out. You said that?" Lewis struggled against the shoulder strap to turn toward her.

"I was talking about beating him in the next election. Taking him out of the game, out of the Senate. The guy's never in New Mexico. That house, it's a movie prop. You saw the yard. He doesn't give a crap. His kids don't go to school here. I hear *los viejos* asking who is this guy, where'd he come from? That's when Pete said Valles is one of those people who makes decisions other people pay for while he gets to live in a safe, make-believe world. An actor on television playing a role. What if, Pete said, what if he was forced just once to live in the real world, where the ones who pay for his bad decisions are us and the people we care about? What if it was his family on the front line? Then we'd see what kind of man he really is."

Lewis said, "Now I see why you're worried."

"And he said ... " Aragon bit the inside of her lip, thinking how she'd picked up steam herself, trashing Valles, turning him into a punching bag to make Cervantes feel better. And herself. Maybe. No, yes, it had felt good. "He said, the only way things will change in this country is when the big people start paying the price for their big ideas."

"I don't want to hear what you said to that."

What had she said? Nothing she could remember. They'd shared enough between them she didn't need words. She'd nodded and jutted out her jaw, telling Cervantes yes sir, he had that right. Everybody knows it.

"Your wife," she said to Lewis, who was drumming his fingers on the dashboard and staring at the ceiling liner. "She works at Game and Fish."

"She's the PIO." That made Lewis stop. "You with this sudden change of direction thing again. I know something's coming."

"Can a public information officer find out if someone has an elk tag?"

"Like Pete Cervantes?" Lewis's fingers started drumming again but his eyes were on her.

"Would you call her?"

You didn't scout for elk in the middle of the season. Her brother headed to the mountains the first week of August, before the early hunt when only hikers were up there.

In a couple minutes her worries were confirmed. Lewis's wife let them know that Pete Cervantes hadn't applied for a hunting permit. He hadn't applied since the year his son was murdered.

———————

Using her cell, Aragon asked Sergeant Perez to meet them here by the puny river, away from the office and the activity at Senator Valles's house. The way Perez drove it would be a while. They listened to the scanner as they waited. Not an all units call to the Valles residence, but close. Most of the patrol cars were instructed to report to an SFPD captain coordinating with FBI. By now the media would be picking up on it. The entire city would notice State Police helicopters in the sky, circling, not moving off. A new voice on the scanner said a helicopter from the FBI's Aviation and Surveillance Section was en route.

"I don't know what Pete thinks he's going to accomplish," Aragon said.

Lewis tried the big AM news station out of Albuquerque to see if they were reporting. "Cervantes comes out of this in cuffs or a body bag," he said. Only talk radio, Sean Hannity with no news bulletins interrupting. Not a word about a US senator being asked to trade his life for his family's. Lewis silenced the radio.

Aragon twisted the steering wheel in her hands, seeing Pete Cervantes over the basket of chips and salsa on the table between them, remembering the light coming back into his eyes when they were done talking. Thinking then she'd helped him get through another bout of rage and despair. Thinking now she should have kept her mouth shut.

They saw Perez's unit, a solid black Ford, waiting for bicycles to cross the street before turning their way. "There's Pop," Aragon said and flashed her lights. She and Lewis got out and moved toward the river bank. Perez caught up and they walked under the trees, away from picnickers and workers from the Supreme Court taking their lunch break. Aragon told Perez why she'd telephoned to set a private meeting.

When she'd told it all, Perez used the same words as Lewis.

"Take him out? You said that?"

He had a couple inches on Aragon, but both of them were more than a foot shorter than Lewis. Pop had dark skin—Indian blood was the word, or part Black. A round head on a round body getting rounder every year. She'd seen him running city streets during the lunch hour and couldn't figure out how he got moving so fast on those short, skinny legs. His hands were thin, too, the plumpness in his arms stopping above the wrists. It looked like there was another man in there slowly getting covered over as layers of fat and age spread from his waistline.

Now Perez's face was darker and he was shaking his round head.

"Denise, he's got Mrs. Valles and two kids in that house with him. And he tells you he'll trade their lives for the senator's? It gets out you maybe didn't give him the exact plan but planted the seed ... you see how this plays out? For you and everybody else in spitting distance?" He gave Lewis a hard look. "Were you in on any of these victim support sessions with Cervantes?"

Lewis shook his head but the glare didn't soften.

Aragon turned away to avoid Perez's look when it came her way again. She gazed down into riverbed lined with stone walls, the trickle of water, trash down there, a shopping cart catching debris.

Always this place had been clean. It added to her sense things were coming apart.

"I want your conversations with Cervantes written up word-for-word and delivered to me within the hour." Hearing Perez behind her, a flat voice, clipped. Birds in the trees overhead, music further up the waterway, a *cajon*, somebody banging a guitar. "I'm going to tell the FBI negotiators we may have something for them. And then you are going to tell them yourself. They're going to investigate you, Denise, as an accomplice until they're satisfied you're just a loose-mouthed fuck-up. You're doing nothing but writing your report. I have to take this to Professional Standards. After I close the door behind me in the chief's office."

When she turned back around Perez was walking to his car, head down, a stiff-legged walk, the hips stiff, too. He kicked a McDonald's bag in his path. A cup inside exploded and splashed his pants. He kicked it harder and it flew into the gutter by his car.

Aragon told Lewis, "You need to get as far from me as you can get. We should split up now."

Lewis had always ignored suggestions like that the other times she'd involved him in one of her messes. But things had always panned out. Sure, she crossed lines. Sometimes big ones. Like felony lines. But they got the bad guys and saved lives. It was good between Lewis and her.

He said, "I'll take you to your car." A deep breath. "There's kids dragged into this, Denise."

Seated behind the wheel, he said, "Don't tell me anymore. I don't want to know." Already putting distance between them.

The scanner wasn't saying anything about Cervantes having hostages. Or about Pete Cervantes's demands. The man inside the Valles house was referred to as "suspect" without mention of a name. The

Santa Fe County Sheriff's Office was instructed to stand down when its SWAT van rolled past the FBI inner perimeter and took its place. Now the FBI were asking local law enforcement to push the street barricades out another two blocks and requesting that news helicopters stay away.

"Valles is a shit," Lewis said as they neared SFPD headquarters parking. "But his family doesn't deserve this."

Miles apart in minutes.

He didn't say anything more when he pulled to the curb by the front entrance to the SFPD offices, the asphalt lot baking in the sun, the grounds a tangle of weeds and rattling trees. Traffic roared by on Cerrillos, so close it felt like she was standing between the lanes of cars on the littered median. He waited for her to get out. He was rolling before she had completely closed her door.

She thought of calling Pete Cervantes again. He would answer this time. She would talk him down. It would end without anybody getting hurt. He would open the front door, send out the family, then follow with his hands on his head.

She started dialing and stopped.

That's not how it would end. If Pete answered, or even if he didn't, they'd find her earlier unanswered call on his cell when they took it off his body.

FOUR

PETE CERVANTES PEERED THROUGH the peephole he'd drilled below the eaves of the Valles house. Flat on his stomach in a space where insulation had been just yesterday, he closed one eye and hoped the police out there would not notice the dot in the stucco exterior. Instead of police he saw people in windbreakers and street clothes moving in and out of his vision. When they turned around he saw the letters on the back. They'd moved fast. Fine. He wanted the FBI here. Damn straight this was a federal case.

He backed away until he felt air below his feet and lowered his body onto the ladder. Across Saltillo tiles his crew had laid down years ago for a different owner, he moved to a hole on the other side of the house. This one was larger, with a fish-eye lens so he could see more. From the outside, the lens blended into a tile mosaic above an outdoor sink. What he saw: big men moving behind dead trees and basalt boulders he'd positioned with a Bobcat. They had earpieces and hands-free microphones near their mouths. When one man stood to change his seating position, he leaned a scoped rifle against a rock. Then he was behind the rock and the barrel looked like part of a lifeless pine tree.

In the dining room he'd set up security monitors on the Valles's long formal table with the twisted pewter and brass chandelier overhead. The FBI would see the cameras he'd installed at the house's four corners. They would be shot out or cut when the FBI made its move. They would want him blind. But he'd had enough time to place smaller cameras in shadows under drain spouts, in gaps between the logs extending from the flat roof, and in a *nicho* between the legs of a statue of a peasant on a donkey. At the end of a cable hidden in a cholla cactus, he'd see what was going on over the hill at the edge of the property.

He'd cleared the trees and brush around the house. Nobody could approach without him seeing. He'd decided against hauling off the cuttings. Instead he'd used them as a second barricade behind the bank of construction waste and landscaping boulders that blocked vehicle access to the house.

He still had work to do. He'd been at it for twenty-four hours straight and wasn't sure how much longer he could go before he had to sleep.

He checked the door to the room where he'd locked Patricia Valles and her sons. A cooler with food and water and a camp toilet in there. Everything she needed but windows. This was the innermost room in the house, built long, long ago to hold grain or drying meat.

Pah-trree-sea-ah.

She made sure you got every sound when she said her name, rolling those *R*'s like she was making fun but serious as hell. Look at me, I'm a proud Hispana. Latina, Chicana, whatever. All these new labels for people he used to just call Spanish, if they'd been here a long time, or Mexican, if they were newbies or you wanted to start a fight. That's all it took when he was coming up, at the drive-in or on the ball field, a boy insulting a girl in line for popcorn, or the runner on base sneering to the shortstop. "Mexican." It had been a cuss word among the Spanish kids who marched in the Fiesta in the armor and sweeping dresses of their ancestors who'd conquered this land for the kings and queens in Madrid.

Now they waved more Mexican than American flags at political rallies, plastered them on the rear windows of Chevys and Fords, canceled school for Cinco de Mayo.

Mojados, too, sometimes slipped across his tongue, though he tried to forget the term everyone his age once tossed off like it was nothing. The wets, they came here to work. They were good people. Honest, hard-working, they showed respect and earned it back. This new wave of invaders ... that's what they were ... they came here to kill and steal and rob. And laugh in our faces.

He'd looked in the refrigerator and seen only gringo food. Bread from a snooty French bakery, no tortillas. No sacks of pinto beans in the pantry. No green chile in the freezer in the garage. Patricia Valles was Spanish, her people an old family from up near Taos who'd been here since this was part of the Empire. Her people had come with the conquistadors, or soon after. But you couldn't tell from this house she kept.

That voice of hers, the usual one: a little girl, a Kewpie doll talking. Squeaky, silly, *que cute.* But since she'd seen the gun, it had changed. Flat, sober, deeper. Like it wasn't the same person talking. Maybe there were two people inside of *Pah-tree-sea-ah* and it had taken this to bring the second one out.

For a fact the woman who'd decorated this house was two different people. The living and dining rooms were Santa Fe Fiesta and Indian Market on parade. Spanish colonial table and oak chairs each weighing a ton. Art on the walls from Canyon Road galleries: blue coyotes to cowboys in yellow dusters to Indians on horseback on snowy mountains with eagles on their shoulders. Coffee table books on Georgia O'Keeffe. Plenty of Rudolfo Anaya on the end tables. An anthology of poems by Jimmy Santiago Baca, and every Tony Hillerman ever published.

Decorative, useless ladders made from saplings, lashed together with leather straps, mock-ups of those used in the pueblos to climb between floors. Navajo rugs draped over the rungs. Hammered tin sconces on the walls. Cowhide and rivet chairs. Hand-carved *santos* by the kiva fireplace. Lots of crosses on the walls, wood, silver, some made from broken mirrors and shards of tile.

The high-beamed ceiling of vigas was ponderosa tree trunks supporting cross-hatched aspen latillas. His crew had done a fine job restoring wood set in place long before the last century began. He knew how many layers of unseen tree trunks were above that, and how many tons of rammed earth separated the wood from the sky above.

In the master bedroom and study, a different Mrs. Valles had done the decorating. Not one thing saying this house was in New Mexico. Photos of Senator Sam Baca Valles, the young city councilman, on the campaign trail shaking hands, on the steps of the nation's Capitol, his swearing-in as a senator, wife and young sons at his side. Newer photos with the president, TV celebrities, shots of the Washington Mall with the Washington Monument in the distance.

And there he was, Pete Cervantes, in the mirror where Patricia Valles dressed. He had to look twice; he couldn't believe he was seeing himself in their bedroom. He had bags under his eyes. But it wasn't worry. He didn't see that in his face. He was looking more like his father since he'd turned sixty. His mouth sagged. He had the same strange gray patch on his forehead, a washed-out lock that always grew faster than his black hair. White hair in his ears, white stubble on his chin, but he wasn't doing too bad up top. They'd buried his father with most of his hair still as dark as night.

But unlike his father, his eyes were weary. He broke off eye contact with himself and saw his stomach pushing against his polo shirt. A few extra pounds, but the way he moved it didn't matter. He had the arms of his workers, bigger forearms even. His men called him for the final torque on a tough bolt or to twist a sewer cap off a rusted pipe.

The dressing table held photos of the two boys looking like their mother, already with big bottoms and going soft, and Senator Sam with his famous chin at Lincoln's feet, all of them wearing *I Love DC* T-shirts.

He'd brought from his house pictures of his own family. Mary, gone eight years from the cancer. Sam in the Santa Fe National Cemetery, where his coffin had ended its long trip from Iraq. And Jacob and Estella and their daughter Ciela—thank God it hadn't been a bring-your-kids-to-work day. Ciela was living in California with Estella's sister and never wanted to return to the city where her parents had been killed.

He had the photos in frames in the dining room by the television monitors. They'd be there when the FBI came.

A voice from outside, huge, loud. He moved to one of the windows he'd covered with plywood and metal sheeting. Someone announcing themselves. Giving a telephone number so they could talk. They were calling him "you in the house," not seeming to know who Pete Cervantes was yet.

He'd been ready for this moment and found his megaphone and turned on the power from the battery. He let it charge, then stood to the side of the front door, behind the thick adobe walls, and cracked it open.

"If you want to talk to us … " He adjusted the megaphone to stop the screeching. There, his own voice booming back louder than whoever had yelled to "you in the house." "If you want to talk to us, call *Pah-trrrrreee-sea-ah's* phone."

A hundred yards away, across the barricades of construction and landscaping waste, at the side of a black truck holding their communication equipment, FBI negotiator Art Helmick turned to his number two, Pamela Magnano.

"Who's *us*?" he asked.

Behind him, Tyson Dix, team leader for the Hostage Rescue Team, a hard guy who looked like a statue inside a compression tee, spoke into his lapel mic and said, "Be advised, we have more than one hostile in the house." And then he called his boss in Washington for more men with guns.

Helmick brought the megaphone to his mouth and heard his voice bouncing back. "What's your name? What do we call you when we talk?"

Later, he'd get to asking what these people really wanted. He had to learn what was driving this lunacy—*your life for your family, Senator Valles*. What crap. What madness. Sometimes it made him weary, playing word games with the nut jobs and trying to understand how their broken minds worked. This one thought he had it figured out. They all did. *Hey, take some hostages, put guns to their heads, and the entire US government will grant your every wish*. But this one, even though it looked like he had put some time into it, wasn't any smarter than the desperate, cornered, impulsive ones.

Because the FBI handing over a man who sat on the Senate Intelligence and Armed Force Committees, who carried in his head hours of security briefings and secrets about the nation's spy programs, its counterterrorism strategies, its own strategic weaknesses—its nuclear weapons—that was never going to happen. Sam Baca Valles with no military background, no interrogation training, nothing at all in his history to suggest he'd stand up to even the threat of physical pain. Helmick had seen him on television during hearings on police and FBI misconduct, sitting next to a senator who'd lied about surviving combat in Vietnam. Two expensive haircuts, two empty suits behind microphones. That's all he knew about the man whose family he was now trying to save.

Helmick got Dix's attention and waved him over. Dix was long, with angular muscles braiding his arms, well-defined so you could see the separation in his triceps. Helmick knew more about Dix than the man showed with his hard looks. Dix, the gun man, loved to garden. He'd unload beets, carrots, parsnips and odd things like kohlrabi on the office starting in late summer and not stop until he'd dumped the last Jerusalem artichoke on a secretary who didn't know what to do with the thing. Dix lived alone with two German shepherds and plants. Helmick had seen the garage with the lights where he started his seeds. Dix brought baskets of produce into his church, leaving them at the door so people could help themselves on the way out. Helmick had learned about that when he attended the memorial service for Dix's wife. Now it was Dix alone in the house with his weapons and dogs and root vegetables.

They'd done this act together before. There always came that moment, when decisions had to be made to take someone's life or risk your own or another agent's, that he'd ask, what were regular guys like us doing making calls like this?

Instead of Dix's plant lights, Helmick had a work bench in his garage. Tools from his grandfather who'd been a master carpenter and had made what he needed. Things you'd never find in a hardware store and that would last another hundred years. He made furniture,

27

fixed cabinets, enjoyed a beer or two with country music playing on the 1960s transistor radio that was built as well as the adzes and awls and tools with names his grandfather created.

Helmick liked flannel shirts in the winter and wished he could wear shorts to work when the humidity in the DC summer made him miss his first assignment in Anchorage. He was fit but softer than Dix; less time for the gym these days. Too much sitting by telephones, in conferences, in classes learning how to get into the minds of the people he tried to make trust him. To trust him just enough to get them out in the open for Dix and his team, if it came to that.

Helmick sneezed, hard. Sneezed again. He was about to talk when he caught himself and prepared for another explosion.

"Good luck with that," Dix said. "You've got your man hanging on every word and you blow out his eardrums."

"Hell's in the air here?" Helmick wiped his nose on his forearm. He was out of tissues. A whole box gone already. "And it's so dry. I haven't been able to breathe since I got off the plane. Listen. The director will be involved in this one personally."

"Not surprised."

Another eruption. "Jesus." Helmick pinched the bridge of his nose, trying to force the sneezing to stop. "The director may show up here. Keep that to yourself. He won't be out front on any call we make." Helmick looked around for what could be waging war on his sinuses. Tall desert plants heavy with yellow flowers bending spiky stalks surrounded their location. He felt another blast coming on and got out fast what he wanted to say. "We're the ones who'll deal directly with the senator. He's got this chief of staff the director hates. Prick's burned the bureau when he thought it would be good for his boss. The director doesn't want that history between them in the mix if this goes bad."

Snort, snuffle, and he exploded.

"Be glad you won't have to hold still to make the shot," Dix said, and handed Helmick an oily cloth he used to wipe his rifle down. "We both know that's where this is going. After he realizes he's not going to get a live senator in the trade, what's this guy's fallback? You can't string him out with the promise of a plane ride to Cuba anymore. It's clear he did this to hurt Valles. When he can't get the man directly, he'll do it through his family. And he's ready for a fight. Look how he's prepped the battlefield." Dix waved his hand toward the yard. "He's cleared lanes of fire. That house, I'm not sure a .50 cal would penetrate. We see gun ports cut into those windows and a couple firing positions under the eaves. And now we learn he's got help. This is terrorism, Art. Not your vanilla hostage situation where there's something to discuss, where your new buddy on the other end of the phone just wants someone to *hear* him for once in his life."

"He said call *Pat-tree-see-ah's* phone," Helmick said. "I assume that's Mrs. Valles."

"He's not giving us his own phone to play with."

Helmick studied the barricades, the cleared ground, the boarded windows. He saw a camera on the house in the corner. Another by the garage. They were being watched.

Another eruption. Helmick wiped his nose and recognized the smell of gun cleaner on Dix's rag. "Why Valles?" he asked. "Why this senator? And if they get him, what then? They force Valles to tell them something, some national secret, then use their communications to get it out? After that, what? They surrender and release the family?"

"Or it ends as soon as Valles steps out of the crowd and goes inside to save his family," Dix said. "We hear shots, then it's quiet, and we look at each other not knowing what the hell to do next."

FIVE

PETE CERVANTES HAD SAID he forgave Teofilo Alvardo. Aragon had
been in court to hear him when he stood in front of the judge and
said he'd prayed and prayed, spent hours with his priest, read about
the Amish who forgave the monster that slaughtered their children
in the little school at the edge of their fields. He'd lost a son and
daughter-in-law, they'd lost an entire school. He wanted what they
had in their hearts, in every breath. He'd looked deep inside and
wrestled the hate and rage living there. Talking through tears, in a
suit and tie, shoes polished, with a fresh haircut, a faint whiff of
Aqua Velva on his face, dignified as he'd been throughout the trial.
He spoke in a shaking, respectful voice, calling the judge "Sir" and
his son's murderer "Mr. Alvardo."

The world needed more people like Pete Cervantes.

Never a statement for reporters, always refusing comment, beg-
ging them to respect his need for privacy in this painful time. He
had attended the arraignment, bail hearing, all the motions hearings, jury selection, and sat through the trial in the same seat, third

row back, five places in. First in the courtroom when the bailiff unlocked the doors. Always last to leave, the bailiff locking the doors behind him with a pat on the back. Getting to know the bailiff's first name but calling him "Mr. Connors."

He'd been patient when the defense lawyer requested continuances, not really unprepared or caught short when a witness didn't show. The lawyer was trying to wear the police and witnesses down by jerking them around, Aragon explained. Seven times the judge had granted a delay. Always Cervantes had shrugged, said a quiet little prayer, and waited for the killer's public defender to pack up and walk to his spot in the courtroom. Always a weak smile for the lawyer, who wore argyle socks under heavy sandals to court, below a cheap suit and cheap briefcase, Pete giving him a "see you next time" until he didn't have to say it anymore.

The sentencing hearing was the only time Aragon had seen Pete cry since he'd seen Jacob and Estella at the Office of Medical Investigator. "Can you identify these people?" He had stood over them while they bled to death on the floor in his office, torn between talking to the 911 operator and pushing his hands into all the places where blood was spurting out. The people in white coats had given him all the time he wanted in the cold room with the cold bodies. He told her later that every second was too much and not enough.

Aragon had been with him both times when he let it out. She'd taken him back to his house both times, as well. Coffee in his living room in the ancient adobe above the city, with the curtains pulled to keep the world out. Cervantes had talked for hours, showed photos of his family, showed his sons' rooms, the one for his boy killed in Iraq the way he'd left it when he signed up after 9/11, with the American flag, photos of a young, fearless, happy teenager heading to a war his father wouldn't tell him made no sense. That stupid war; sick to his stomach listening to the news about Americans getting shot eating ice cream on the streets of Bagdad, the dogs with explosives up their ass, the explosions in traffic, the sniper they couldn't stop who had a gun that could pierce armored Humvees. You can't tell a boy his war is a stupid war.

She took time to answer his questions, explained police procedures, how they would investigate the case, how they were going to catch the killer. And after Alvardo was convicted she explained the pre-sentence investigation and report, the final hearing, what Alvardo could expect in the State Penitentiary south of Santa Fe.

Cervantes and Sons Construction had built three houses within sight of those prison walls and high fences. One was their first job installing solar panels. That got the attention of the warden, who gave them a no-bid contract to do the same inside the chain link and razor wire. Now the prison had acres of solar panels to keep Teofilo Alvardo warm in winter, cool in summer, with the smallest carbon footprint of any prison in the country.

Yes, he told the judge, he'd wanted to kill Alvardo himself for gunning down Jacob and Estella in the front office of Cervantes and Sons. He had to sell that building and relocate operations to where he wouldn't be thinking about blood soaked into the concrete. He'd moved forward in life and could not keep looking back. He had a family of employees now that needed him.

Don't let the sun set on your anger, Cervantes had quoted St. Paul, his priest nodding yes in a seat behind him, his brothers and sisters, nieces and nephews filling one side of the courtroom, solemn, sobbing quietly. Dignified like the man they'd come to support. Not one said a word to the reporters pecking at them when they stepped into the hallway. Not one made a sound when Alvardo, at his turn to address the judge, said he hadn't meant to shoot anybody, it had been an accident. He wasn't a bad person. Really.

Alvardo had shot Jacob Cervantes three times as they fought for control of the pistol until Jacob lost his strength. Estella's hands were tied behind her. Alvardo shot her through the roof of her mouth. Forensics found saliva with her DNA on the gun sight.

Pete Cervantes told the judge he couldn't let Alvardo kill him, too. So he did the hardest thing he'd ever done, harder than burying his wife and sons and a woman he called his own daughter. He forgave him.

But that didn't mean the judge should go lightly. The tears gone now, Cervantes clear-eyed, steady. Alvardo was going to kill again, he said. The judge needed to think of other lives that had to be saved. A maximum sentence, Cervantes said. It wasn't for revenge. It was common sense. Alvardo was a murderer. The judge had a job to do.

The judge did all he could. Alvardo would die in prison.

That was Pete Cervantes's future if he wasn't killed by an FBI sniper.

Alone now, SFPD's main office quiet with everyone pulled into the Valles hostage situation, Aragon wanted to hear Cervantes's voice. She wished her phone call at the start of this madness had gone through. She wanted another talk with him, this second before it went any further. To ask what he thought he was going to accomplish, what he was going to change. He may not have his children, but he had a granddaughter. All those people behind him in the courtroom. *Pete, think about what you're doing to them. And you're not going to leave a scratch on someone like Sam Valles. People like that never bleed.*

Her phone rang. She almost answered, "Pete?"

It was Perez, wanting to know if she was done writing up her conversations with Cervantes. An army of Feds at the Valles house needed her information. He was with the chief, trying to make the kind of wise choices she had failed to make for herself. Hurry up, Detective. We need your report.

Wise decisions she had failed to make for herself. Like not thinking about leaving her number on Cervantes's phone in the middle of a standoff with all of law enforcement for fifty miles around plus whatever had flown in from other states. What the hell, Denise?

She typed, edited, typed, and there was Perez in the doorway to her office wearing a tactical vest over his short-sleeved uniform shirt, a light blue swatch across the shoulders above a black midriff. A dorky shirt she always thought looked like a bad high school basketball uniform. He had an extra vest for her.

"We decided. The chief said forget writing anything for the FBI. You and I are meeting with the hostage negotiators. Let's go."

They took his Crown Vic, beads on the driver's seat, a fuzzy seat cover for the passenger. When Perez flipped down his visor against the sun Aragon saw photographs of children taped to the underside. His grandkids, a few great-grandkids. He had three sons and three daughters and they all had their own big families.

He drove under the speed limit, hogging the middle lane, cars coming up on his bumper, going around on both sides of them.

The seats were filthy with some kind of red dust. All day long Perez ate Mexican peanuts coated in chile powder. A plastic bowl of his *cacahuates* nested in a sandbag holder on the transmission hump.

"How far did you get on your report?" he asked, tossing nuts into his mouth with one hand on the wheel. They were taking critical information to federal law enforcement. Seconds counted. But Perez was taking it slower than usual. He wanted time to talk.

"Close to printing before you had other ideas."

"So when Cervantes said Senator Valles should be taken out..." Perez was missing his mouth, dusty red peanuts dropping between his thighs. "Let me get this straight, you said you hoped someone strong ran against him in the next election. Did I hear you right?"

"The other way around," she said. "I said he should be taken out and talked about the people I hear bitching about him. I told Pete that Valles was a true piece of shit and nobody would miss him." She adjusted the vest so it closed under her armpits. "I didn't sugarcoat what I said to Pete. You'll have it pretty much word for word in the report."

"A piece of shit or a waste of skin, what you told me before?"

"Probably both."

"You sure it wasn't Cervantes who said the 'take him out' part, and then you got talking politics, thinking that's what was in his mind? I was sure that was what you told me. That's what I told the chief. That made sense. Cops can talk politics on our own time. We can hold strong opinions about dirtbag politicos. We don't stop being citizens because we wear a badge. So when Cervantes said 'take him out,' you picked up the thread. The other way around, you suggesting someone should take out a United States senator, not just saying he should go down in flames at the polls, that wouldn't make sense, would it? And, another way: you thinking his 'take him out' stuff was about anything but politics, you would have done something besides dip your chips in salsa and keep the conversation going, right? You would have grilled Cervantes about his intentions and reported a threat against a United States senator."

Perez reloaded a fist with peanuts. He missed. A peanut now rode the collar of his bulletproof vest. They drove without talking for a mile or more, now off wide streets onto residential lanes with no traffic.

"I mention we got new computers?" His aim improved and he spoke with full cheeks, chewing between words. "That antique PC giving you headaches won't be your problem after today." His hand going for more peanuts. A pause while he tossed several in his mouth. Another pause until his mouth cleared, giving Aragon time to wonder what computers had to do with this. "You're getting a new one. It will be on your desk when you get back."

"I get it," she said. "You'll get rid of the old one for me." And the hard drive with her report the way she'd written it, with what she'd really said to Cervantes.

Perez pointed to the bowl with peanuts. "Help yourself. These aren't as hot as the last batch. I make them myself, chile colorado and garlic. Vinegar to add bite." Two SFPD patrol cars blocked the street ahead, their lights strobing, bright even in the daylight, men in FBI windbreakers beyond the cars where the road turned to gravel then dirt. "You talk about the laser sight on your cheek, they're going to want to know about Cervantes's family and friends, maybe someone they can reach out to who can show them how to handle the man, paint the picture of what this is all about. See what buttons they can push to make him do what they want. What else you got to tell them?"

"He's a hell of a shot with a rifle," Aragon said as they were waved round the barricade.

"How do you know that?"

"I've been hunting with him."

Now Perez was looking at her, slowing to a stop by the black FBI panel truck.

"Your brother's guiding business?"

She nodded.

"This comes out wrong," he said, "they hear things that don't make sense, you understand it'll be your friends and family they reach out to next, filling in notebooks about you?"

"I know Pete Cervantes. He would never hurt Mrs. Valles and her kids. He wouldn't hurt a fly."

"Denise, you met him on a hunting trip. You know he's a hell of shot because he missed Bambi?"

"It was an elk hunt."

Perez flipped the sun visor flat against the ceiling liner, then killed the engine and had his door open, one foot out in the heat. A man in black-rimmed glasses looked out from the FBI truck like he'd been expecting them.

Aragon said, "I need a minute."

Perez said, "I'll tell them you're finishing a call and will be right in."

She studied the hands in her lap, her mind numb, knowing what she was facing. Two taps on the window. Perez had come around to her side of the car.

She rolled down the glass.

He said, "Your open homicide with Lewis? Not the combo plate caper, we know who did that one, just not exactly why. I'm talking about how Mr. and Mrs. Easterling deserve justice for their dead boy? You're my best, and you do your best playing the Lone Ranger. Now you're alone for real so I'm expecting great things."

"There's my partner."

"What partner?

She saw Lewis's back walking away from her, telling her what he wouldn't say with words.

"Cops without your smarts," Perez was saying, "without your drive, your commitment to whatever it takes, they fuck up. Bad guys will get away to kill again if you're not on the job. Lots of innocent people will get hurt if you don't make the right decision in the next seconds." He took two steps away and turned around. "Cervantes isn't coming out of this. Who's going to contradict anything you say?"

He gave her his back and walked up to the man with the black-rimmed glasses. Helmick, she remembered his name was. Shit,

Perez handing over a bag of his homemade chile-garlic peanuts. With vinegar for bite. Slapping Helmick's arm, laughing about something. Making friends before the lying started.

———

That looks like Denise Aragon, Pete Cervantes almost said out loud as he watched the screen on the dining table. The FBI had its command center in that black panel truck she'd entered; he had his command center here. He could see them, but they were blind inside this house.

For now. Something that worried him: the secret tools they had. Something to stay worried about.

He'd had time to set a camera on the hillside above the house, hidden in a spiny cholla cactus, the wires buried six to ten inches under the soil and entering the house through a drain pipe. It gave him a view over the rise he was certain the FBI would use to screen themselves. Sure enough, that's where they'd moved the black truck after showing it to him, letting him know who he was dealing with.

He tried clearing up the image of the woman at the door to the truck. Short, stocky, a fireplug with no hair. A bulletproof vest over a T-shirt. The way she carried those arms, like a guy proud of his biceps. Yep. That was Aragon.

"What's she doing here?" He heard the words in the cavernous room coming back to him.

He knew the answer. She'd said, "Pete is that you?" She'd recognized his voice. She was in there telling them about it.

"Not good, mister." Talking to himself already. Damn. Now the FBI knows who I am. I'm not ready for that.

SIX

THE NEGOTIATORS WITH THE eyeglasses waited inside the command center. This time Aragon got their first names, Art Helmick and Pam Magnano, the woman with the single eyebrow across her forehead and the fuzz on her lip. Aragon tried not to stare and wondered if Magnano knew people had that tendency when they met her. Maybe Magnano used it in interrogations, catching someone staring, making eye contact and not letting go. Like the way some people stared at her own nubby scalp and the scar that showed when her hair was cut to nothing.

When Magnano introduced herself to Perez, she again pronounced Magnano like *manyano*. Perez repeated it twice to make sure he had it right, but he kept saying *mañana*.

The four of them sat in a kind of circle, Perez next to Aragon on a padded bench by the window, Magnano at a fold-down table, and Helmick in a captain's chair that swiveled, by a box of tissues with an overflowing waste basket at his feet. Perez nodded to Aragon and she told them about Cervantes, from hunting trips to court hearings to him pouring out his heart over salsa and chips.

"Why didn't you tell us immediately?" Helmick removed his glasses and showed cold gray eyes. "It makes me wonder." He sneezed and blew his nose while he waited for her answer.

"I had to be sure," Aragon said. "Before it was just guessing. I wanted—"

Helmick cut her off before she could say more. He instructed Magnano to obtain the transcript of Cervantes's statement at the Alvardo sentencing and she got on the phone. He swung back to Aragon.

"Who's with him?" Helmick asked.

Aragon had been looking at the small smile on Perez's face, a satisfied smile that made her hate herself. Just now she'd betrayed a man she considered a friend and committed a federal felony, all in a single sentence: *When he said 'take him out,' I thought Mr. Cervantes was talking politically, taking Senator Valles out of the Senate in the next election. If I'd correctly understood what he was saying, I would have ended the conversation at that instant and called the Secret Service or the Capitol Police. Or you, the FBI.*

What was the punishment for knowingly or willfully making a materially false statement to federal law enforcement? How much time did Martha Stewart get?

Helmick was now giving her something to consider besides the lie she'd just fed the FBI. "Cervantes keeps using the plural form when he talks about trading for the senator's life. He says 'we' and 'us.' Tell me about his brothers, the ones you said came for the court hearing."

So Pete Cervantes had someone willing to go down with him. Aragon's mind raced, like thumbing fast through an index file, seeing all the people who'd ever been around Pete.

"They live in Texas. Dallas area," she said, trying to remember the name of the town. "Denton." Cervantes had introduced them in the hallway before going in to face the judge and his son's killer. "Big families. They work in banking, one of them. The other, I think he's an exec in a trucking company. I don't see them doing this."

"Do you see Pete Cervantes doing this? President of a reputable construction company, family man, no priors, a fellow who spends a lot of time at mass and listens to his priest about forgiveness?" Helmick adjusted his glasses and she noted the bifocal line and the red eyes behind the lenses. His nose was running. "Friends. Who was with him on the hunting trips?"

"His sons, the first time. Later, after Iraq, just Jacob, the last one. I don't know Pete's friends. He might not have any. Why was he calling me to talk out his troubles?"

Helmick swiveled to Magnano. "Contact Dallas, have them visit the brothers." Three sneezes while everyone waited, then back to Aragon. "He told you he'd remodeled the house for the previous owner. So he knows the place. He's had time to prepare. We've been hearing a drill and hammering. Sometimes two power tools at once, so he definitely has help in there. The weapon he pointed at you, what was it?"

She'd seen only the tip of the barrel but that was enough. "A handgun with a laser sight. Large caliber. Not a revolver."

"On the hunts, what weapon did he use?"

She told him about Cervantes's CZ-USA rifle, something special that made the other men gather round. A bullet she'd never heard of back then, the .338 Lapua. Magnano hadn't heard of CZ-USA rifles and Aragon explained how precise the gun could be and the kind of energy its bullets delivered. Two thousand foot pounds at 800 yards, enough to drop any big game on the continent. Enough to penetrate body armor. Cervantes had gone to a private ranch outside Chama and stopped a bison with a shot across a valley that went through a small tree first. She'd heard that story one night around the campfire, men telling hunting whoppers she didn't believe. She had believed Cervantes.

Helmick knew the gun.

"That's the rifle he's mastered? That gun uses the same round as military snipers. Fantastic." Back to Magnano. "Tell Dix what his team's dealing with." Back to Aragon. "So he's got money. Guided hunts aren't cheap. Or the guns he uses. Are you aware of other weapons in his arsenal?"

Cervantes knew guns. He'd tell other hunters about their weapons. He'd helped Javier sight in rifles for the clients who'd never fired their toys before arriving in camp. The bourbon and beer flowing at dinner, the men talking about guns instead of women or politics. Pete would say things like, "I have a thirty-aught-six semi-auto Remington. I got it for hog hunting. I'm not sure my AR-15 would do the job on a big boar." And, "I carry a .45 when we go up in the mountains by Truchas. More for the people than the bears. Bears run away. The locals will burn your car while you're hiking. The people hanging around trailheads aren't there for bird-watching."

That was when his sons were alive. After, he'd once told her he was going for his concealed carry permit. Something smaller than a .45, but he never said what. Only that he'd qualify on a large caliber so he could carry anything he wanted.

She told Helmick everything she knew about Cervantes and his guns, but didn't repeat the "wouldn't hurt a fly" line that had made Perez snicker. Helmick gave Magnano another order—contacting ATF for everything Cervantes had ever bought—then came back to her.

"If you paid for your meals with a credit card we can nail down your meetings with Cervantes. It would be great if you have the statements. Or we can get that ourselves." Helmick took off his glasses and wiped them with a cloth he unfolded from a pocket while Magnano squinted behind her own smeared lenses. Probably that eyebrow brushing against the glass all the time.

Helmick was talking to her but Aragon didn't seem to hear him. She found herself blinking to break off eye contact with Magnano. That brow thing would be effective in an all-night interrogation. With blue eyes that didn't match and pulled you in.

Helmick said, "And we'll be speaking with your brother to get his perspective. Do you have other family?"

She heard that.

Across from her in the circle, Perez stared at his feet. The slight smile on his face was gone. She noticed that the FBI team hadn't touched their gift bag of homemade *cacahuates*.

"It's just the two of us," she said. "I have a brother in Portland or Eugene, Oregon. We haven't talked in a very long time."

"We'll find him."

"I have a question." Magnano flipped backward in her notebook, dragging a finger across a page, stopping and looking up. The black eyebrow wriggled when she squinted. "In your last meeting with Cervantes you said Sam Valles was a piece of shit and/or a waste of skin. Why so hostile?"

Perez had said they would look at her hard if they picked up any signals.

Aragon said, "He was a jerk in college. You know. Guys."

The eyebrow twitched. "Strong feelings from, what, twenty years ago?"

"Not that long. Some things stay with you, I guess." Shoulders rising to her ears, then dropping. "College memories, like yesterday, you know?"

"I let the bad memories go," Magnano said, and Aragon wondered what was behind all the frowning. "But maybe that didn't work for you." Magnano went quiet, waiting for Aragon. She sensed Helmick and Perez sitting back, surrendering the silence to her.

Bad memories like those didn't go away. You just learned to live with them, made them work for you so they didn't eat you alive. Aragon wasn't going to open that door. But she knew nobody was going to speak before she did. She had to say something to get out of here.

"Those years leave impressions," she said and rolled her neck. Just a little, not so much they'd read anything in it. They'd been sitting for a while. Anyone would be getting restless. "The silly things that stick with us. Nowadays I can't remember what I did at the start of the week. Know what I mean?"

"I don't," Magnano said. "But I can see you don't want to talk about it."

"Nothing to talk about." She shouldn't have said *nowadays. Know what I mean?* That was worse. In her own ears it rang false, probably louder for these seasoned interrogators. "Some people rub you the wrong way. Sam Valles, the college boy, was one of those. Never imagined he'd be a United States senator. He surprised all of us."

"And you grew up to be a cop."

The blue eyes were ice. Aragon had to look somewhere else. But then it would appear she was avoiding Magnano's gaze. She caught herself blinking when she didn't want to.

"That surprise you?" Magnano asked.

"I would have been surprised if I'd been anything else. And you an FBI agent?"

"Same here." Magnano smiled for the first time and Aragon saw her trying another approach to keep this going. "All I ever wanted to be, since I was a little girl watching cop shows on TV." Magnano showed good teeth. Full lips, Aragon noticed for the first time. Take away the brow and the face fuzz and the frown lines, Magnano could be very pretty. "I'm not working," Magnano said, "I'm not happy. I bet you know what I mean."

Girlfriends, now. Sharing.

Aragon could come back with, "Right, the job is what matters. This is why I breathe." Magnano was inviting her to keep talking, discover what else they had in common. She'd pull more out of her. They'd chat about … stuff. And then she'd find herself wondering how they hell they were back to why she hated Sam Valles.

It was past time to shut up.

"That's really all I have to say about Mr. Cervantes," she said, forcing herself not to call him Pete. "If you're done, I've got an open murder case on my desk. A little boy, disappeared from his backyard a day before he was found up the mountains ten miles away."

She poured on details she knew by memory to make them follow her lead now: the height of walls around the backyard, the boy's missing pocketknife and Boy Scout bandana slide—he'd been backyard camping, practicing for a Scout troop backpacking trip—the total blank from canvassing the neighborhood, how they'd put the parents under a microscope and found nothing but the discrepancies in their story that wouldn't go away. What was missing from the boy. The condition of his body. What she saw at the autopsy. An unexplained substance on his sneakers. The theories they'd tried and rejected.

There. Magnano looking to Helmick, closing her notebook. Helmick trying to appear interested but his hands twiddling a pen saying otherwise. She'd be out of here soon.

———

Already making mistakes, Pete Cervantes told himself. One little slip bumps the next move off course and down the line it builds. Progressive error, buddy. Like laying tile, not keeping the lines straight, trying to eyeball it, skipping the spacers and seeing the mess when you got to the far wall.

This is not my line of work, he remembered.

On the monitor he watched Aragon stripping off the bulletproof vest as she walked from the black FBI truck back to the Ford with a man who could be her uncle, but darker. A round man with little feet and hands in a police uniform under his own vest. Not a regular uniform like the cops who gave you a ticket. More like a dress uniform and without the calf-high leather boots. He got behind the wheel and Cervantes guessed he was Aragon's supervising officer. He'd brought her to talk to the FBI.

Mistake number one: putting a laser sight on Aragon. That broke the rule he'd taught his sons—never point a gun at anything, on four legs or two, unless you intend to shoot. He would never harm Aragon. She was the most stand-up cop on the rough road of the past couple years. He would have killed Alvardo. Santa Fe judges couldn't be trusted. But she'd assured him his judge would do the right thing. He'd been appointed to the bench by the last governor, a former prosecutor herself. His judge wasn't one of the criminal defense fraternity, ACLU lawyers in robes who thought the real victim in the courtroom was sitting at the defense table.

She'd helped him hold it together. Helped him find the courage to get on with his life.

She knew that what he said in court had been an act. The words had been forced, things he'd thought would honor the dead. He'd said the word "forgive" and still wanted to kill his son's murderer when the man turned around, scripted by his lawyer, to face the family and say "sorry." The judge said, "That's all you have to say to these people you hurt so much you changed their lives forever?"

Alvardo shrugged his shoulders, like, what else you want from me? Forgiveness. It hadn't stuck.

Whenever he'd needed to talk, he turned to Aragon. She was always there to hear him out, no matter the time, night or day. But the last time, when he was ranting about Senator Valles calling people killed by the Alvardos roaming the country "bumps in the road," she'd done a lot of talking. More than ever before. Not cop talk. Talk from her heart that got him thinking.

And now she'd been in the FBI van making him pay for his mistakes. She had a job. He couldn't blame her for that. What he was sorry for—Christ, he'd grown to hate that word. What he didn't *like* was dragging her into this.

A phone rang. It wasn't one of the prepaid cells he'd stocked up on. Or his cell phone. Or the house phone. It was the cell he'd taken from Mrs. Valles.

The screen said *FBI*. No number. Just the letters.

How did they manage that?

"Pete Cervantes," a voice said when he answered and waited. "This is Art Helmick. I'm a negotiator for the FBI. I want to talk with you, to find a way for you to get what you want out of this without anybody, that's including you, getting hurt."

"You know my name."

"We do. I know about your son and daughter-in-law. I've worked with too many victims of violent crimes. I want you to know I appreciate the pain you feel. I will never understand it, but I do appreciate it."

Helmick told him right there he was real. The people saying I understand your pain … he never heard the rest of what they had to say. He'd drift off, or get angry. Mostly he went numb to be nice. Aragon

47

said she understood his pain, but that was different. Like she really felt it inside, but couldn't share it completely, words not coming close. It was the way he felt when he was talking to anybody besides her.

Okay. Pay attention here. "You know what I want," Cervantes said. "That's why we need to talk. I need to understand exactly—"

"Senator Valles's life for his family. Call me when he's ready to trade."

Cervantes hung up. No more mistakes. Maybe he was tired. Sure he was. He was exhausted. He checked his watch. He'd been working now for almost thirty hours straight. Almost done with the priority work. The windows were secured, plywood outside, metal sheeting inside. Not enough to stop a high velocity bullet, but it would block the infrared detection equipment the FBI would use to see inside the house. They wouldn't know what to aim at.

Those infrared sensing cameras—he'd studied up on them. They would only see what he wanted to show.

Food: plenty. Water: fifty-gallon barrels in the garage with his construction van and tools. He'd fill the bathtubs now. Flashlights charged. Extra batteries in boxes. Candles, too, to keep a steady light at night when they cut the power. They would do that, along with water when they decided to pressure him.

Two generators with jerry cans of gasoline. He'd need to keep his phones charged and the cameras running, and lights on outside so he could see if they were making their move.

Now, concrete to mix and pour. He had an idea for reinforcing the doors. He chewed ice cubes to stay awake and got back to work.

———

Helmick closed the phone, thinking about what he'd learned from hearing Cervantes's voice. He had a photograph Magnano had obtained from the New Mexico Department of Motor Vehicles: Steady brown eyes, a strange white patch of hair at the forehead, the rest of the hair still black at his age. A strong neck with a little jowl under the chin. Cervantes looked amused, one corner of his mouth pulled back, a dimple in his chin.

The face didn't tell him much he didn't know from Magnano's lightning research and Aragon's statement. He was looking at a working man who had made it. High school education, starting out paving driveways and stuccoing houses, working side by side with his crews even when he'd gotten big enough to need an accounting firm to keep his books straight. Some sun damage on the bridge of his nose. No need for glasses, lucky guy. He had clear eyes, a confidence in them. He knew how to get things done.

They'd found his will in a search of his house. Helmick had never written a warrant in less time nor used fewer words, but no federal judge was going to block the FBI from searching the home of man who'd taken hostage the family of a United States senator—especially a judge who owed his nomination to Senator Valles.

He wanted to know if Cervantes's will showed pre-planning and he got his answer on the first page. It had been updated only this month and passed a lot of money to the only grandchild. Cervantes had liquidated everything, according to financial records found in the envelope with the will, with everything in a money market but the house, which was listed for sale. A million was split between his brothers for the benefit of their children. A quarter mil went to an organization for the families of Americans killed by undocumented immigrants. Cervantes's vehicles and a lot of weapons, including expensive shotguns and muzzleloaders, had been sold, according to records from the Department of Motor Vehicles and the ATF. Only one vehicle remained from a small fleet of trucks and Jeeps: a large cargo van.

Peter Cervantes had made things easy for the executor of his estate.

AFT records confirmed he still owned the high-powered rifle Aragon had mentioned, as well as a Springfield Armory .45 and a pricey Fort Discovery AR-15. These were the weapons Dix's teams would have to contend with if they assaulted the house.

What had he heard in Cervantes's voice? Minimal use of words. The man wasn't a babbler. He'd had many first calls with hostage-takers who gave you their life story in the opening minutes, trying to sell you on how justified they were in their desperation.

Not Cervantes.

He'd heard a man who knew exactly what he wanted. He wanted Valles.

They wanted Valles.

His team had captured the landline in the Valles house and the cell phones subscribed to Mrs. Valles and Pete Cervantes. The US Attorney for New Mexico had people chasing a judge to get a warrant to pull Cervantes's phone records for the past two years, both his personal and business lines. Somewhere in those numbers they'd find out who "they" was. He'd get as much help as he needed culling those records. The director had told him the entire bureau was his backup on this. Managing the resources rushing at him would be a separate challenge. He needed someone to act as his executive so he could concentrate on getting inside Cervantes's head.

"Art." Magnano handed him a folder. He opened it to copies of newspaper articles on Santa Fe Police Department Detective Denise Aragon. She'd taken down some front-page criminals, been injured on duty, suspended, reprimanded, sued many times. A couple outright dismissals, two jury wins, one undisclosed settlement of an excessive force claim. There she was with Pete Cervantes, a man thinner and older than the one in the driver's license. Exiting a courtroom, eyes avoiding cameras. She was wearing a skirt, and a wig to cover her buzz cut. She was holding his hand.

Magnano said, "Aragon is lying about something. She hates Valles. You could see it in her eyes. Shoulders lifted, hands turned up, telling us the feelings were just residue from college years. *Nothing to see here, folks.* But the eyes, they showed something else. And her neck, hard cables along her windpipe."

"Fighting to hold something back," Helmick said. "You know the drill. Tell me who Denise Aragon is. And get her sergeant back here. You catch that sly smile passing between them?"

"When she got to the part about Cervantes saying somebody should take Valles out? It was Perez smiling. Aragon went robot there. Then she was back, talking easy."

"Sure, Pete, take out a US senator. Would you please pass the chips?" Helmick looked more closely at the photo, Aragon's arms almost as big as Cervantes's, but her hand was swallowed inside one that had worked construction for a lifetime.

He'd read the folder later. "When is Valles touching down at Andrews? Before he leaves the plane I want someone asking him about Aragon without anyone else around. What happened between them during their college days? Did he do something to make her hate him?"

SEVEN

"GET BACK IN YOUR world," Sergeant Perez told Aragon on the drive to the office. "You can't help Cervantes."

He looked hard at her as he drove, cars all around them and Perez driving almost on the stripe in the middle of the road.

"Sarge, eyes front."

He didn't turn to the windshield. "You think you're a shit for what you did in that black truck. You think you betrayed someone who trusted you. But you stayed what you need to be, what we need you to be, and that is an active duty detective of the Santa Fe Police Department. That matters more than anything you're feeling. You are now going to put all your attention on finding the person who dumped a boy in weeds and thorns in a place where people go to hear birds sing and pick flowers. You've done other things to get the job done. This isn't the first time you haven't told the truth when it stood in the way. Stop." A hand came off the wheel but thank God he'd at least looked forward for a second, nobody in front for a block.

"I'm not calling you a liar. You're a good cop. Good enough not to get caught in your lies."

Traffic was heavy on Cerrillos moving south from the center of town, like it had come from a dam breaking upstream behind them. Perez drove slowly, ignoring the guy on his bumper leaning on his horn.

"The truth that matters. That's what you're good at. What you never waver from."

"Lewis knows," she said.

Finally he put both his eyes on the road and kept them there.

"Lewis knows a lot. Don't kid me. The things you get him into. Listen." Perez pulled over and let the driver behind pass. It was a car full of boys, the mad-dogging freezing when they drew even and saw Perez in his uniform. He lifted a finger off the wheel and smiled at them. "What you said about Valles being a waste of skin. That part you got dead right even if you didn't tell the rest of it straight. Pete Cervantes is the better man in spite of this madness and I can't say I hope the senator gets away without a nick. His family unhurt, yes. But if Cervantes can take Valles down a notch, I won't hold anything against him other than charges."

"We have this thing between us now," Aragon said. "Me lying to the FBI. What you just said about a hostage situation involving a US senator, your real feelings."

"You want me to go on about Valles? You want more, to be sure I'm never going to burn you for not revealing it was you that said what you said?" Perez pulled back into the center lane, ten miles an hour below the limit. "Here it is. If there was a way we could take Valles down to save Cervantes's life, I'm for it. Senator Sam's screwed cops since he got the power. On the way up, he was true blue. Thank you very much for your endorsement, FOP, Santa Fe Police and Firefighters Union, Border Patrol Agents, State Police, my dear, true friends, the heroes among us who go out there every day putting your lives on the line. Did I mention the tens of thousands in campaign contributions from our friends in blue? Since he's had 'US Senator' in front of his name we're out of control, need oversight, a DOJ investigation to make cops better people and score points with the social justice billionaires. Fuck him. Maybe you want to tell me why you hate him all these years?"

"I don't hate him."

"Bullshit. And that FBI with the eyebrow, she called bullshit, too. There's something deep in you with him. Give me a hint."

"What's the statute of limitations on rape?"

"He raped you?" She felt the car slowing even more. His foot was off the gas and he was looking at her as the front of the car drifted across a dashed line.

"Sarge, you're going to kill someone." When his eyes were back on the road she said, "He didn't rape me. He raped a friend of mine. Her name was Amy McSwaim. It killed her."

"I want to hear this."

"Only if you pull over and park."

———

Perez had his turn signal on for two blocks before they drove into an empty lot for a seafood restaurant that was out of business. *Mariscos Chihuahua*, said the sign missing letters. Selling dirt-cheap shrimp and tilapia from God knows where. It had been a scary place to eat.

"You know there's no statute of limitations for rape. It's a first degree felony," Perez said, putting the car park. "And if it killed her, why aren't you talking murder?"

"It wasn't homicide, but he killed her just the same."

Aragon had handled the case that closed the seafood restaurant. Five men from Juarez eating ceviche and raw oysters looked up at a nine-year-old wearing a Tweety Bird hoodie and holding a .22 Ruger. They couldn't believe what they were seeing. The kid was missing a front tooth. The gun was shaking. They talked about it later with her at the Christus St. Vincent ER, the five of them hooked up to saline bags. The kid emptied all eight rounds, speed-loaded and was firing again—*chinga,* he knew what he was doing—before they reached their own guns. Nobody was killed. The kid ran before their guns came out. Tweety Bird the assassin was still out there and the men, none of them licensed for concealed carry, all of them wanted for other crimes, were still in Santa Fe. None of them in the country legally but not going anywhere. SFPD was following the city's law on not notifying DHS that these guys needed to be eating their scary seafood back in Juarez. She'd charged them with illegal possession of a firearm. She never got notice of a trial date and saw them again at the new super-cheap seafood place, Playa La Paz, no guns or hoodies allowed according to the sign taped to the door.

She had let her mind run to that old case because she didn't want to talk about Amy McSwaim.

"You tell any of this to Lewis?" Perez asked. "Why you hate Valles?"

"What's the point?"

"Why am I having to drag this out of you?"

"Saying Senator Sam Baca Valles raped a friend, with no proof, not even a complaint on file, that kind of stuff will end your law enforcement career right quick."

"Saying to a distraught victim someone should take out Senator Sam Baca Valles, and then the victim runs with it, and then you lie to the FBI about how that conversation went—that will end your law enforcement career quicker. But we got past that, didn't we? You'll get over feeling lousy. You've got your whole life ahead to use your fire to make a difference in this screwed-up world."

"What are you, Pops, my *abuelo*?"

"I'm your sergeant and don't call me Pops. You do what I say. I say, tell me."

"Yes, sir." She started telling him what only she and two other friends from college knew. One of those friends was inside the house with Pete Cervantes. She was Mrs. Patricia Valles.

———————

Danny Luna boarded the US Air Force C-21 with a female FBI agent whose Anglo name kept slipping his mind. Adams, that was it. She was looking cool in a navy blue suit while his only suit and almost-clean white shirt stuck to his skin. They walked across the hot tarmac, the agent with a roll-on overnighter and Danny with a backpack. The superhero characters on the flap and sides had been cool when he bought it. At age 12. He felt ridiculous but it was the only luggage he owned.

At the bottom of the stairs they were met by another FBI agent who had flown with Senator Valles from Geneva. "Enjoy the trip," he said and handed a folder to Adams. He threw a critical look at Danny's cartoon backpack, knotted his tie, and walked, shoulders slumped, to the terminal. He was done. Adams and the two men with sunglasses crowding the top of the stairs would take over from here.

Danny had only ever answered phones for the senator and set out glasses and napkins at fundraisers. In exchange he got to put "intern" on his resume. Maybe his next summer job would pay something. Until then he got to show a badge every morning to security at the

Hart Senate Building. He got good seats in the Senate chambers when the senator was giving a speech. And he got leftovers when the fundraisers were done and free drinks while they cleaned up.

Now with the news showing Santa Fe police cars blocking streets, a crazy man holding the senator's family hostage, he was chosen to be with the senator himself at the most important time in the senator's entire life. The other interns in the dump they shared off U Street had gotten up early to watch the latest reports, nothing else on the television or Internet. And to see him off. Jealous. They were going to their cubicles to answer phones and categorize letters to be matched with form responses. He was jetting to a crisis at the side of the great Sam Baca Valles.

In the sky with guys with Uzis under Pierre Cardin jackets. These FBI people sure dressed well.

The heat followed them into the plane through the open hatch. Danny recognized some of the people who looked like they'd slept in their clothes during the flight from Switzerland. The senator's executive secretary. His legislative director and legal counsel. The communications director and his assistant. The woman who scheduled every minute of the senator's life. And his chief of staff, Martin Kilgore, no more rumpled than he always looked. He slept in the office in the Hart Building in a sleeping bag rolled out on the floor. He showered in the senators' washroom with a handheld sprayer attached to a sink's faucet. He had a nose that looked like it belonged on a street drunk—but Kilgore didn't drink. Not anymore. Pockmarked cheeks, eyes that weren't level, a chin somewhere in the folds on his neck. The Ugliest Man in the World. Kilgore gave that title to himself and said it referred to more than his appearance. Fuck up and see.

"Tuck your shirt in," Kilgore said. "The senator wants to hear it from you." To Agent Adams, "Wait here. You're next. Meanwhile, call your director. I want to talk with him personally and not any brain-dead deputy."

Danny's shirt had been tucked in when he stepped onto the tarmac. How had it come loose just walking? Now he was worrying about his socks, whether he'd matched them right, dressing in his dark apartment trying not to wake his roommates who got up anyway when he'd made coffee. Digging in boxes on the floor instead of a closet, a bathroom down the hall shared by everybody on this floor. Eating a dry bagel, all that was left from the last run to the food pantry over on R Street, all the good stuff from the senator's reception for the billionaire enviros long gone.

He was happy with a hockey puck for breakfast. He was flying with the senator into history.

He'd bought an apple from the stand at the top of the moving stairs at the Metro, but he was still hungry. Then he realized it was the smell of bacon in the plane making his stomach growl. Real bacon on a plane. He could only hope.

And there was Senator Valles, leaning back on a padded seat, hot breakfast on a tray table folded out from the arm rest.

Crap. Danny saw his fly was open and reached to pull it up. Quick. Before anyone noticed.

"Sit." Kilgore pointed to a seat opposite the senator.

Danny stole a glance at his ankles as his pants rode up his shins. Sure enough, his socks didn't match. At least he'd covered the scuffs on his shoes with a black marker. There was a shoeshine stand under the House office buildings. A cool place to hang out, see great men and powerful, scary women with their high heels and hard eyes. Chatting about nuclear weapons, a trillion dollars here and there, and sometimes sex. The basic shoeshine cost more than a lunch in the House cafeteria. The government subsidized food for worker bees, not shoeshines.

"Tell it to me, word for word, exactly as you heard it," Valles said, cheeks filled with potatoes and eggs, eyes steady and fixed.

Valles was the kind of guy you didn't want next to you flying economy. His shoulders would take half your space. His elbow would be in your ribs. He worked at keeping the weight off, sometimes in the Senate gym twice a day. But his muscle was covered with a layer of soft flesh that made him look rounded at the edges. No rolls at the waist, yet sitting his stomach was doubled in his lap. On the walls in his office Valles had photos of himself on the UNM cheerleading squad looking like a gymnast, squared off, short but powerful, balancing a girl with killer legs on his shoulder. Danny wondered what it would be like to have his own hands on those thighs, a palm under that perfect butt. Girls like that went for men like Senator Valles, not sweaty schmucks with saggy socks and superhero backpacks.

The senator's black hair was streaked with gray and brushed back at the temples. It usually stood up off his head, a cliff of thick hair. Something you'd expect on a man with swagger. But today it was matted and flat, and Valles needed a shave. The collar of his white shirt was folded under and Danny didn't feel so bad about the shirt he'd worn twice already this week.

A shove to his shoulder. Kilgore glaring at him.

"What did Cervantes say?"

He'd been staring at Senator Valles. He'd never been this close, knee to knee, the focus of attention.

Danny repeated what he'd told the FBI. Now Kilgore was sitting next to Valles, their shoulders and arms crowding each other.

"I got the call, routed from the receptionist. He didn't give a name. I only learned that today when the FBI questioned me. He said, 'Tell the senator this: We'll take your life for your family.' Some kind of prank, for sure, but I thought I should call somebody."

Kilgore leaned forward, elbows on his knees. "*Senator.* He said that?"

"The man said 'Valles.' I always say Senator, or Senator Valles. I know"—Danny turned to Valles—"you want us to call you Sam, but I feel funny doing that."

"The senator's name," Kilgore said. "How did he pronounce it?"

"He had that right. *Vye-yes.*"

"He should have it right," Valles said. "He's been getting checks from us every week for a couple months. My wife hired him for the remodel." Valles wiped his mouth. He had full lips, like a woman. Perfect teeth. Crazy white. "Had you heard his voice before, this Cervantes?"

Danny had been thinking of that. Because there among his notes in his desk, the scraps he shoved in there at the end of the day because Kilgore insisted they leave nothing out for the cleaning staff to see, was a record of a call from a Pete Cervantes complaining about one of the senator's speeches. Going on about his son and daughter-in-law not being any politician's "bumps in the road." Senator Valles would never use such language for a personal tragedy. Danny had believed that when he'd told this Cervantes he must be wrong. And Cervantes had come back with, "Listen, you," and a two-minute rant. That's when Cervantes moved from concerned constituent to the wingnuts column, anger rising in his voice, telling Danny how Valles didn't give a shit about the little people, he'd forgotten who gave him his job, he was no more New Mexican than Taco Bell.

Did he recognize the voice?

"We get so many calls," Danny said. "But a couple months ago he did call the office." He'd brought that note with him in his jacket pocket. He unfolded the torn sheet of paper and handed it to Kilgore. "He didn't ask the senator to do anything. He just vented and then he hung up."

Kilgore spit a sliver of fingernail on the floor as he read.

Senator Valles waved a hand and a woman in an Air Force uniform stopped as she passed. He raised his plate for her to take away. She tapped the pilot's wings pinned above her left breast and shook her head. Valles handed the plate to Kilgore, who took a strip of untouched bacon and then placed the plate on an empty seat. Danny pushed his hand into his belly to quiet his stomach.

He had forgotten he was in a military plane. It was plush, lots of wood and soft fabric. Something the Air Force used for jetting VIPs around the globe and back from Switzerland when their family had been taken hostage.

"Every voter's concerns, no matter how irate, how irrational, are important," Valles said. "You made a mistake not informing your supervisor. You should have let them decide how to respond to Mr. Cervantes."

"Yes, Senator."

"But that was early in your internship," Valles said. "Now you know. When Cervantes said 'we,' did you think that was intentional? He was speaking for more than himself? Or just loose talk?"

"The royal we," Kilgore said, and Danny didn't know what that meant.

"Soon as he said it, he had me wondering," Danny said. "He seemed to pick his words very carefully, not like the time when he was really angry. I got the feeling he'd worked out what he wanted to say ahead of time."

"How the hell would you know?" Kilgore slid bacon across his lips. One bite and he swallowed.

61

"People sometimes take a while to get going. The regular people calling from New Mexico to their senator's office in Washington, D.C., they want to introduce themselves, make a connection before getting down to business. They thank you for taking their call. Some ask if I'm related to the Los Lunas, the ones the city's named for. Not this man. Soon as I said hello he went straight to what he wanted to say."

"How did his voice make you feel? Did you get a picture of the person speaking?" Valles unrolled his sleeves and buttoned his cuffs, stiff as paper, while Danny thought about how to answer.

"I heard my father when he was in his no-nonsense mood. You did exactly what he wanted. Or else. And that's what I saw, someone like my father. A strong Hispanic man who knows who he is, knows he can handle anything because he's done it before. And if he hasn't, he'll figure it out."

"Your family, they're from Tres Piedras?"

"Still there, all but me. I moved to the big city. Some of them have never been to Santa Fe and don't see any reason to go. Taos is big enough. They drive through town to get to the supermarket on the other side, they're done for the day."

Kilgore pushed himself up from his seat and moved to the front of the plane, leaving Danny alone with the senator, something he'd be sure to tell the other interns. Women and young people, they were never alone with the senator. A precaution, he'd heard, so no one could ever lay a sexual harassment claim against him. That was weird, a powerful man afraid to be alone with his employees. But he'd heard it was that way with other interns, all the politicians terrified of the power kids had to bring them down. Weird.

"As I remember, your father had a problem with VA," Valles said.

"Yes, sir. He wasn't getting his checks. My grandmother saw your ad, about calling you directly with problems like that. She didn't get her Social Security once and called you. Us." Danny paused to see that Valles got it, that they were a team. Valles smiled with the perfect teeth under the woman's lips. "She got on my dad to call us and we got it done. That's why I wanted so much to intern with you. But now, all I want is for your family to be safe."

"Thank you, Danny. I'm glad we could help your father. That's why I'm in this business." Valles inched to the front of his seat. He was ready to get up. "Don't feel bad about keeping that first call to yourself. You know better now. Be sure to apply for next summer, okay? You can show the other interns how it's done right."

Danny had expected him to follow Kilgore. Instead, Senator Valles swung his hips around and sat next to him, his shoulder pushing Danny over a little, his elbow in his ribs.

"What Cervantes wanted, this trade he talked about, who have you told this to? I know you reported everything to the FBI. Did you share details of the calls with other interns, anyone back in New Mexico?"

"No, sir. With the FBI in the picture, I figured it wasn't for me to say anything to anyone."

"Good boy." Valles patted Danny's knee and was back up, looking down at him, a big hand flattened on the bulkhead. "I'm glad you took that call, Danny. You have some real street smarts. Lots of kids would have been blabbing everything on Facebook. You didn't do anything like that, did you?"

"No, sir. I'm smarter than that."

"Yes, you are. Or Twitter? Or Snapchat?" He waited for Danny to shake his head. "Like I said, you're smart."

Valles followed Kilgore and Danny wondered what he was supposed to do, alone now in the back of this fancy jet. Everyone was at the front of the plane with the FBI agents. The FBI lady, Adams, handed a cell phone to Kilgore, who started chopping the air and turning around in place as he talked. Then she was alone with Senator Valles. He saw her ask something and the senator blinked. Squeezed his eyes shut and open hard. Then he was shaking his head and pushing past her to follow Kilgore, who was moving through the open hatch, his lumpy body half in sunlight, half in shadow.

Across the space between the seats was the senator's breakfast plate. Danny looked over his shoulder, then back at a strip of bacon between egg yellow and red ketchup soaking cold home fries.

The coast was clear.

Damn, real bacon on a plane. Burned just right. Danny licked his fingers. What was for lunch?

———————

Down on the hot tarmac, Valles ducked under the wing of the plane even though the clearance was greater than his height by a couple feet. Kilgore swung wide around the wing and caught up.

"So that's Jerry Luna's nephew?" Valles asked. "We're still paying for him swinging Taos County our way?"

"It's an unpaid job," Kilgore said. "Costs us nothing and Jerry's happy. Look, when he says he's backing a candidate the entire clan up and down the Rio Grande votes together. They make lines at the polls. That kid is related to everyone in New Mexico."

"His grandmother and her social security? The father with the VA problems?"

"It was our friend in the Post Office holding back the checks. People call you, you say you'll find out where the check is. We call our friend to put it back in the mail. Senator Sam comes through with a miracle and has a supporter for life."

"Wish the guy hadn't retired. It was a good play while it lasted." Valles slapped the landing gear and Kilgore flinched.

"Don't do that."

Valles slapped again, harder. "You truly hate flying, don't you? You can't find an excuse this time to take Amtrak across the country. I love it, especially this ride where we don't have to mingle with the masses. Danny Luna." Now Valles was out in the sun, staring into the sky, shielding his eyes. "He hasn't told anyone but FBI about the trade Cervantes wants. How long do you think he'll keep it bottled up? The kid's gonna talk."

"I'm putting Lorna on it. We're not staying at the Eldorado, where the FBI wanted to park us. I've got a donor vacating their house. No neighbors, a high wall around the property. You need a place where reporters won't bother you. We'll keep Cervantes's terms under wraps and Lorna will make Danny Boy the happiest lad on the Rio Grande."

"She's okay with this? We usually put her on someone with power or money."

"She said she'd do anything for you in this crisis. This will be child's play. Her words. She'll catch up on other work when the boy nods off."

"Where's this going, Marty?"

"We'll find out more when we get to Santa Fe. With the media in the dark, we've got room to maneuver. Right now, I don't see a good way out of this for you. Either you really do give your life for your family, or you don't and you're just as dead for all the things we've been working for. A man who won't give everything he has for his family, he's a spit magnet."

"So I have to make that call—walking up to my house, me shouting to Cervantes, 'take me instead of them'? 'You've got what you want, now let them go.' And I hope for the best?"

"Something to consider. Let me think about that."

"Getting myself shot?"

"Tackled, maybe." Kilgore held out his hand shoulder-height and swept it right to left in pace with his words. "The desperate father defies over-cautious law enforcement, exposing himself to a madman to save his family. The father dashes across the open space. 'Take me, take me. My life is nothing compared to my love for my family.' But faster FBI agents tackle him. He's dragged away sobbing, pounding fists on the backs of large men. Or a shot in the meaty part of the thigh, nothing serious, but enough to give you a limp to remind voters of the heroic sacrifice you made. The FBI could use a small caliber that won't break the bone. You'd barely feel it. Well, not that much."

"You're nuts."

"I'm a genius and you know it."

"You're so smart," Senator Valles said, "tell me what I did to this guy."

EIGHT

She got the "dried beans" speech from Perez. She'd given him what he wanted to know: how Sam Baca Valles, during spring break of his freshman year at the University of New Mexico, had raped Amy McSwaim because she'd rejected him. Laughed at him. How the rape had definitely changed and probably killed her. How Valles cut the hair he could once tuck into the back of his pants, married Patricia Garza, one of McSwaim's best friends, never held a real job, and was now a United States senator she hated. Yeah, she admitted it. Hated. She rolled the word around her mouth and it tasted good.

Here it came. She'd heard it before when she brought Perez cases she believed in but knew were going nowhere. "Dried beans," he said. "You can't chew on them. You don't want to swallow them. No, sir. They're no good unless you soak them, then boil them till they're soft. Then you've got something you can live on through good times and bad."

Pops dispensing cop wisdom in parables.

"What you've got is a girl dead now, how long?" He'd moved from the speech to her feeble facts. "Just her word to you and your friends that Valles raped her. No police reports. No witnesses. She go to a rape crisis center? A doctor?"

Aragon shook her head. "We saw the scratches and bruises."

"So show me the photographs you wisely took to preserve evidence. Right, you were mush-headed college freshmen not familiar with use of your brains or the rules of evidence. I'm telling you, Aragon. Dried beans."

She wasn't going to argue and get another parable he'd take ten minutes explaining.

"You say it killed her?" Perez wasn't done. "But it wasn't *someone* killed her? Not Valles to shut her up?"

"It wasn't murder. She got herself killed in the Sandia Mountains. Running in almost one hundred degrees for thirty miles. She pushed herself way too hard. We'd been worried about her extreme stuff. It caught up with her. Hikers found her collapsed by the trail. She died on the way to the hospital. She could have died up there and her parents would still be looking."

"Something sounds wrong about your friend. That's not for you to think about. Until it's closed, you have the Easterling case to keep you occupied." Now he was done. "Lewis is assigned to the hostage situation to assist as needed. I don't want you anywhere near that. So forget your dried beans and find who killed that boy."

Reread the file. Check witness statements against each other. Review the evidence. Flyspeck the timeline. Look for similar crimes in Santa Fe and the region. Study the autopsy … for the fiftieth time.

Hours later, she sat in the dark backyard where Chase Easterling had been playing at wilderness camping before he disappeared. Cinderblock walls all around connecting to the sides of the house. No lights reaching from the street. No lights in the Easterling house. Nobody had been home for a year. The parents couldn't live there anymore and had moved into an apartment. Their realtor wanted to leave the place empty, give people time to forget, before she put it on the market.

In the night sky, helicopter searchlights and beacons pushed out stars. She guessed she was a mile or two from the circus Cervantes had drawn upon himself, but the air overhead was busy. News choppers buzzed at the edges as State Police and Army helicopters in the center kept them from the airspace directly over the Valles house.

This dark backyard, no different than a thousand backyards in Santa Fe. A cement patio at the foot of the sliding door into the family room of the single-story wood and stucco rancher. A picnic table and grill on the concrete. Flowers had once grown by the house where there was shade. In the yard the landscaping was past dead. Indian squash and goat head weeds had taken over. A sandbox in the corner conquered by ant hills. Iron poles set in concrete for the clothesline. No trees in the yard but pyracantha blocked the wall, their tangled branches and thorns better than any fence. Nobody could get through without shredding themselves.

Chase Easterling had made his tent from sheets strung over the clothesline. He was a Boy Scout, Troop 1120, Great Southwest Council, swept up reading *Boys' Life*, preparing for his first weekend camping trip, a backpack into Bandelier National Monument to reach Painted Cave. He insisted he needed to practice sleeping outside, away from his nightlight and the toys he'd grown up with. Chase spread his official BSA sleeping bag on a plastic sheet and brought his pillow from his room after he'd given up bunching his jeans under his head. He'd been out there when his parents turned off the television and headed for bed. Both had peeked through the curtains to see his silhouette against the sheets and thought he was up reading. He'd taken a book about the early explorers of the Southwest into his tent. Chance

Easterling, the father, rose in the middle of the night and saw the light out. So did Ginny Easterling, the mother, several times, as she had trouble sleeping. She always had trouble sleeping since they'd moved to Santa Fe.

In the morning, overriding her son's instructions to leave him alone—because there are no moms in the wilderness—she'd started wondering how her son could still be sleeping as the sun scorched the yard. She decided to deliver cereal and milk as an excuse to look in on him. His book on explorers was there, with his flashlight hanging on a bungee. Chase was gone.

A couple walking their dog through the Santa Fe Canyon Preserve found his body on a crushed prickly pear cactus. He'd been beaten to death, hit so hard on the side of his face an eye hung from its socket. He was wearing the shirt from his Boy Scout uniform with its Bobcat patch, what looked like a peeled cornhusk inside a golden diamond.

Sergeant Perez had shifted the case to Aragon and Lewis from another detective team that had stalled out. Since then Aragon had been in this yard a dozen times, staring at the wall of thorns and the table pushed to the locked gate in the corner of the yard, right next to the house where his parents' bedroom was. That was the only way Chase could have gotten out. Climbing onto the table, pulling himself to the edge of the wooden gate and dropping down the other side. She had tried it herself. The gate squeaked and groaned under her weight. She had one of Lewis's daughters, older than Chase but lighter, give it a go. The gate squeaked and groaned.

The Easterlings said they heard nothing all that night until the newspaper slapped the front door around six a.m.

Time of death was the early morning hours. Chase could not have walked to the canyon preserve. It was over ten miles away. His bicycle was in the garage, locked to the wall because his first bike had been stolen when the overhead door was left open one night.

The first detectives interviewed every resident on the street in front of the Easterling residence. The hinky ones got return visits. The registered sex offender at the end of the block received surveillance until his alibi checked out. He'd been in Thailand. He said he'd found a way to satisfy his needs without ever again breaking American laws. He'd learned that "Thai hot" made New Mexico's hottest chile boring. They weren't sure if he was talking about food or making some twisted joke.

Several people had security cameras trained on driveways and approaches to their front doors. None had picked up a kid in a Boy Scout shirt.

They worked the street with houses having backyards the other side of the Easterlings' pyracantha thicket. Mostly older couples, a few rentals, nobody with a police record. Aragon had looked at the Easterlings' rear wall from the other side. It was higher there, the neighbor's yard a foot lower with pretty ornamentals in a carefully tended garden at the base. No footprints had been noticed in the turned soil. No plants crushed by a kid dropping off the wall. The table pushed to the gate remained Chase's most likely stepping stone out of the backyard.

Forensics found fibers on Chase's clothes from his sleeping bag and his cotton sheet tent cover. His shirt was torn in the back. There were signs he had been dragged to the spot where his body was found. Burrs from weeds by the road but not near the creek clung to his pant cuffs, as though he'd been dragged by his arms.

No defensive wounds on his hands. Gravel and tar in the treads of his sneakers puzzled the technicians. The Easterlings' street had a few spots where the pavement oozed chip seal on the hottest days.

But the petroleum product in the chip seal didn't match what was found on Chase's shoes.

Aragon and Lewis told each other they'd hit the same dead end as the previous team of detectives.

Something she hadn't done: spend a night where Chase had practiced camping out.

Right now, listening to night sounds in the Easterlings' backyard, she heard televisions, the clinking of dishes, dogs barking, dragging their chains over concrete, winding them around metal stakes. A car, no, an old pickup now that it was closer, a V-8, rumbling on the street beyond the house. In the distance she could hear the white noise of traffic on Cerrillos and choppers in the sky. The helicopters hadn't been here when Chase lay on his back under his bedsheet tent. She had to filter that out. She hoped their racket wouldn't drown out something she needed to hear.

Smells. Night flowers opening. Moonflowers, the white trumpets Georgia O'Keeffe made famous. They thrived on the poorest soil in the harshest conditions. She'd seen their large, deep green leaves in the abandoned yard during previous visits in daylight. The white flowers would be opening now and stay open until after sunrise. Beautiful things, and deadly. She remembered yanking them from the dry, hard ground of her family's house as a kid and watching her skin turn black, go numb, and scare her mother to tears. Stupid kids still made tea from the seeds, wanting to experience the hallucinations they'd read about in Carlos Castaneda. He called the plant jimsonweed. Others called it sacred datura. That didn't help with the stupid kids. That word, "sacred," it gave them the idea they'd have a life-altering religious experience when they left their skin and flew over mountains. What they did was wake up in the ER with tubes in their arms and puke on their chest.

Someone sneezed from the same direction as the sounds of the television and dishes. A pine scent drifted on the breeze and she remembered the juniper and pinyon trees in neighbors' yards.

The air was cooling but she wouldn't need a sleeping bag. It had been a warm night like this when Chase had staked out his backyard camp. Maybe he'd crawled out of his sleeping bag when he got hot and lain on top. Maybe he'd pulled on his pants for the little warmth his legs would need. His mother had seen him rolling his pants up before he'd crawled into his sleeping bag, but he was wearing them when dog walkers found his body on the crushed cactus.

A whiff of ammonia. A cat jumped from a neighbor's roof onto the wall. Orange eyes glowed, then the head turned away and she saw the animal in profile disappearing behind the skeletons of thorn bushes.

A garage door banged shut. A car alarm sounded and someone cursed. The alarm went silent. Laughter. Kids on skateboards in the street, hard wheels clacking on rough pavement. No, they were on the sidewalk. Bang! Three times. Three kids on skateboards launching off a curb.

They'd looked closely at the Easterlings. The table Chase had used for a ladder—he had to have pushed it into place. The Easterlings said it was usually next to the grill. But they said they hadn't heard just outside their bedroom window the awful scraping and grinding of metal against concrete when Lewis had repeated what Chase must have done. Even with the swamp cooler running and the windows closed you could near the sound indoors.

They were not heavy sleepers. Mom admitted to having trouble sleeping that night. They both used ear plugs and eye shades. Sometimes they used a sleep aid, over the counter, nothing very potent. Not accustomed to the sounds of the city, they said. They'd moved up here from empty Catron County down south, their ranch fifty miles outside

Reserve on the Plains of San Augustin where their trucks were the only vehicles on the dirt road ending at their corrals. Where there were thousands more elk than people. Down there they slept with windows open. In Santa Fe, they locked everything tight before lights out. For air they ran the swamp cooler, fan only, all night.

Chase's teachers reported no reason to suspect mistreatment. He was always well dressed, a hot breakfast in him when he came to school, unlike classmates who got their cereal in the school cafeteria. From neighbors what detectives heard most often was, "More families should be like them. We wouldn't have so many bad kids on the street."

Medical records showed no history suggesting physical abuse.

Dad and Mom didn't drink or use drugs except the Advil PM or Benadryl to help them sleep. They attended a Baptist church regularly. The marriage was good. Both parents had jobs. They were better off, if not happier, with steadier incomes from city jobs than when they had tried ranching.

But Dad had a temper and had threatened federal officials.

That came from the Catron County Sheriff, who used to have coffee with Chance Easterling. *A hundred men with a hundred rifles* is what Chance had sworn he'd have waiting for the Forest Service when they came to round up his cattle. He'd shot up the sign at the Forest Service office in Reserve, the sheriff was sure but couldn't prove it. He'd jammed potatoes in the exhaust of USFS vehicles at wolf hearings so they wouldn't start. He'd stood up at those hearings and said a revolution was coming, people could only take so much.

USFS Law Enforcement had a file on him, but not enough to take to the US attorney. The closest he came to being arrested was when a dead wolf was found on his allotment in the Aldo Leopold Wilderness. Shot with a thirty-aught-six from a Remington Model 700. Chance Easterling had that kind of rifle and wouldn't let it be test fired. The LEOs didn't have probable cause for a warrant to seize the weapon. Another wolf was shot in the Blue Range in Arizona with the same kind of rifle at a time when Chance was in Truth or Consequences at a wolf hearing, standing up from his chair calling on men with rifles to join him on his ranch.

Something flew low overhead, buzzing and clicking. Aragon felt it stirring the air and ducked. It happened again, another shadow across the stars for a second.

Drones. They were bringing in drones to watch Cervantes. She wasn't sure where they'd come from. Cannon AFB in Clovis remotely controlled drones in Afghanistan and Iraq. Another shadow passed, coming from the direction of the Santa Fe airport and heading east.

More sounds Chase Easterling had not heard. She forced herself to concentrate on the space enclosed by the cinderblock walls and the back of the house, and the sounds coming at her from the city beyond.

Damn. More of that ammonia smell. This time a fat bully boy of a cat on another wall, swaggering, spraying the thorn bushes, hissing at something she couldn't see.

She poured coffee from a thermos and ate a second cold Lotaburger. The first one, with fries and still hot out of the bag, had been her dinner hours ago. The Coleman lantern she'd brought hissed and roared when she fired it up. She wouldn't hear anything. She killed the gas and strapped a headlamp over her buzz cut.

Spread on the sleeping bag she wouldn't use were aerial photographs of the Easterlings' neighborhood. The photos were several years old but little had changed. The Easterlings' patio was identifiable, as was the dot that was their outdoor grill. Even the sandbox in the corner could be seen. The weeds and the moonflowers hadn't sprouted yet. The yard looked like a place where you might want to spend time. The walls were blocked from view by the pyracantha, but in the aerial view they spread like a maze across backyards to the edge of the street. And there was an aerial view of the Santa Fe Canyon Preserve, the dirt parking lot, trees, foliage thickening where water flowed. Where Chase had been found.

She didn't know what she'd expected to find and put the photos aside. Better to reread interviews of neighbors, the newspaper carrier, the municipal waste workers who'd been on the street that morning.

Better to think about the tar on Chase's sneakers that no one understood.

The house she'd grown up in had a flat roof. She remembered her father and brothers fixing it after a snowy winter when melt water made their living room ceiling bulge. Gravel and hot tar finished the job.

Back to the aerial photo of the neighborhood. She saw only pitched shingled roofs.

What would the boy have been doing on a roof anyway?

Maybe the killer had transported him in the back of a truck used for roofing work. The equipment for heating and spreading the tar, it could make a mess. She made a note to learn if anyone in the neighborhood was having roofing work done at the time.

Now cats were fighting. She couldn't read. She went to the cinderblock wall and yelled for them to shut up. More cats joined the fray. She picked up a rock and climbed onto the table against the gate. One foot, then another on the wall. Where were those critters? There in the bushes ... and she nailed one. It shrieked and bolted, two other cats chasing after it.

Man, the ammonia smell. These cats claiming territory. It was unbearable back here. How could people stand it?

Wait. It hadn't smelled this bad when she and Lewis had looked over the walls before. It hadn't smelled this way when she'd rolled out her sleeping bag before dusk. That terrible cat smell, it didn't come and go with the sun.

That was when she heard the rush of air, like steam escaping, and a fresh wave of the ammonia stench, her skin a little sticky like there was suddenly moisture in the air.

She sidestepped along the wall to get past the pyracantha and came to an intersection dividing four backyards. The rush of escaping steam came from straight ahead. A stretch of wall fifty feet long led in the direction of the sound. She gave up sidling and walked it, heel to toe, the same walk she'd ordered hundreds of drivers to do when she'd worn a uniform, but not on a cinderblock wall seven feet in the air. Another yard, another fifty feet of wall. Then another stretch, looking at dark windows on the backs of houses, some branches in the way, an arbor vitae that needed pruning, and she was seeing a flat roof just a little higher than the wall, with an open hatch, thick steam rushing into the cooler night sky, lights inside there, and she knew what it was.

Someone was cooking meth.

The aerials had not shown this building. This was too new. Now she saw Chase Easterling doing what she had just done. A curious boy, lying there under his sheet, hearing new sounds, strange smells, and going exploring. Maybe having an easier time of it on the tops of stacked cinder blocks than she did and coming to this same spot but not understanding what he was seeing and smelling.

Voices in there. Heavy metal from a cheap radio. She pushed through the thick branches, sap on her hands—

Holy crap, there was sap on Chase's palms and pants and they thought it had been picked up when he'd been dragged to the side of the creek—

Inching forward now on hands and knees, the light in the hatch coming closer, feeling warmer air, hot even, rising against her forehead.

Eyes over the edge. Two men below her. Work tables. Beakers. Scales. Propane tanks. What looked like a carton of cold and allergy medicine. A lot more smells than ammonia. The idiots were smoking as they worked.

A guy with stringy hair, a bony face, drew hard on his cigarette, head tilting back ...

She pulled away from the opening and heard, "Fucking kids again." A door flew open below and she saw the edge of the ladder now against the roofline. A hand coming up. Another hand holding a gun. The top of a head. Rising. Eyes locking on her.

"Hey, you!" yelled the guy with stringy hair had who tilted his head back when he sucked hard on his cigarette. "Don't fucking move."

And she remembered her gun was locked in her car in the East-erlings' driveway.

NINE

LEWIS HEARD ARAGON'S CALL, patched through to every cop in Santa Fe. Officer taking fire, shots in the background, her voice full of pain. The dispatcher shouting, then controlling herself. Are you hit? Aragon saying she was bleeding bad. Have you been shot, Detective? What is the nature of your injuries? More gun shots. Aragon, quieter, giving her location close to an address he recognized, the Easterling house, but on another street, the one beyond the family's backyard.

He didn't check with the FBI before he ran to his car, abandoning the roadblock down the hill from the Valles house and accelerating without lights until he'd covered several blocks and blown all stop signs.

SFPD cars appeared in the rearview, leaving the Feds alone with the hostage scene. Overhead one of the helicopters, State Police most likely, moved with him, its searchlight sweeping ahead. Now another helicopter following. He saw a television station's letters on the underside.

Aragon's voice again on the radio. She'd broken her arm, a compound fracture, she said, couldn't move her legs. She was losing blood. The dispatcher was back to shouting, are you hit? Aragon kept repeating she was bleeding and getting dizzy and cold. Static, the sound of things breaking, crashing. You could hear her struggling for breath, long pauses between her words. *I've … locked them … out. Meth … lab in here.* Men's voices shouting. Shots fired, pinging off metal. A groan.

And no more of Aragon's voice.

He knew exactly where he was going. He and Aragon had both canvassed that street door to door. He remembered the one house he'd gone to with the ugly yard, weeds, dead hedges, standing out from the green lawns and pretty gardens. At the painted doors with flower pots on the stoop older people had answered, polite, glad to help the police, horrified at what had happened to the Easterling boy. At the house with the dead yard, a woman with the side of her head shaved, long orange hair brushed over the bald, had talked through the screen. That wasn't unusual, but he remembered it because it was the opposite of how the neighbors had responded. That unsightly house was a rental. The other houses were owner occupied.

He led the patrol cars, using his emergency lights instead of taking a hand from the wheel to slap a flasher on the roof. The three patrol cars on his rear bumper shooting white and blue light in every direction gave enough warning to anyone ahead.

He was in the right street now. His headlights picked out two men running from behind a house to a Japanese car at the curb. He stopped in front of the vehicle just as the driver put it into gear. The patrol car that had been behind him swung sideways to keep it from reversing. The other patrol cars hemmed in what he now recognized as a Nissan Sentra, pinned against the curb by a semicircle of police cars. Officers crouched behind doors, behind hoods and engine blocks.

The shooting started before he could get out from behind the wheel. He saw a muzzle flash, a gun out the Sentra's driver's window, the door opening and a leg emerging. A bullet through his windshield and he dove for the blacktop as cops fired back. When he came up to his knee, aiming his own weapon, the shooting was over. The driver, a man with long stringy hair hiding his face, was dead on the sidewalk. The passenger was trying to crawl, collapsing, now pulling himself with his hands and dragging his legs along the ground. Stopping when a police officer put his boot on his gun hand.

Aragon.

A flat-topped building, a guest-house, a mother-in-law quarters, something like that, was burning in the backyard. Sparks shot through an opening in the roof. A window shattered and flames curled into the night. The door was locked from the inside. The handle burned his fingers.

Lewis sensed people behind him. "Is she in there?" someone asked.

Lewis threw his shoulder into the door and staggered back. It was solid core. The door jamb was steel.

"Denise!"

The roar of flames venting from an opening in the roof drowned out his voice.

A female officer had a hand axe. What she was doing with an axe Lewis didn't stop to ask. He took it from her and swung it against the door handle. The axe rang in his hand. He swung again and a space opened between the ring holding the handle and the door. Another blow and the handle pulled away. Lewis twisted it loose. He reached inside with his fingers, feeling for the lock pins, realizing the door knob on the other side had fallen off.

He heard a voice, Aragon calling for help, very close to the door.

"I need a screwdriver," he shouted to the uniforms behind him. "Pliers. I can't get the lock free."

A crowbar came over his shoulder and he took it, wedging it into the remains of the lock and leveraging it against the door. He felt it give. Metal hit concrete and the door eased open and Aragon was there on her stomach, blood all over one side, something white tearing through her shirt. Jesus, that was a bone.

Lewis and another officer pulled her out of the doorway. Lewis cradled her in his arms, careful not to jostle the mangled arm. She was mumbling something about her back and legs. He shouldn't move her but he saw propane tanks inside, flames spreading toward them, something flowing across the floor. He turned for the street with Aragon in his arms, tight against his chest, as the little building exploded, searing his back. Officers behind him screamed but he forgot them and ran.

Sergeant Perez was in his Crown Vic, in pajamas, on his beaded seat cushion, engine running, the back door thrown open. Other officers stood over the body of the dead shooter. The wounded man was still in the street, an officer applying pressure to a hip wound.

Lewis looked at his own car, blocked by police vehicles that had arrived after him. Perez was yelling he'd take her and Lewis was thinking he could walk Aragon faster to the ER than Perez would drive.

"Come on, Rick, let's go." Perez waving him forward, looking angry. Lewis laid Aragon out in Perez's back seat, making sure she was flat. He threw the door shut and slapped the trunk. Perez took off, burning rubber to get going, the Ford's big engine revving loud.

Lewis's phone rang.

"Sarge?" Lewis answered the call, Perez's taillights moving away fast, not slowing as he weaved through cars where officers had stopped and jumped out.

"Denise did it again. I knew she would. The dead shitbird had a Boy Scout thing in his pocket for a money clip, I guess you call it a slide for a bandana. It was the boy's, with his name. The Easterling kid."

Down the street, Pop Perez took the corner on two wheels, still talking.

————————

While Martin Kilgore argued over the phone with the FBI director, this other FBI agent, a woman named Adams who had come on the plane with Danny, caught Sam Baca Valles alone and asked him not about his wife, his two boys who must be terrified, the maniac in his house, or how he was holding up. Instead it was, "What can you tell us about Denise Aragon? Can you think of any reason she might harbor hostile feelings toward you? When was the last time you had any contact with her?"

Valles wondered what Denise Aragon looked like now. He'd seen photographs in the newspaper, what, a decade ago when she'd moved up from driving a patrol car to detective? A couple times on the television when she broke a big case. A lot of coverage for that Cody Geronimo business, proving New Mexico's all-around favorite and very, very wealthy artist liked to put pieces of women in his freaky statues. *The Santa Fe Mexican* also gave her front page attention whenever she'd been sued for knocking somebody in the head.

What had happened to her hair? In college it had been long and thick, almost as long as his own the end of freshman year. Now it was either boot camp buzz or a black wig when she was in court. The baby-big eyes, too, they'd changed. Still pretty enough to keep your focus on her face instead of drifting down her body to see what was there. Denise never had huge tits. But she'd been cute, a tight, trim figure with enough curves to make you wonder what she looked like without clothes.

Now, as with her hair, she'd changed her body. So many of the girls from college had grown fat and round. Aragon had turned into all shoulders and arms. He remembered her looking good in shorts throwing a Frisbee on UNM's Johnson Field. She'd spend her weekends running the Sandia foothills or biking the Turquoise Trail just for a beer at the Mine Shaft in Madrid. What was that for a cold Coors, over a hundred-mile round trip? A "century," Aragon called it, and a lot of it was climbing out of the Rio Grande Valley into the mountains. She was lean then. The muscle she carried now must have come with being a cop.

Denise Aragon a cop. She had talked about "her dream" but he'd never believed it. He got busy campaigning for student council, building his base, working on city council campaigns, getting to know the congressman representing Santa Fe, the job he wanted as soon as he turned twenty-five. Instead he'd run for the Senate, after the white guy who'd held the job for decades retired soon after being spotted wandering the Senate chambers late at night in a nightshirt. He'd lost track of her except when she popped up in the news, and that's what he told the FBI agent. That and, sorry, he had no more to say about Denise Aragon.

She shot people now. Last year she killed the Silva twins, guys who'd contributed to his campaign and private charity through their wives, never in their own names. The Silvas could be counted on to deliver some key precincts. The widows weren't letting their money go anymore and had quit politics. Martin said they still didn't have anyone reliable to deliver the Agua Fria neighborhood in the next election but he was working on it.

And here he was, flying in this VIP Air Force jet to a situation he never could have imagined. Some maniac holding his wife and kids hostage, demanding his life in exchange. He'd been told not to call his wife's cell phone. That was the line of communication with this Cervantes lunatic. But he wanted to ignore the FBI and talk to his family and know they weren't hurt. He was worried about Patricia and Clint and Jimmy. God, they must be terrified.

He hoped a sniper shot Cervantes in the head.

He saw his Santa Fe house, where he hadn't slept in close to a year. Patricia said it needed new windows and a lot more. She was going to hire the guy that had done the remodel for the prior owners. He'd worked all the houses on the street. She'd seen his van in neighbors' driveways and they said good things about Cervantes and Sons Construction.

He'd been in the room to hear her end when she made the call: *Mr. Cervantes, this is Patricia Valles. Yes, the senator's wife. We'd like you to come to our house and give us an estimate on some work we're thinking of doing. You've come highly recommended.*

Since then, Patricia had expanded the scope of work to the point where he was thinking maybe just tear the old mud house down. Build something modern, with electrical outlets in every room, square rooms, floors that were even, plumbing they could count on to work. Everyday for months Cervantes had been showing up on the job to replace the windows, retile the bath, put in new countertops—visions coming into Patricia's head every minute. With each swing of his hammer, each squeeze of the caulk gun, Cervantes was getting closer to making that insane call Danny Luna took.

He'd been using all that time in their house to get ready for this. The Valles family had been paying him to do it.

Denise Aragon.

He went to the back of the plane where Martin Kilgore was snoring, strapped into his seat, mouth open and cheek against the window. Across from him the Luna kid was wide awake, listening to earphones. Perking up now. Slipping the earphones off, tinny music escaping.

Valles said, "Danny, you got everything you need?"

"Yes, sir, Senator Valles. It's all good."

No it isn't, you stupid kid.

"That's great, Danny. You need to eat, just help yourself in the galley. Booze, too, if you want. They stock good Scotch on these planes."

"I couldn't drink now."

"Whiskey for breakfast. After listening to some Dixie dum-dum read Dr. Seuss and Webster all night because he's so short on votes and friends he has to filibuster, after watching all-night returns—I won by a thousand and one votes my first Senate race—you get to like a jolt in the a.m."

"You want me to drink."

"Enjoy a good snort on the American taxpayer, then find a seat to sleep it off. Somewhere else," Valles said. "Martin and I need to talk."

When the kid was gone, Valles tapped his foot on Kilgore's ankle. Kilgore burbled, rubbed his face, and was awake. He could do that, fall into deep sleep for five minutes, an hour, then be instantly alert. Like a cat.

"Someone from my past has come up," Valles said. "She knows things."

———

Tyson Dix, wearing his tactical vest with extra magazines velcroed to his thigh, caught Art Helmick dozing at the desk in his panel truck. Helmick's head lay between two cell phones, with a notebook for a pillow. He started at the sound of Dix closing the door and adjusted the glasses on his nose. He must be near blind, Tyson thought. Lenses thick like safety glass. Don't count on him making a close shot at distance. That's why he's a talker.

"Where's Magnano?" Dix asked, wondering if she was sleeping on a bench in the back behind the bathroom closet. His men on the ground, ordered to stay alert with eyes pressed against scopes, were getting irritated. Watching constantly for scorpions they were told came out at night and sought warm places, like pant legs. During the day the sun frying them, and getting colder at night than you'd think after roasting for twelve hours. And the jaw flappers were dozing in air conditioning waiting for a call from the loon in the house.

"Making inquiries," Helmick said, standing now, stretching his arms to the ceiling, bending side to side. Now wiping his nose with the back of his hand. "We're starting to get a picture of Mr. Cervantes."

Next he's going to tell me how hard it is sitting in a chair for hours fighting boredom. What did they call it, cauliflower ear? A job-related injury for people who worked phones instead of bolt actions.

Helmick polished those thick lenses with a soft cloth from his pocket and said, "Want coffee? How do you take it?"

"Intravenously," Dix said. "Nothing from Cervantes?" But he knew the answer. Last report, Helmick had been the one calling repeatedly to Patricia Valles's phone and the house's landline with none of the guys in there picking up.

Guys in the house. That's what he'd come to tell Helmick. But Helmick had something for him first.

"You hear about that Detective Aragon, the one who was Cervantes's grief counselor?"

"I heard about the firefight. Was that her, the one who was in here not long after we set up?"

"She nearly got killed in a meth lab explosion. But looks like she got the shits who killed a little kid. She's in the hospital and not leaving soon. We'll know where she is when we're ready to talk again."

"Magnano's inquiries, they're about this Aragon?"

Helmick poured two coffees, his in a mug that said *Listen, Understand, Act*. He held a cup out for Dix, who took it without using the handle.

"You have something for me?" Helmick asked.

Really, this duty wasn't too bad. The desert was dry, no bugs. The sky was pretty, the wind calm. Thin air, and hot, but not like the jungle where your sweat made a trigger slippery. Excellent conditions if they had to take a shot. And you could get good coffee just by knocking on the negotiators' door. Last time, in Maine with the fisherman holding his family in his leaky boat at the end of a rotting dock, it was rain and sleet. When the sun broke through so did the black flies and chiggers. Every man had a stitch line of chigger bites inside the waistband of his underwear and blood on the back of his neck where the flies ate while he stared through the scope. Positions too far from town to get hot food. Slugs crawling up your sleeves when you stayed still.

The food here wasn't bad. He'd order Mexican for his men. Or take-out from this Lotaburger outfit he'd seen in several places driving in.

"We did an IR scan with the drones," he told Helmick. "The infrared is blocked by most of the plywood Cervantes put up in the windows. That's unusual, as if he's added insulation to blind us."

"So he knows what he's up against?"

"Or it could be thicker wood, or metal. But a couple windows we could see through the plywood. The drones got in close above that courtyard in the center of the house. Two significant heat signatures at opposite ends of the building."

"There should be more than that."

"I'd bet the hostages are locked inside an inner room where we can't see. That leaves us with two bad guys to worry about. The body-heat images are too big for kids. I understand Mrs. Valles is rather large in the seat cushion department, but pretty short. These are too tall for her."

"Two men?"

"Count on it. One is huge, a big dude."

"Where are they now, these large heat signatures?"

"We knew where they were a half hour ago. But they've disappeared. We can't get any IR read inside the house. It's as though the peepholes we had were closed."

"Now you see me, now you don't. The only windows we can see through and they show us two images to make us think two men. Now we're blind."

"They can take shifts. They can sleep."

"This could last longer than most situations." Helmick drained his cup and poured a refill. "And don't think I was sleeping, Ty, when you walked in. This medication to make me stop sneezing might keep me from operating heavy equipment. That wasn't it. I was trying to see this Cervantes."

"I'm trying to see him, too." Dix held his empty for a refill. "With crosshairs on the base of his skull."

"Is that how we should be talking? I haven't exchanged ten words with this guy yet."

"You know the words that matter to him. *The senator for his family*. One life for three. How does Mr. Pete Cervantes come off that opening offer?"

"You just told me it's two guys." Helmick slid a sheet of blank paper into the center of the round table and drew the outline of two heads with question marks inside. "Two guys are going to have to see this through to the end. Those dynamics give us something to work with. It's always harder dealing with one determined loser. That's what they are, losers in one way or another."

"As in, lose your son to a man who shouldn't have been in this country if the politicians had let law enforcement do its job? The entire country failed Pete Cervantes," Dix said. "There's nothing to debate about that. The easiest way to end this is blow out his medulla. That may be the hardest trigger pull my guys are ever asked to try. But they'll do it because of the kids in there, and a woman who doesn't deserve this just because she's married to one of the culprits of Capitol Hill."

Helmick let that go and taped his drawing to a wall of the truck, next to photos of Pete Cervantes with his sons, the dead wife, and his employees posing for an ad that ran on the back of telephone books.

"You and I were at Waco," Dix said. "Young pups. Lots of potential dissenting voices inside that compound, lots to play with. Long conversations with a couple of the loons."

"I remember."

"So how many walked out after all the talking?" Dix dropped his cup in a plastic tub with other dirty dishes. "Thanks for the joe. I'm gonna do my rounds with my gun teams, make sure nobody's been bit by scorpions." He paused at the door. "A US senator walking across that open space, us knowing there's a chambered .338 Lapua magnum in a rifle sighted on his face. Neither one of us is seeing it. The director isn't either, I guarantee you. Find some way to get Cervantes and his sidekick out in the open."

TEN

CERVANTES DIALED ARAGON ON one of his pre-paid cells. He had a sock full of them from Walmart. He'd read how the FBI would "capture"—a word that said a lot more than "intercept"—all calls from any phone lines inside a hostage house. He knew they'd capture the cell subscribed in his name, and Patricia Valles's phone, and the house's landline and anything over the DSL. They might detect a signal from any cell phone he'd used just once and be able to capture that, too. He didn't know what all they could do. He'd paid cash in Santa Fe, Espanola, Albuquerque, Rio Rancho, he couldn't remember where else, for a bunch of phones he'd use once and put under a sledge hammer.

He was still seeing Aragon going into the FBI truck, a superior officer escorting her to even higher authorities. He wanted to tell her he was sorry for pointing a gun at her. Maybe he could explain himself so she'd understand. Remembering her across from him at the restaurant; ignoring the waiter wanting to go home, she'd listened without any sign she noticed anything but the pain he was sharing. The sudden softness in her eyes, a change from what was usually there. But it had been that other look that told him she understood, the one she wore while he talked of his anger, his sense of helplessness, of wanting to hit something that counted. More than cop's eyes. He saw her understanding pain and rage. Knowing what it was to lose someone and be dumped on by, what do you call it, "the system"—a phrase that seemed so Sixties. That system was supposed to be on your side. We were supposed to believe in it. It was what held everything together, what kept us from being animals tearing at each other. In exchange, we gave it our loyalty, our taxes, the life of a son dying in a stupid war so far from home.

She'd never revealed what was buried inside, but it wasn't far from the surface when they got away from other cops and lawyers and courtrooms. In their quiet talks she let it show. Almost tears a couple times. Almost. He didn't think she let anyone see her cry.

She'd helped him and now he'd hurt her. The way her superior held the door for her, like a father telling a kid get in here, I want to talk to you.

He'd never let anyone know she had given him the idea for this. He didn't want her ever getting that idea either. His call was ringing, ringing when a man answered.

"This is Detective Aragon's phone. May I help you?"

In the background, excited voices. Somebody shouting, "Nurse!" Another voice, "Get this one to surgery." Cervantes listened to the sounds, wondering who was answering for Aragon and where she was.

The male voice persisted. "Hello, who is this?"

Cervantes hung up and put that phone aside for the sledgehammer in the garage.

He checked the cameras to see if anything outside had changed. In the books he'd studied about how the FBI handled hostage situations, he'd learned something that had him worried. Somewhere in the South, a man had taken a kid into an underground bunker and the FBI had been able to see and listen to everything going on. The books, written by FBI men who'd been there, made a point of not saying how they'd done that. Some kind of probe, fiber optics, he didn't know.

He did know the FBI had men with rifles pointing at the house. He'd located the ones behind the landscaping rocks at the corner of the property, another team on the neighbor's house behind a swamp cooler. Probably there were snipers concealed in the arroyo that ran on the north, just deep enough to hide a man squatting on his haunches.

He checked his monitors. For now, the FBI was keeping its distance. It was good he could follow the news on television, showing him things his own cameras couldn't pick up. So far, he hadn't seen the man who had called, Helmick, talking to any reporter. He wanted to see Helmick's face. He always met the clients, the subcontractors, suppliers he was considering before going another step. The picky homeowners, the wives who would be looking over his shoulder, the old men setting up lawn chairs to watch him work, take their own tests of cement, drop plum lines along the framing his crews raised, they thought they were interviewing him. They had it backward. He was sizing them up, deciding how much of a headache the job would be, whether he should charge weekly for time and materials or trust them with a down payment now, the balance later. And whether he needed to add an aggravation adjustment to his bid.

He wanted to see Helmick. More than that, he wanted to see Valles standing in the driveway.

The news reports gave him a sense of what was out there. From the books, he had a pretty good idea. He knew about the division in the FBI forces, the negotiators—Helmick's crew—being one team and the shooters the other. He knew about some of their tools. The high-resolution lens that would allow them to inspect every inch of the house without coming close. Another kind of camera, the infra-red imaging that let them look through walls to identify warm bodies. This old adobe, he was positive, with its thick mud walls, some two feet thick, would block any heat fingerprints except from the windows. He'd just now covered the last two with insulation on the inside, behind the plywood and tin he'd put over the glass. They'd had a peek inside. He hoped so. Let them know he wasn't alone.

This secret probe thing, that he had to stay on top of. Let them peek and guess. But he didn't want them watching and listening to him inside this house.

There at the bottom of the screen on the television a banner scrolled about a gun battle involving a Santa Fe Police detective. One suspect killed, another critical. A meth lab exploding. A detective taken to the hospital with multiple injuries and burns.

More going on in Santa Fe tonight than his show. He hoped the detective in the news wasn't Aragon. But the sounds on her phone, they made him feel the way it was in the emergency room when his son had been shot.

Time to make his rounds then get some sleep. Four hours. He'd set his watch. He left his control room, what he was calling his bank of monitors in the dining room, and went down the hall to the door where he had Patricia Valles and her sons. He'd expected the boys to cry. He hadn't expected them to be angry at their mom for what was happening. Like it was her fault, the man meeting them inside the house with a gun when they got back from Ojo Caliente where Mrs. Valles had been taking the spa and hot springs. The nice man who had been working on their house now marching them to the windowless room, telling them to shut up. They were mad at Mom. Brats. His sons had never behaved like that.

He checked the lock. Secure. No way in or out but this door. An interior room, built for storage, none of its walls connecting to the outside. He'd given them their bathroom break an hour ago, the boys no longer whining, now scared. He let them out one at a time, Patricia last. She had looked at him and said, "Why?" She was past "don't hurt us." Now she wanted information.

He rattled the door so she would know he was here but faced down the hall to the other half of the house. He shouted, "Bobo, you doing alright? You want me to bring you something to eat? Sandwich or tamales? There's still pizza." He headed back to his control room without an answer. He wanted another look at the gun team in the arroyo. A pipe that drained rainwater surfaced about where they were hiding. It ran inside the walls, then underground; an opening he couldn't see led back to where he was standing. Maybe that was how they were going to get eyes and ears inside the house without coming closer. Who knew what they had to play with?

————

Patricia Valles heard Cervantes on the other side of the door yelling to Bobo. She'd been hearing voices in the hallway since their contractor had put a gun in her face, told her boys to shut up, and locked them in the storage room. She'd called him Mr. Cervantes every time they'd met to discuss the remodel. She'd trusted him, giving him the run of the house. A key, the security code, the password in case he tripped the alarm and had to explain when the home security company called.

He'd been busy while they'd been away at Ojo Caliente for her mud and massages. He'd started off by installing energy efficient windows, low-flow toilets, LED lighting, and replacing the forced air with ductless heating and cooling. Radiant heating for the master bath. She'd been looking forward to that. This ancient house froze solid in the winter. The floors were an icy pavement.

In the storage room he'd rolled out futons. Toys from the boys' rooms. Extra underwear for all of them and a hamper for the soiled stuff. A five-gallon water jug and plastic cups. Huge packages of snacks like you see at Costco. Five pounds of cashews, five pounds of Twizzler red licorice, two pounds of Triscuits.

The book from her night table, too. Thoughtful guy, this one. But it creeped her out picturing him sneaking around her bedroom, thinking of her, planning, completely at liberty to do what he wanted to get ready for this.

Shouting outside the door about sandwiches and tamales. Cervantes wanted to know if Bobo was hungry. She hadn't seen the other man yet but felt him in the house. They'd rolled something heavy down the hallway and she'd heard them talking to each other and Cervantes saying the name "Bobo." It was what she called her uncles. There'd been a country sheriff down south named Bobo, more a politician who delivered the old Hispanic families to the polls than a lawman. Her mother's neighbor up in Taos had a pit bull named Bobo. It's what they'd called the stupid kids in school.

Who was this Bobo?

Pete Cervantes had introduced the men on his crew and the subcontractors. He'd had that nice, friendly way that led you to think you could trust a man like that. She didn't remember any of his crew though he'd introduced them like family. She dealt with Cervantes. He was in charge of all those men. They were his concern.

She wondered when she'd see Bobo and worried that might not be a good thing.

"Mom, I need to pee."

Clint grabbing his penis through his pants, a chocolate smear at the corner of his mouth.

Pete Cervantes had been considerate to give them a camp potty for emergencies between scheduled walks to the bathroom. Such a nice man, smiling, waving the gun.

She led the boy to the miniature crapper with the plastic bag under the seat. She told him to pretend they were camping. Clint didn't like it. He wanted a real toilet. Jimmy wanted a sandwich and milk and a television. He didn't want to sleep on the floor. This wasn't real camping and he didn't believe her.

More shouting in the hallway. Clint now joining Jimmy in demanding a sandwich and milk. Jimmy throwing his Game Boy across the room, saying he wanted to go out. Clint wanting out, too, looking for something to throw, kicking the potty instead but she caught it before it went over on its side.

She had some shouting of her own to do.

With her face an inch from the door to the hallway, she shouted, "What do you want? We've done nothing to hurt you. Please let us go. At least my children." She pounded on the door. "Mr. Cervantes, this is madness. It's not right."

She heard hurried footsteps. They stopped on the other side of the door.

"Mr. Cervantes, you're a better man than this," she said. "Whatever is bothering you, this won't fix it. You'll only make things worse."

Speaking clearly, taking his time so she could hear every word through the door, Cervantes said, "It's not me you need to be worried about. What kind of man is your husband?"

ELEVEN

Sergeant Perez was covered in red cowboys and Indians. He sat on an orange plastic chair, legs crossed, cheaters on his nose, reading a file.

"Are you in jammies?" Aragon asked, and the back of her throat was raw.

Perez pushed the glasses further down his nose and squinted. She blinked back. Her throat felt like it had been raked. Here was somebody who might be Lewis, a big wavy thing with light behind him. It was a waterfall. No, an ocean on its side. What the hell. She concentrated. Was that Lewis? He came closer and she saw his face and was sure it was him.

"What did you say?" Perez, pulling the orange chair to her bed, cowboys and Indians dancing on his shoulders.

She tried talking again and Lewis and Perez looked at each other and shrugged.

"They pumped her full of some very good shit," Lewis said and she realized she was in a hospital bed. The ocean on its side was a green-blue curtain; the waves were folds.

Perez said, "How do you feel? Do the burns hurt?"

Hey guys, she tried. Nothing came out. *What burns?* Her throat hurt and she was wondering what had been shoved inside her.

Lewis turned his back and she saw bandages on his head and neck. His ears were taped except for little holes so he could hear.

"You're not driving, Rick. They pumped you full, too. Call for a ride when you're ready to go." Perez now leaned in close to put a hand on her shoulder. "Denise, you in there?"

She tried again for words and squeezed out, "I can't feel my legs." She heard it in her ears, not just inside her head, and knew it was real because Perez was yelling for a doctor.

She couldn't move her right arm but had that figured out. A cast ran from her arm pit to her wrist, the elbow bent so the limb lay across her chest. Perez had turned into a bear. No, he was gone. That was her brother Javier sleeping in the orange chair. Snores came from the other side of the room. Dim light from a cracked door to the hall showed Perez slumped on the floor, his back against a wall, case files on his legs. He'd fallen asleep, his chin on his chest and, yes, those were pajamas with cowboys and Indians.

A cart rolling in the hall woke Perez. He stirred, lifted his chin, and cast a sideward glance at her brother.

"He's been here all night," Perez said. "Your sister-in-law took a shift but had to get the kids to school."

"When did you get here?" Aragon croaked.

"I brought you. Sorry for the rough ride."

Perez pushed himself up, feet in socks slipping on the floor. He came to the end of her bed and touched her shin. She saw his hand there on the sheet but couldn't feel its weight. He read her mind and shook his head.

"You jammed your neck, the docs say. Compressed vertebrae. And you broke your arm. But you know that."

"Who needs x-rays? I saw the bone through my skin."

"How did you fall?"

"I jumped." She told him about diving into the hatch on top of the roof, going straight down, bouncing off a hard bench, hearing her arm snap. Looking up at two heads against the night sky and hearing, "Don't shoot, you idiot. The propane." But shots pinged off metal, concrete chips flew into her face, and she heard pressure releasing and knew the gas would settle on the floor, where she was. One arm worked but not her legs. She pulled herself around a work bench for cover and stalled out. She couldn't reach anything to drag herself forward. It must have been the propane exploding that threw her against the door. And there was Lewis, pulling her outside, and they were running and she felt his body shielding her from the heat of another explosion.

"Your right foot's burned," Perez said. "You got some of it. Lewis's back got all of it. We thought you'd been shot."

She tried to see her foot, so far away at the end of the bed. "How bad is Rick?" she asked.

"He was lucky not to be wearing one of his polyester shirts. A tropical-weight wool thing his wife got him. It didn't burn. His ears are going to peel for a month, and he's got no hair from sideburns back. Now he looks like you. But no permanent damage. I've got six other cops out with burns. That lab blew sky high. The cinderblock wall in the backyard toppled like Legos kicked across a floor."

Javier groaned, stretched, a bear stirring from hibernation. "Lil Sis. What the fuck did you do to yourself this time?"

She'd tell him later. She needed to ask a question. She needed to know.

100

"What's wrong with my legs?"

Perez and Javier did the same thing: sucked air through their teeth and avoided her eyes.

"I was hoping for better than that," she said.

"I'll get the doctor." Javier shuffled to the door. "Let him tell you so I don't get it wrong. You need clarity."

"It needs an official explanation?"

"It does," Perez said. "You could be here a very long time. But you won't get bored. I've been reading reports on the McSwaim homicide. Your friend who said our good senator raped her."

"There was a homicide investigation?" Somehow Aragon pushed herself off her pillow. The sheets slid down her chest. Did she feel something on the back of her calves? "They said Amy died of dehydration, heatstroke. She pushed it too hard on the wrong day."

"Police never looked at the medical reports. I'm telling you, Denise, it wasn't running that killed her. Something stinks. I want you to figure it out. Lewis and I will be your Runaround Sues until you're better."

"What's it take to get time off? A coma?"

"Every time you get suspended, soon as you're taken off the rotation things happen."

"You see this as an opportunity to reopen a case, not a tragic situation where one of your officers may never walk again?"

"A little fall is not going to stop you."

"Ten feet onto hard concrete is a little fall?"

Perez shrugged his shoulders. She'd never noticed how narrow and thin they were, narrower than the swell of his belly.

"You just don't want me lying here feeling sorry for myself."

Perez shrugged again. "I'll leave the files in the drawer in your bedstand."

"That case is outside our jurisdiction. Sixty miles from Santa Fe."

"Where did your friend say she was raped?"

"Valles was driving her back home to Santa Fe for spring break. She lived up by Museum Hill, before it was all built out. She said he pulled into an empty lot and locked the doors."

"A possible homicide following a rape in our jurisdiction, we've got us a case. And you've got something to think about besides your legs."

———————

She heard the doctor, a Turkish or Iranian woman with an expensive hairdo, twelve inches of lush black curls piled on top of her head and heels below her white jacket, say she might be able to walk again. The trauma to her spinal column would resolve in time. Or it wouldn't. Or it would take longer than they could predict, spinal cord injuries being great unknowns to the world of medicine.

Clarity. Just what Javier said she needed.

Then her mind was on what Perez hadn't explained before this woman brought her long legs and olive skin into the room. Thinking about a case was better than being scared by what the doctor was saying: "We must address substantial inflammation to prevent a buildup of scar tissue that could impinge the spinal column and induce sensory loss."

But she was hearing again the news that Amy McSwaim had died on the way to the hospital. Amy had been found on the backside of the Sandia Mountains near the end of a marathon-plus-ten at almost two miles elevation in the middle of a crazy hot July day. It had been Amy's way to celebrate her birthday and laugh at another year closer to the end of it all. Amy ran south to north along the entire mountain range, starting in Tijeras Canyon, climbing, climbing, skirting South Sandia peak at the alpine meadows, dropping into passes and gaps, climbing back into the sun on rocky slopes. Then the killer hump to the Tram, the halfway point. This was the harder way, because of that lung buster. Most people who attempted this went the other direction.

Amy threw in loops to add mileage. She ran alone because that was her only option. No one else could keep up or wanted to try.

With gal pals, Aragon had hooked up with Amy at the top of the Tram. They took the cable car up, bought themselves beers, and waited for the girl with strong legs and red hair to trot out of the woods. They had a pint ready when she found their table. She tried to resist. They made her join the toast to the strongest, toughest, nuttiest, prettiest woman in New Mexico above 10,500 feet.

They'd shuttled her car to the Tunnel Springs parking area at the northern terminus of her run, a beer cooler waiting on the back seat. The keys were hidden atop the left rear tire. That was over eleven miles past the Tram, not counting Amy's add-ons, just about all of it at high elevation before hitting the full force of the mid-afternoon sun during the descent. Amy would meet them after showering, for dinner and more beer.

Patricia had taken the call on her cell phone. Amy would be missing dinner.

"After the inflammation subsides," the doctor was saying, "and we ease you off steroids, we hope to have you walking. Unless there was damage to the spinal column we can't see right now." More clarity. But Aragon's mind was in the mountains on a blistering hot day. "You should remain off your feet for at least a month, Miss Aragon, if all goes well. Please do not sit up again on your own. That may guarantee you'll be immobile for the longest term, which is permanently. Let me adjust your pillow. It should be supporting, not turning, your head."

Aragon lifted herself on her elbows, then let herself down with a gasp at the stabbing pains in her lower back.

The beautiful doctor smiled. "Enjoy the pain. It's a gift."

"Pain is clarity," Aragon said. "I'll take it."

She said no more so the doctor would leave. Then she thanked Javier for coming from his place in the mountains and told him to give her love to his wife. He had to get to work. Clients from Chicago were waiting at the airport and then it was a long drive to the hunting camp in the mountains.

With only Perez left behind, she said, "What are you seeing in those reports that's wrong?" Back to talking about Amy McSwaim, her mind never really registering what her physician said.

"You know the La Luz run?"

"I've run up it twice. Ran back down once. That was a mistake. My quads were jelly the next day. I rolled out of bed and collapsed on the floor."

"I was one of the guys that started the La Luz run. Never set a record, but it was a couple of us in Converse high-tops running with Indians from Jemez Pueblo. Ten miles uphill. We started lower than they do now, so we had a full mile elevation gain. Why? So we could brag about it like you just did. Then someone got the idea to have an official race with judges, stop watches, ribbons. The Indians always won. Al Waquie set the record like forty years ago. He did it in under an hour. No one's come close, even with these high-tech trail shoes and paid coaches."

"You ran La Luz?" she asked, not believing him.

"Every weekend."

Still she wasn't buying it. "What's that got to do with your seeing homicide?"

"Before La Luz became a big deal I ran the Sandia crest trails, end to end, in sweatpants and tube socks, carrying water in old Coke bottles. We munched raisins and jerky. I don't buy that someone with experience and the best equipment died the way they say Amy McSwaim did. You get to that level where you run those mountains for fun, you learn how to take care of yourself."

The Sandia crest run was right at marathon distance, and except for the first minutes, hot as hell the whole length in summer. She'd never seen any reason to give it a try.

Amy said she was going to add the ten miles so she wouldn't get bored.

"She knew the trail," Perez said. "She was in shape. Even if she was stressed or hit the wall, she could walk out. No way her death was an accident.

A women's hiking group found her off the trail, flat on her face, eating dirt, singing nursery rhymes or what they thought were nursery rhymes. None of them had the strength to carry her. It took forever to get her down the steep rocky canyon to the parking lot. Then the bumpy ride on the road the Forest Service wasn't maintaining to where a crew of EMTs could meet them. Amy died three miles out from University Hospital in Albuquerque.

"After the Tram, when you think you've reached the highest point, you've got a climb for another mile," Perez went on. "It can surprise the hell out of you; you think the ascents are all behind. Yeah, you're getting hotter. Eighty at the crest, it can be a hundred in the open spaces. But you're cruising. You make it to the end and flop in the stream with the water you can't drink because of cattle once upon a time. Cold as hell and it'll give you the shits you take a sip."

"And you got this hunch sitting on the floor in your jammies?"

"You haven't been much for conversation. Read the EMT records, the skimpy boilerplate police report. Nobody gave it a second thought. Stupid girl goes running forever in the sun in the desert, drinks a belly of beer. You shouldn't a done that, you know. Drinking with her in the middle of a marathon."

"We were college kids. It was her birthday. She'd had a hard year."

"The year you say she'd been raped."

"She'd been pushing herself to do crazy things since it happened. Extreme stuff, the running, rock climbing, mountain biking. All alone, something harder, more dangerous each time."

"I read that. The coroner thought she'd finally pushed too hard. And that was that."

"Let me ask, why are you interested? It wasn't in Santa Fe. And it was years ago."

"Because I made you do a shitty thing with the FBI. Sure, I'm a genius now, keeping you on the job so you could close the Easterling file. But I know what I did to you. Maybe I'm trying to make it up somehow."

"And show me I have a valid reason for hating Sam Valles."

"Oh, you've got your reason, like me. I was thinking maybe there's something we can do about it."

"I look like I can do anything about anything?" Aragon forced herself to stay still. Fire raged up her spine. Knives cut through her hips. Breath came harder all of a sudden.

"Pain again?"

"Takes me where it wants to go," Aragon said, "and I just follow."

"Keep telling yourself pain's a gift, like the doc said. You should be happy you're feeling anything. Here's something more to read between your joy rides."

He moved a file from his spot on the floor and laid it on the rolling bedside table next to the pill cups and glass of water. She hadn't realized he was wearing bedroom slippers until she saw his feet in the light of the doorway as he was leaving. They were red, with black-against-white goo-goo eyes that jiggled when he walked.

"From my granddaughter," he said, catching her smile. "They also happen to be the most comfortable things I own."

And just like that she tensed. She couldn't feel her legs again. Or her hips and back. She couldn't feel anything. She'd never wanted to hurt as much as right now.

TWELVE

LEWIS BROUGHT THE NEWS about the two men on the roof.

The one shot and killed was Taylor Fredericks. He'd arrived from Arkansas a couple years ago, enough time for him to become known to police in New Mexico. He'd been arrested for choking a store clerk who caught him slipping a family pack of ribs under a T-shirt. He'd been arrested for stealing a bicycle from the St. John's College campus. Another arrest for three auto burglaries, stealing personal identification from glove boxes. He'd tripped up by handing over one of the stolen IDs instead of his own at a traffic stop. All that in three years, and the only time he'd spent in jail was awaiting bail hearings. The store clerk didn't show for trial. The DA diverted Fredericks into a pre-trial program for the bike theft. The stolen ID charges were dismissed when Fredericks's lawyer convinced the judge the traffic stop lacked probable cause.

The one with a bullet in his kidney but still breathing was Luther Partigan, of Missouri, in the Ozarks by the Arkansas border. He'd been in New Mexico longer and had devoted more time to building

107

relationships with law enforcement. A couple fights outside bars and a fracas inside a strip joint on Cerrillos. Busts for possession and possession with intent. Later, possession of stolen property, specifically, Indian rugs taken from a house near the governor's mansion. A curious patrol officer had pulled him over. What was the buckled Mazda pickup without fenders doing with beautiful rugs like those? Partigan said he'd got them at the flea market, which proved to be partly true. Partigan was running the stall as a way to unload what he'd taken from east side mansions.

Most recently, it was aggravated assault on a young woman. She claimed Partigan had threatened to kill her if she showed police photos he took of her face so she'd always remember what it cost to talk back.

The thing Fredericks and Partigan shared in common jumped out at Aragon. Not one had been taken off the street for longer than it took to sign the terms of pre-trial release. She brought it up and Lewis said, "CMO. That's why we missed them."

The last arrests, and the most serious charges, Partigan's agg assault and Frederick's auto burglaries, had occurred in Albuquerque and ended in dismissals. They'd had their best fun in Duke City during the time the state Supreme Court had imposed a case management order on cases in Albuquerque and the surrounding county. To reduce the jail population, the justices had said. What it did was reduce prosecutions because police and prosecutors couldn't satisfy the crazy-tight deadlines. Missing a discovery deadline no lawyer could meet and leaving out something like an irrelevant 911 call the defense decided later it wanted to investigate would result in dismissal. So what the cops did was arrest violent felons, get them off the street for seven days until arraignment, then watch them walk out of the courtroom with the right to have their records wiped clean.

People, none of them wearing fake velvet robes, had been footing the real price of the program. A little girl had been killed in a high-speed tantrum that stretched for miles on I-40 through the city, the shooter being one of those turned loose under the rule. A police officer had been murdered outside a drug store by another beneficiary of the justices' bright idea. Those stories made front pages and led the news. Hundreds more kept police busy running down people for another seven-day rest with free food and old friends.

"The rule was implemented to avoid delay while providing fair and timely justice," said the Director of the Administrative Office of the Courts, playing PR flak for justices under fire. "Resolving criminal cases in a timely fashion benefits all New Mexicans and improves public safety."

Dismissing charges and turning people like Fredericks and Partigan loose was one way of "resolving criminal cases in a timely fashion." You dropped charges and crossed your fingers. And some defendants, like Partigan and Fredericks, used the opportunity to expunge their records.

Fredericks and Partigan moved north to Santa Fe. The woman Partigan was abusing had rented the house over the wall near the Easterlings' backyard.

"Her head shaved on one side, orange hair combed over," Lewis said. "I remember her at the door. She said she lived alone. I didn't get anything from her that made me want to look closer, so I moved on to the next house. I screwed up."

"She didn't seem suspicious?" Aragon asked.

"I read her as victim, not perp."

"We had a hundred doors to knock on, Rick. I would have crossed her off my list, too."

Fredericks had Chase Easterling's Boy Scout bandana clip on him. Partigan had a Boy Scout pocket knife matching the one Chase's parents said they'd given their son for Christmas. Fibers on Chase's clothes resembled fabric in the trunk of Partigan's car. They'd know for sure after some lab work analyzing dried blood found on the spare. They already knew fingerprints on the lid of the trunk belonged to the boy.

Chase's father wanted to take a hundred men with a hundred rifles and assault the Supreme Court building. He said the chief justice should be hung from one of the elms in front of the courthouse for turning loose monsters who killed good little boys. A pair of State Police troopers spent nights outside the justice's house to make sure it didn't go beyond crazy talk from a distraught father.

Lewis previewed Partigan's defense: A lawyer could argue Fredericks used Partigan's car, he had nothing to do with killing a neighbor's boy. He got the knife from Fredericks. All of the bad stuff was on a dead friend. And it was Fredericks who shot at you, Partigan would say. Count on that.

"But I saw the shooter," Aragon said. "Tell me Partigan has long stringy hair."

"Disgusting long stringy hair."

"And Fredericks?"

"The premature balding of a long-time meth user."

"Bingo."

"Partigan will be wearing a piss bag on his hip in prison, always worried about someone yanking it out for thrills," Lewis said. "Add a federal weapon enhancement to the meth charges, attempted murder of a police officer, and he's got a lifetime of protecting his bag from bored guys in prison orange looking to entertain themselves."

"I'm glad we got them." Aragon said.

"You got them, Denise. We only cleaned up after you."

"I wish I could feel my feet."

THIRTEEN

"*Pah-tree-see-ahh.*"

Cervantes stood outside the storeroom door with a dinner tray thinking, why did I say that? He tried again. "Mrs. Valles, would you like to eat?"

From the other side of the door, "Yes. The boys are hungry."

"I'll nuke some pizza. We're eating what requires electricity before they cut us off. Then its beans and potatoes over the Coleman in the garage."

This was changing him. Hell, he'd been changing since he got the idea from Aragon's words, tossed off without thinking how they landed in his head. To do this you had to be someone different than you'd been your whole life, getting married, raising a family, walking the straight and narrow because your reputation was everything. That kind of person wouldn't have put a gun in a senator's wife's face, told her kids to shut up and march the fuck down the hall. That door. Get in. Bang. Click. Locked.

He didn't talk like that to women or children.

"*Pah-tree-see-ahh.*" Yeah, the attitude helped. "Bathroom break after you eat. Still no word from dear hubby. You understand, how this goes is all up to him?"

Down the hallway he yelled, "Bobo, you want pepperoni on your pizza?"

Pounding on the door from inside. *Pah-tree-see-ah* shouting, making the door shake. Now he was hearing himself mocking her name in his own head. It was how he was starting to think of her. Less a person than a tool, his bait for getting Valles at the front door to make the trade, or showing who he really was by abandoning his family to save himself. Either way, Valles would pay. One of the wastes of skin who hurt other people with their incompetence, their arrogance, their indifference, one of the untouchables, the high-and-mighties. One of them finally would pay.

He walked the rooms along the outside walls looking for little wires or whatever they'd sneak into the house to watch and listen. He wondered if they could mount cameras on robot insects and send them under doors like spiders and ants. Or through drains into showers and sinks, crawling at night and roaming the house. Little red robot eyes watching him in the darkness, from under the furniture, climbing the walls to hide in corners up there above the fireplace.

Maybe he'd call that Helmick and find out where Valles was, speed this up before he was the one climbing walls.

Patricia Valles put a fist to her lips. It hurt, banging this old door with the thick metal nails. It scared her boys. It got her nothing but a sore hand.

Cervantes the contractor, diligent, always with answers on what to do with this ancient house, had called her Mrs. Valles. Now it was *Pah-tree-see-ahh*. Where did he get that?

Listen to yourself, she realized. That's how you correct the reporters saying your name. Sending a message to all those Hispanic voters out there, *los viejos* and the activists. *I'm you.* Now Cervantes throwing it back in her face. And needling her about Sam. Of course, this *was* about him. Cervantes wanted something you could only get from a senator. But he was fooling himself. Senators had the title, the suite in the Hart Office Building on Capitol Hill, satellite offices all over the state, television time whenever they wanted it, slots on Fox or MSNBC. But they weren't like the president. They couldn't order anybody around except their own staff.

So Cervantes must be trying to hurt Sam for something he'd done. Take his family hostage because of how he'd voted? That was nuts. But this was all nuts. Something Sam had done in New Mexico, maybe. Stepping on somebody on the way up. Screwing someone out of a job, damaging someone's career at the VA, the Forest Service, DHS. Sometimes senators could do that by scaring administrators or calling in favors. Senators had a lot of stroke on who became judges or the US attorney. Did one of the people Sam put on the bench do something to Cervantes? So go after them and leave her family alone.

The boys were back at their electronic games now that Mommy wasn't banging the door. They'd heard pizza was coming. They would be good until it arrived and was gone. She tried to rest on one of the futons, arms behind her head, staring at the ceiling of the storage room. No fancy vigas and latillas in here. A solid surface except where lights had been punched in. No air vents even. She and Sam had joked about making this their safe room for when the revolution came and the mob with pitchforks and torches wanted politicians' heads on stakes.

Cervantes hadn't had any work to do in here as a contractor. What'd he done was search out the best room in the house for holding prisoners.

When was she going to hear something from Sam?

Her youngest stood above her now, the distraction of bright lights and sounds gone. He had wet cheeks. She reached for him and he folded himself into her arms. Her oldest son came to her other side and put his head on her shoulder, his body angled away because of her wide hips. Together they looked up at the plain ceiling, so thick and heavy that no sounds entered the room except when Cervantes stood outside the door playing with her name, sneering, no longer anything close to the nice man they'd hired to put in new toilets and windows.

———————

Danny Luna watched the crop circles pop into view as they flew over the Colorado plains. Green circles inside brown squares where water didn't reach and it remained desert. Then the first glimpse of mountains, the Sangre de Cristos, two big peaks by themselves, pointing at the sky like tits somewhere just west of Walsenburg.

They suddenly turned north. They were going to an Air Force base, he wasn't told the name. They spent the night in a kind of barracks on the edge of an airstrip in the middle of nowhere. The senator was on the phone all the time and then behind closed doors in a conference room, Danny outside in a chair to make sure no one interrupted. Small jets arrived and FBI came and went. Danny was put in a two-bunk room with Kilgore. He tried to call his parents but his cell phone couldn't get a signal.

Order room service, drink up, he was told, and men and women in uniforms brought him a steak and beers in a bucket of ice. Kilgore was gone most of the night. Danny didn't leave; he hadn't been given a key card to get back in. When Kilgore returned sometime around three in the morning, he was talking on the phone. He never stopped and Danny couldn't get back to sleep.

At least he got a good breakfast. The senator came by with a bottle of Scotch and said he could use a drink, it had been a long night. Danny joined him for a couple rounds while Kilgore yelled at someone over the phone about keeping their arrival in Santa Fe secret.

They crossed over the mountains and he glimpsed the Great Sand Dunes, a sea of white at the foot of towering mountains. Man, they were flying fast. And no stops. He sipped the drink Senator Valles had ordered for him, deciding he could like Scotch if he could afford it, and Martin Kilgore was squeezing his shoulder. The Ugliest Man in the World had a hell of a grip. It hurt.

"Move somewhere else, kid." Kilgore crowded him, making it hard to get out of his seat. Then Senator Valles was there, not looking like the man in his campaign ads. This man looked worried, exhausted.

Danny moved to a seat in another row beside a dozing woman, the senator's scheduler, if he remembered right, the next most important person on staff after Kilgore. He found a miniature of Johnny Walker in a seat back, half empty, and added it to his cup.

Just like that they were in New Mexico, Kilgore saying that's Wheeler Peak. We're coming in over Taos. There, the Rio Grande Gorge. That's the Jemez. And Santa Fe. All those helicopters, Sam. At two o'clock. That's your house under that traffic.

Danny got up to find the head, his stomach churning, telling him whiskey for breakfast had not been such a good idea.

He didn't make it but he didn't puke. The captain's voice through speakers in the ceiling told everyone to take their seat and buckle up, they were on approach to Sante Fe. That was different. He'd always flown out of Albuquerque's Sunport. Who used the Santa Fe airport? Movie stars with private jets. And US senators rushing back from Europe to deal with an armed wingnut holding their family hostage.

If he pushed his cheeks out and breathed hard it was better. He turned the air jet above his head wide open.

Danny watched Senator Valles, his face to the window glowing from the light outside. A double chin he hadn't noticed before, sagging skin in front of ear lobes. He must have been weighing the terms of the trade, his life for his family. A man on his way up. Talk of him on a national ticket as vice president to pull Hispanic votes. All of his life ahead, unbelievable, a golden dream. He looked like it was falling out of the sky.

Danny could see it ending, too, like a movie finale: Senator Sam Baca Valles stepping out from a cordon of police, rifles pointed over his shoulder at his house. Crossing a no man's land to his own front door. Calling out, the door cracking open. Then his children squeezing through, wrapping their arms around his legs. Him prying them loose, pointing for them to run to the police. Then his wife standing there, the two of them hugging, the end of everything they've known, their final farewell. He lifts her hands from his neck, kisses her one last time, and steps into the house. The door closes behind him.

What happens next? The cops storm the house? Or days passing, everyone wondering what's going on inside but knowing Senator Valles wouldn't be walking out. Or maybe walking out after he convinces the bad guys to surrender and his life soars again. However it ended, Danny was sure Senator Valles would come out of this a national hero.

The small jet stopped like a car braking and the door opened. He hadn't felt the wheels touch down. He slapped his face. Sucked air. He didn't want to stagger when he climbed out of his seat but his head was spinning.

Men with guns came in and waited for Senator Valles to move to the front. Kilgore went first, had a word, then came back for the senator now looking at the floor between his feet. Valles met Danny's eyes as he stood, and they connected. Danny felt his sadness but no fear.

He dug his cell phone from his back pocket. He had to tell his parents about this. No, his girlfriend, Ciela Bustos. Not quite a girlfriend. Not close. He was dreaming. But when she heard what he was doing she'd stop ignoring him

Something crushed his hand. Kilgore was quick. He'd been at the front of the plane a second ago.

"Give me that." Kilgore breathed and loosened his grip. "The FBI wants no cell phones they don't control. No communications in or out that don't fit their program. Did you bring a lap top?"

"A tablet."

"Hand it over." Kilgore waited while Danny pulled his backpack onto his lap from under his seat and dug out the tablet. "You'll get this back later. Head for the limo when you get to the bottom of the stairs."

"Limo?"

"You're coming with us. The senator needs someone around the clock. You'll have the guest house until this is over. You'll do whatever he needs done."

"What guesthouse?"

"We're staying at Las Campanas, outside of town. The senator will need peace and quiet."

The place where rich people lived southwest of Santa Fe. The big houses at the end of private drives. The private clubhouse. Two Jack

Nicklaus Signature golf courses. He had never been past the gates except on a summer job delivering furniture. Past tennis courts to an empty house as big as his school, windows all around, the mountains and blue sky behind Santa Fe, other mansions on hills in the short trees. The bathroom in that house had a tub you could wash a horse in.

"You'll be sharing the guesthouse with Lorna Pierson. She's doing the cooking and playing secretary."

The lady from the DC office, somewhere short of forty, with the good legs and the straight long brown hair, always wearing something cut low on her chest. Danny was never quite sure what her job was. She'd been away for the summer. Vacationing in Europe. He'd heard she was going to meet up with the senator in Switzerland. She must have flown back ahead of him.

"I expect your best behavior," Kilgore said and Danny saw the black limo rolling across the tarmac toward the plane, two men in sunglasses in the front seat, two brown Fords with more men in sunglasses following. "Here. Your breath stinks." Kilgore dropped a roll of mints into Danny's lap. It rolled under his crotch and he felt stupid hunting around under his balls with Kilgore watching and the plane starting to empty as people disappeared into the bright hole that had opened at the front.

His backpack with the cartoons went in the limo's trunk with compact roll-ons and suit bags. He sat facing backward, Kilgore and Senator Valles across from him watching the landscape slide by as the limo entered traffic on Airport Road. Next to him one of the men in sunglasses studied the other cars. He spoke into a microphone clipped to his collar, an earbud giving him the response. Then he told the limo to slow so one of the following cars could come alongside.

Kilgore opened a cabinet and poured orange juice for himself and the senator. Danny was glad when a glass came his way. The men in shades shook their heads when Kilgore offered and Danny, cold orange juice clearing the fog a little, guessed they would have said they needed their hands free at all times.

When he twisted in his seat to look where they were going, Danny saw helicopters in the air, one passing over the glass in the roof, really low. Then the car turned south and found its way to the Santa Fe Bypass and the exit for the Las Campanas golfing resort.

He wanted to say something to Senator Valles but kept his mouth shut. Kilgore gave him a look every now and then that said pretend you're not here.

At a gate the driver punched in a code, metal bars rolled to the side, and they were in, climbing a winding drive to a Spanish-style, mud-brown house that covered the top of the hill. Flagstone patios spread on every side to meet low walls before the hillside dropped away. The door was open with an older man and woman standing there, coming forward, stepping just past the shadow of the portal into the light and stopping. Two white people looking pale in the sun. Danny got the impression this was their house. The woman held a black notebook to her chest. The man started checking a ring of keys in his hands.

Stepping from the door behind the pale couple, floating into sunlight, came long brown legs, long brown hair. Lorna Pierson in white shorts, wiping hands on an apron, a sleeveless top showing her fine long arms and top cut low as always. Long fingers flicking hair from her face. Danny saw how tall she was when she stood next to the homeowners. He guessed his head would come up to her chin, his own chin at the level of her breasts, his eyes on the two points in her collarbone where her soft neck started, but he'd never get close enough to find out.

The FBI teams exited their cars before any doors opened on the limo. The man next to Danny was first out. Then Kilgore was tapping his foot against Danny's ankle, telling him go. The wind blew his hair in his eyes, and he was conscious of his sticky fingers patting it back into place as Lorna Pierson watched him.

"Luna, you're blocking the door." Kilgore nudged him forward. A small smile spread on Lorna Pierson's face. He smiled back but she was looking over his shoulder as Senator Valles came out of the car.

"Luna, Jesus. Get out of the way." Kilgore pulled him aside and Senator Valles stepped past. What was this? Lorna Pierson coming forward and stopping so close to Senator Valles their toes were touching, the two of them separated from everyone else for a moment. He thought they were going to hug. But she took his briefcase and went back into the house. Danny could see he wasn't the only one watching the muscles on the back of her legs.

The pale couple handed over keys to Kilgore. The woman gave the senator the black notebook and Danny heard her saying it explained how everything in the house worked. Sometimes she needed to check the book herself, some of the electronics were so complicated. The man said the Jeep in the garage was theirs to use. Then the couple left in a white Cadillac they backed from the garage, leaving a shiny red Grand Cherokee in there.

A man in sunglasses dropped Danny's bag at his feet. The limo left. He heard the mechanism of the gate opening and closing. Danny saw the limo again on a bend in the road far below, and again after that, smaller, crawling across the vast landscape that swept away from this hilltop.

Now he was alone and Danny wondered what he was supposed to be doing.

"Luna, bring the bags to the living room." Kilgore yelling from the doorway. "Then give Pierson a hand with lunch."

She was in the doorway. A hand on a cocked hip inside those white shorts, head tilted, her shoulder splitting her long brown hair, smiling, waving. Come here, you.

"Yes, sir, Mr. Kilgore," Danny said and swung his superhero backpack over his shoulder.

FOURTEEN

"The way I do pull ups..." Aragon was saying to Lewis. Perez had left her hospital room to grab some sleep. Soon Javier would return with Serena and the kids. Serena would bring something she shouldn't eat, a red enchilada casserole, green chile stew with elk, chicharon burritos. She was telling Lewis about jumping through the roof hatch. "That's how I looked as the floor was coming up fast. I had my legs straight out, bent at the waist, my hands above my head trying to grab onto anything. I landed hard on my tailbone."

"Shaming every man in the gym. That's how you do pull ups." Lewis scratched at the bandages on the back of his head. "With your knees to your chest almost, throwing abs in with upper back. But this time you were falling down instead of pulling up."

"I started in a dive, head first through that roof hatch. I had to move. That gun was coming around on me. My plan was to rotate to get my feet under me, then I'd spring forward onto my hands, roll onto my feet, ready for whatever comes. That was the idea."

"The Denise Aragon action figure."

"My former self." She lifted the sheets to see her lifeless legs. "Instead I was spinning, and wham! My tailbone hit first. My arm got caught on something. I heard it break. I bounced, you know it? Then I couldn't move. Now my face hurts." She touched her cheeks, round, swollen. "The steroids they're pumping into me. I must look like a plump brown baby."

"You look cute. The no hair goes with the chubby newborn look."

"This is not what cute looks like."

"Rivera wants to know if he can stop by."

Tomas Rivera, the FBI Special Agent and former lover. The living likeness of her true love, a teenage boy she couldn't save, her reason for becoming a cop. The story she'd gotten very close to sharing with Pete Cervantes to show she really did understand his pain.

"He wasn't sure and wanted me to check," Lewis said.

Tomas wasn't pure like the boy in her nightmare. Tomas had cheated on her. They were back to talking, but trust hadn't caught up yet.

"The more the merrier," Aragon said and pressed the button that gave her another drip of pain killer through the needle in her arm.

"He's on the Valles thing. Or do we call it the Cervantes thing?" Lewis paused. She had her eyes closed now, starting to float away. "When he comes it will be unofficial, personal. He says the FBI asked him about you. He wanted me to pass along a heads-up. They asked about me, too. I can expect a visit from Agent Pam Magnano."

"Remember, don't stare at her eyebrow. It's a trap," Aragon said, dreamy, a vague memory of the FBI agents she'd lied to.

"Eyebrow."

"Right."

"I see you're not taking this opportunity to forget work."

She lifted an eyelid to see Lewis with a folder Perez had left behind.

"Who's Amy McSwaim?" He turned a page. "This isn't one of ours. It's not even Santa Fe."

"Close the door," Aragon said.

Before he got to the door Serena came from the hall, a casserole dish wrapped in aluminum foil, her girls rushing to the bedside, Javier's bulk filling the doorway after them. All the hospital smells were gone. Aromas of onion, cumin, oregano, red chile fiery enough to heat the building claimed the room. The smells took her out of the hospital. She was in her mother's kitchen, windows open to an autumn breeze, both of them blinking tearing eyes as they chopped onions, meat frying in the pan, her father over a pot with a wooden spoon, in charge of the chile. Another time, with these same smells bringing up good memories, she was on the porch of her brother's ranch in the mountains, food piled on the table, cold beers in buckets, wind making the ponderosas dance.

Lewis and his family were going to score this feast. No way she could get a mouthful down.

"Put that by my good hand," she said. "Peel back the foil." She dipped a finger and tasted. Yeah, she was far away from here.

Something on her leg. Her thigh. Javier had his big hand on her shin, giving her a squeeze. Maybe it was the weight of his big paw she'd sensed.

"I love you, bro."

"Love you, too, Sis."

"I think I feel something. Try the other leg."

Serena was crying. She dipped her own finger in the casserole and put it to Aragon's lips. "It's the chile, girl. You know how your mom said it cures everything? Have another taste and we'll watch you dance around the room."

Then Javier was looming over her, one of their daughters in his arms and riding his hip.

"You hear about that craziness at Senator Valles's house? Some guy has his family, they don't know what he wants. I keep hearing Pete Cervantes. I'm thinking no way that's our hunting buddy. Then this FBI lady is at our house, coming up the steps, I thought she had on two pair of glasses. I know dudes with the unibrow. Never seen it on a woman."

"She was at your place?"

"And she asked about Pete. All the times he hunted with me, what guns he had, was he as good a shot as they heard? And then she was on to something else."

Here he put his daughter down and knelt by the bed, his face close to his sister, his voice low so it didn't travel.

"She got to asking about you. Wanting to know if you've ever talked about hating Sam Valles and what the reason would be."

He didn't talk low enough for Lewis not to hear. She saw him mouth something and turn his eyes to the ceiling.

"I know you hate that pretty boy," Javier said. Lewis had turned his back and was looking at ... the closet door. No get well cards taped there, just white pressboard. "But you never said why. I remember you cursing when he got elected to City Council. Getting drunk and walking out in the woods when he went up to the Senate. Serena and I took hours to find you."

Lewis was moving to the door.

"Rick, stay," Aragon said. "I want to show you something. When we're alone." To Javier she said, "And you told Magnano this."

"I told her you don't care shit about politics or dirt bag politicians, and what the hell was going on with Pete Cervantes? He's a good guy, I told her. There's a mistake."

"No mistake, Javier."

125

Serena tugged at Javier's shirttail. "I think we need to go," she said.

"There's some shit going on," Javier said.

"That's one word for it, bro."

The EMT report was handwritten and difficult to read. Ink mixed maybe with sweat had bled on the cheap, faded paper.

"How'd Perez get this so fast?" Lewis asked, the orange plastic chair creaking whenever he shifted his weight. They were alone. He had closed the door after Serena and Javier. A nurse stuck her head in to say it had to stay open. Lewis showed her his badge and said it had to stay closed. She gave them an hour, then she'd be in to wash Aragon.

"Twenty-plus years with Albuquerque and Bernalillo County. He made friends down there," Aragon answered.

"I can't make sense of most of it."

"Perez translated for me. He knows the abbreviations. This came out of Sandoval County, the emergency crew assigned to cover Placitas. They had their own system for reporting." She raised her good arm with the needle and tube connecting to the bag on the stand. "She was dehydrated. Acting goofy, trying to kiss the EMTs and saying there were birds inside the ambulance. Racing heartbeat, dilated pupils. A hundred and one outside, getting hotter as they came off the mountain onto I-25. Amy's body temp was above a hundred, too, but she wasn't perspiring."

Lewis slid a finger down the page. "Okay. I think I can make sense of these notes. I see I-25, anyway. They went to UNM Hospital."

"Amy was dead before they left the interstate."

"And this was how long after she told you she'd been raped?"

"I've been thinking about that. She died on her birthday. Nineteen years old. She'd first told us about Valles—God, it's been fifteen years—I'm going to say two, three months before."

"And she hadn't reported it to police?"

"She was moving in that direction. She knew the problems the delay caused, but it took her that long to work through everything. She spent a lot of time talking it through with us. She was worried about what he would do, and getting dragged through the courts."

"You didn't say when she'd been raped."

"The day before she first told us. We were back in Santa Fe during spring break. I think we were at Amy's house or someone else's. Not mine. My friends didn't like that part of town. Look at that report. What did Perez see that makes him think it wasn't accidental?"

"Those physical conditions you ticked off, how long would a person have to go without water to get there?"

"Maybe a day or two."

"You're guessing."

"She was strong, in fantastic shape. She tanked up when we met her at the Tram, the halfway point. She took off with a full Camelbak."

"She emptied it, obviously, and needed water."

"We don't know she emptied it. There's nothing in the EMT report about her gear."

Lewis studied the handwritten scrawl on the pages in his hand. "Not that I can read."

"She should have made it to the bottom of the mountain without dying from thirst. That's what got Perez reading between the lines. Do me a favor?"

"You got it."

"Squeeze my feet."

He reached over and his big hand cupped the sole of her closest foot.

"You ever imagine you couldn't walk?" Aragon asked. "Losing a hand, eyes getting weak, other things seem small when your legs may never work again."

"You'll be jogging up Baldy by the end of the summer. You said Amy McSwaim told 'us' about the rape."

"Girlfriends. Our little beer-drinking, boy-chasing, sharing-ups-and-downs gal pal circle. Patricia Garza, now Patricia Valles. She was one of us."

"Get out."

"She and Sam were in student politics. All of them but me played at it. Sam was the bright, shining prince. He was running for student council president, and bigger things after that. We all knew it. He talked about running for president and believed he'd live in the White House one day and change the world. They called him The One years before anyone called Obama that. More was taken from Amy than what a rape does to you. She'd been a true believer."

"Patricia Valles, she's been carrying around what Amy McSwaim told her?"

"There was another one in our circle, but she won't talk. She needs to keep her state job. Last I heard she's a single mom with three kids."

"So we don't have any proof of a rape. Two of the three gal pals who heard about it would never testify. And only Perez sees a homicide in old emergency records. No wonder you've never talked about this."

And she hadn't said anything about his hand around her foot, being squeezed she guessed by the motion of the biceps in Lewis's forearm. She didn't feel a thing.

"Do something for me," she said. "Get me the names and telephone numbers for the women who found Amy."

"I'll get this EMT report translated, too."

128

"And a map of the Sandia wilderness. I want to see the trails. I don't know that mountain except to run up La Luz, drink beer at the top, and take the Tram down."

"One Sandia Mountain Wilderness trail system map coming up. Anything else, like a stack of good books to read?"

"So you're on this with me?"

"I don't even know what 'this' is. I'm only providing reading material to fill the empty hours of your long recuperation. For once I'll know where to find you. When was the last time you were still for more than a couple hours?"

"Can you get me one of those grip strengtheners? I can at least get some exercise."

"What was I saying? Just take it easy."

The door opened. A women's head appeared. Lewis scowled at the clock above the doorway. "You said we had an hour."

"Rick." Aragon watched the woman step into the room, coming forward like she didn't want to be there. Aragon not sure she was seeing right. "This isn't our nurse. Meet Margaret Baldonado. I was just talking about her." He gave her a blank look. "The one with the state job."

Lewis nodded and studied the woman, short as Aragon but with spread hips, weak shoulders above arms that would flap if she waved them. Her pepper-and-salt hair was piled on her head and she wore a mask of makeup.

"Denise." Margaret came to the foot of the bed. "It's been a long time."

"Years. I'm glad but I've got to say I'm really surprised to see you."

"I'm so sorry you got hurt. I follow you in the newspaper and on TV when you solve a big case. This is you without your wig. I like it. Your eyes pop out. You always had beautiful eyes." Margaret inched closer and Lewis stepped back to give her room. "You really meant what you said in college, about all you wanted to be was a police detective. But why I came, I have to admit, it isn't because I read about you getting hurt."

She shuffled her feet, white footies inside flat pale purple shoes. Aragon saw a friend who'd grown older faster than the years behind them. Margaret looked around the hospital room, touched the corner of a bed sheet for no reason. Her nail polish matched her shoes. Ball earrings dangling from tiny ears. Cheap earrings. Plastic beads on a chest much larger than Aragon remembered.

"I thought you should know," Margaret said. "There's this woman who came to see me at work. It was to ask me about you and our college days. She said she was with the FBI, showed me a badge, but I'm not sure and I didn't write down her name. I was kind of stunned. Why would the FBI be asking me about you? Maybe she's a fake, trying to dig up dirt, to hurt you on one of your cases. I thought you should know right away."

Aragon asked, "Any distinguishing features?"

"She should get her eyebrows plucked and do something about the cat hair on her shirt."

Lewis threw looks between Aragon and her friend. Soon he'd be rolling his eyes to the ceiling again.

"She had a question out of the blue that hit me like I'd been slapped. She caught that, my reaction, and didn't buy my first answer, that I didn't have a clue."

"About my feelings toward Sam Valles."

Margaret's eyebrows, plucked into a thin line high on her forehead, rode higher as she wrinkled her brow.

"They're investigating you. What's going on, Denise?"

"What was your second answer?"

"I had to tell her about Amy. And how we all felt about Sam, how we wanted to cut his dick off. We had a hundred ways to do it. You came up with the best, make him do it himself with a dull butter knife." She put a hand over her mouth and looked under eyelids at Lewis. "Excuse me."

"He's heard worse," Aragon said.

"Even Patricia joined in. We all hated Sam," Margaret said. "I never understood how she could marry him. But hey, look where she is. She's doing alright for herself."

"When she isn't being held hostage," Aragon said.

———

Senator Valles was back in Santa Fe. Pete Cervantes knew when the camera hidden in the cactus showed the FBI operations truck emptying and people climbing into black Suburbans. The one who might be Helmick got in the front seat of the lead vehicle, carrying a briefcase and water bottle. A man in a bulletproof vest got in back with the woman with jet black hair and thick glasses. The man in the vest he guessed headed up the Hostage Rescue Team. He moved like a soldier. All the important people leaving together at the same time.

Cervantes pulled up the most recent call on his phone and hit send. No number showed, just the letters *FBI*. He wasn't sure it would work.

Helmick's voice answered. "Mr. Cervantes. How are you holding up? I was hoping you'd call. I really do want to have a longer conversation with you."

"I bet you do. Tell Valles when you get there, the terms are non-negotiable. There's not another thing I want in the world but him walking up to the door saying here I am, let my family go. Matter of fact," Cervantes said, "tell him those are the exact words I want to hear. Bring him with you when you come back. I've got three lives to bargain with, one by one if I have to. He doesn't want to be regretting he had only one life to offer. One little life, just a bump in the road on the way to something better."

Helmick on his end would be wondering how he knew they were going to see Valles. Let them understand they didn't know everything. Let them believe he was ahead of them, that maybe he had help on the outside telling him what was going on. Let them tell Valles how bad this really was.

FIFTEEN

WHEN LORNA PIERSON PASSED the tray of sandwiches and salad, Danny saw only her green eyes. "It's nice working with you," she said and aimed him at the living room where Senator Sam and Kilgore and the FBI guards were waiting for lunch. He smelled her then. They'd been making tuna salad and now he inhaled flowers blooming at night. When she gave him a little shove her boobs tickled his back.

FBI guards with earpieces stood outside the front door. Danny left their sandwiches on the bench of the big Steinway under the window. Valles and Kilgore kept talking as he placed plates and glasses on end tables by their chairs. This house was something. The living room alone was bigger than the house he'd grown up in with four brothers and sisters. He hadn't seen any of the bedrooms, down long halls where the floors were sealed bricks laid out in a cross-hatched pattern. He'd had a glimpse of the guesthouse he'd be sharing with Lorna Pierson. Probably a couple bedrooms out there, one for sure just inside the sliding glass door by the hot tub sunk into pink stone.

"They could shoot you as soon as you step into the open. You might not get ten feet," Kilgore said and took half a sandwich. Some of the tuna salad spilled into his lap but he didn't notice. Danny put out a basket of blue corn chips. Kilgore pushed it away. "Get me real potato chips."

"Before they release my family?" Senator Sam sipped a whiskey and ice Danny had brought minutes ago. He shook his glass to say get me another. "Then what? They shoot my family and themselves? Or it's a gun battle. Or they're done once I'm dead and Cervantes and his friend walk out with hands in the air?"

"Or they let your family go and kill themselves to avoid life in max security, the best scenario. We wouldn't have to war game this if the FBI could get a good shot. But they'd need to get both bad guys at the exact same time. One survives, it could be worse for your family." Kilgore gave Danny a hard look. He'd stopped moving and stood behind the senator's chair. "Get the chips, kid. And the senator another drink."

Lorna threw him a smile and a wink in the kitchen and helped him find potato chips in the dozens of cupboards above unrecognizable appliances he didn't know how to work. Lorna found them in a cupboard he couldn't reach. Into a cut glass tumbler she poured three fingers of single malt from the distillery owned by the people who lived in this house. She reminded Danny the senator liked lots of ice.

Back in the living room Kilgore was saying, "The FBI team leaders are coming out to talk. We'll have the director on the phone. They need to understand your interests in this."

What was there to understand? Danny wanted to ask. The lives of Mrs. Valles and the children. Wasn't that his only interest?

Kilgore went on. "This is about embarrassing you. That's how I see it. They're gambling you won't be willing to trade your life for your family. We need to play that back on them. Save your ass and your family's. You become legendary and, zoom, nothing is stopping you ever again. When was the last time a certifiable hero ran for the White House?"

"McCain."

"He was shot down and gave the Viet Cong the taped statement they wanted. Those hits on you for never serving in the military, you'll prove your courage in front of cameras with all America watching. Sam, we pull that off, you can begin the launch countdown. Forget the number two slot. Just think what… Hey, kid, go clean something up."

Kilgore yelled for Lorna as Danny returned to the kitchen. They met at the doorway, face to face. He backed to let her pass and noticed she'd put on makeup and eyelashes in that short time since she'd poured whiskey. She brushed his arm with her breasts—every time she got close that happened—and said, "Don't you go anywhere. I'll be right back." He tried hard not to turn around and watch her walking away.

———

She didn't return to the kitchen. He cleaned everything and wondered what to do next. He stepped outside onto an open patio and watched thunderclouds boiling over the mountains behind Santa Fe. A wind blew in his face and he knew they'd get a downpour before nightfall. Lightning flashed, touching the outline of the Sangre de Cristos. The dark clouds turned orange, then black-green and he felt the thunder in his gut.

Lorna was crossing the sidewalk by the pool to the guesthouse, lightning in the distance flashing as she climbed steps. She saw him and gave him that "come here, you," wave again. He stepped back into the kitchen and got his knapsack.

The door to the guesthouse faced away from the main house. It was open and dark and cool inside. The air was stale, as though the building had been sealed for a long time.

"Let's get some air in here." Lorna opened windows just as the leading edge of the storm reached them. Wind blew the curtains from the screen. A lamp with a shade went over and the bulb broke. Danny dropped his bag and stepped forward to pick up the pieces. Then he was looking up the line of Lorna's legs.

"There's only one bedroom," she said and shrugged. "Big place like this. Doesn't bother me. We're grown-ups. But the sofa looks nice if you'd rather."

The wind kicked up and the front door banged. Danny went for it, an excuse not to stare at her. One of the FBI guards was down at the gate by the road. It was open. A pair of brown Fords came in and rolled to a stop at the walk to the front door. Men and one woman got out, leaning into the wind and running to the house. One of the men looked like a professional soldier. He had a gun on his hip that he took off and put into the car's trunk. A man and woman, both in glasses, went to the front door together, the man going first, a briefcase in his hand arcing with the motion of his arms as he ran. The woman in glasses swung her gaze his way and Danny quickly stepped back inside as fat raindrops exploded on the dry soil in the yard.

The storm came on fast. Danny threw the door shut and went around closing windows Lorna had opened. Where was she? The guesthouse had a teal tin roof, very stylish, with solar collectors up there. The downpour grew and he couldn't believe how loud it was on the metal roof. Then the light from the windows was gone and it was dark in the house. Thunder boomed. Lightning flashed, showing furniture around him, then it was dark again. He tried a lamp. They'd lost power.

But there was light in the bedroom. He went in there. Lorna was bending over lighting a candle, the muscles in the back of her legs stretched taut, her white shorts standing out in the shadows. She'd already lit two other candles. She turned to him with a match burning down to her fingers. It burned behind long fingernails, the flame showing through, and she said, "Oooh," and dropped the match on the tile floor.

She came to him and put her burned fingers on his lips.

He couldn't hear what she was saying as thunder shook the house and she took his hand and was leading him.

On the bed, she made him lie back and undid his belt. Her mouth close to his ear, she said, "I'm going to make you the happiest boy on the Rio Grande." His heart was racing and she sensed it. Her hand went up under his shirt to his chest and she laid her warm palm over his ribs. She kept it there, holding his eyes, her face down by his thighs, her knees on the floor at the foot of the bed.

She needed both hands for the belt buckle. Somehow in the racket of the storm he heard his zipper. And then she said, "Danny."

His mouth was dry. He worked up saliva, swallowed so he could talk. "What?"

"Oh, my." She wasn't moving anymore. She was very still.

He was worried he'd worn dirty underwear. Or that he smelled. Something.

"What's wrong?" he asked, not wanting to hear the answer.

"My, oh, my, Danny." And she pulled his pants with his underwear inside off his legs, lifting his feet at the end. She tugged at his socks, laughed. "They don't match. How cute."

Now she was standing. Taller than ever, the dark ceiling behind her, candlelight showing her pulling her top above her head, then pushing her white shorts down her legs and he saw she'd been wearing no underwear. She left her bra on and he wondered why as she crossed the room to bring a candle closer. Then the bra was off and she stood naked looking at him lying back on the bed, his shirt still on but nothing else. He tilted his head to see her dark patch and she came close and worked her hands up the bed until her face was above his.

She kept saying that, "My, oh, my." Or "oh, my, my." And then just "my" stretched out. When they started again right away she added, "Oh, Lord." And when they started again in only minutes it was, "Mine, all mine."

She was snoring softly when Danny got up and put on clothes but no shoes. He was thinking of the Scotch in the bottom cupboard in the kitchen. He didn't smoke, but he had to follow this with something and Scotch was on his mind. He'd done it. Really done it. He'd been worried when they started that he would be done in a second. But it was Lorna who went still first.

It had stopped raining and was quiet outside. He smelled sage in the smooth, damp air. The wet concrete of the sidewalk was cool under his feet.

He didn't turn on a light in the kitchen. A meeting was underway in the living room, voices besides Kilgore and Senator Sam. He looked at the clock on the stove. They'd been talking a long time; he and Lorna had been going a long time. He found his way to the cupboard he wanted and hoped it was the Scotch he'd seen when he put his hand around the neck of a bottle.

Footsteps coming close. He moved fast and crouched behind the counter by the back door. The ceiling light came on.

"There are other interests here you're not seeing."

The words Danny had heard before. Now Kilgore was repeating them for someone else.

"You want us to protect Senator Valles's political position. What about his family?"

Danny didn't know that voice.

"The FBI should not let itself be used by terrorists," Kilgore said. "The object of this mad act is to destroy an important member of the United States Senate, a potential resident of the White House, a man who could be your next boss. That concern should weigh heavily on your scales."

A cupboard opened on the other side of the counter. He felt it in his shoulder when the door was kicked shut. The next sound was a cork being pulled.

"Join me," Kilgore said. "This is some serious stuff. The people that own this pad own a distillery in the Highlands. This is what the owner gets to drink."

"I won't be touching alcohol until this is over."

"Then end it soon. You don't know what you're missing." Danny heard Kilgore exhale and smack his lips. "You should see the wine racks in the climate-controlled room. Something we need to know … " Kilgore paused, exhaled, smacked lips, taking another sip. "Who knows about Cervantes's demands? There's the Luna kid. Right now he should be the happiest boy on the Rio Grande. He won't notice he's being kept away from the world and reporters and curious friends. He'll be happy to be locked up here."

Again the voice Danny didn't recognize: "There's the Santa Fe detectives who stumbled into this. Cervantes repeated his demand to them."

"And you're investigating one of them, the woman, as a possible accomplice?"

"Looks like she had motive to hurt the senator. A long simmering hatred, then she connects with Cervantes with his own axe to grind. After we talked to her, she got in a scrape with some bad guys. She's incapacitated for an undetermined time. She could be paralyzed, they don't know. We've instructed her partner not to release details of their encounter with Cervantes. We're sure he'll toe the line. He's got a wife and kids to think about. But from what we've learned, better not tell her not to do something if you don't want that something to happen."

"She's one of those." The cupboard opened, bottles clinked, the cupboard closed. Kilgore was done with the Scotch. "You've learned something to discredit her if she does open her mouth? What is it?"

"I can't disclose that."

"She's delusional. She thinks Sam Valles raped a friend in college, is that it?"

Danny, on the floor behind the counter, wanted Kilgore to repeat that. *Senator Valles raped someone?*

Fingers drumming on the countertop. "You were ready for me," said the voice.

"Sam racked his brain. She made that charge years ago and they've never spoken since. His wife knows about it and told her they'd sue if she ever repeated it."

"We didn't get it from the detective."

Danny waited for Kilgore to say something. It was quiet in the dark kitchen. Finally, Kilgore said, "So she's been defaming the senator and it got back to you."

"We're looking into it."

"Mind telling me who's spreading these lies? It's a political hit job. Some woman saying a US senator raped her?"

"The alleged victim passed away long ago. But you already know that."

Pacing. The faucet opening, closing. More pacing, squeaky shoes on the tile floor.

"Agent Helmick." At last, a name. Agent? FBI? "If you were able to speak with Patricia Valles, you would learn that the detective has repeatedly threatened to destroy Sam Valles's career. Apparently she takes the threat of lawsuit seriously enough she's resorted to a whisper campaign. It will spread like a cancer unless we stop it now. Tell me, who is spreading these lies?"

"Let's talk about your idea. Pour me some water, would you?"

Danny looked for somewhere better to hide. There was a table and chairs across an open space … that wouldn't work. He needed to get out of here.

Helmick talked first. "I'm not going to let Senator Valles expose himself to either getting killed or being taken prisoner."

"Of course you won't," Kilgore said. "We get an actor. The right makeup. The right build. Put him in one of the senator's suits. Maybe an FBI agent. You've used decoys before, I'm sure. He'll never be close to anybody but a few of your most trusted people. He steps into the open and starts walking toward the house. You'll have video running. He has his hands up. We can put a hat on him. Yeah, Sam wears a black Stetson now and then. Hat on, hands up, he walks to the house. But the FBI isn't going to surrender a member of the Armed Services and Intelligence Committees. He gets far enough to convince anyone watching he's going through with it and from nowhere an FBI agent, maybe you, rushes him, tackles him. It might take two. You're going to drag him back behind cover while his hands reach desperately, futilely for his loved ones. You meet your needs. We meet ours. Senator Valles was ready to give his life for his family, but the FBI, appropriate to its mission and responsibilities, stopped him."

"And when Cervantes calls and says, the fuck was that, we tell him … ?"

"You tell him there's something he did not factor in. National security. Sam Baca Valles holds in his head secrets too valuable, so critical to our national survival you can't give him over to a terrorist. You've just changed the ground under Cervantes and can start negotiating for real. What does he want that you *can* give him?"

"And if he decides it's all over and shoots the family and himself?"

A door opened. Good, they were leaving. But Danny wanted to hear Kilgore's answer. He didn't get it. Why would Senator Valles even consider playing games? He heard the door close and voices on the other side, but he couldn't make out what they were saying.

It was raining again and he ran fast, scared of the lightning. He entered the guesthouse through the sliding glass door and heard a voice in the darkness.

"Danny, come back to bed."

He stripped off his wet clothes and brought the bottle with him. Lorna was on top of the sheets, her long legs pushing the thin blanket to the floor. Danny stood above her, loving the look of her pale body in the weak light. He twisted the cap off the bottle he'd brought from the house. He'd puzzle out the questions in his mind later. But he got why they'd taken his cell phone and tablet. He got the part about Lorna Pierson, too, and that was okay by him. From her reaction, the way she kept coming at him for more, he was getting the idea that those girls who wouldn't look at him or return his texts didn't know what they were missing. And he was sure those girls didn't know half of what Lorna Pierson had shown him while the storm raged overhead.

He took a swig. Cough medicine. He spit it out and turned the label to candlelight. Gold and black letters told him he'd tasted Grenadine. Now he could see the red syrup inside the bottle. He was about to leave the bed, head back to the house and get what it was Kilgore had been drinking, but Lorna got a hold on one of his ass cheeks and pulled him backward. He was able to put the bottle down before he fell across her hips, feeling wiry hair tickling his back. He smelled Lorna again. The perfume was gone. She smelled like sweat and sex.

"You weren't supposed to go in the house," she said rolling him down her legs as she sat up. "How long were you in there?"

He was across her knees now and it didn't feel so good, the way her shins split his ribs. But he liked looking back along those legs and up her body.

"Long enough to learn why I'm in a one bedroom house with you," he said.

He paused, not sure he wanted to tell her how he felt. Senator Valles must know what he was doing. The FBI, too, were experts in this. A man's family always came first. But Senator Valles didn't seem in any hurry to rush to their defense.

He let a little out. "Something's wrong," he said.

Lorna rolled him off her legs and now had her face above his, elbows locked, the straight hair framing his cheeks. "Whatever's wrong," she said, her arms bending and her face getting closer, "it's definitely not this."

———

"The storm gives me an idea," Helmick said, up front in the lead Suburban as the FBI drove away from Las Campanas. The wipers whipped water from the windshield and still the driver was leaning into the steering wheel, pushing his eyes closer to the glass as if that helped. "Somehow Cervantes knew we were leaving. He took a wild guess we were meeting the senator. Unless he has someone inside the bureau or Valles's staff? No, he threw a dart and got lucky. But for certain, somehow he knew we were heading out."

"You didn't tell him he was right?" Dix in the seat wiped fog off the window to look out at the stormy night. "My men are out in this. Those teams in the arroyo had better get to higher ground. How much rain does it take to cause a flash flood?"

"Enough to flood the road, sir," the driver said and slowed. Headlights showed a river surging across the blacktop, the culvert under the road blocked with debris. He put the transmission into four-wheel-drive and rolled forward slowly. The force of water pounding the wheel rims and bumper caused the Suburban to reverberate, a low hum spreading through the vehicle's frame.

Helmick ignored Dix's question. Of course he didn't give Cervantes the satisfaction, and the confidence that would go with it, of confirming his information. That wasn't how you laid the groundwork for later negotiations.

"Somebody could be watching us beyond the range of those cameras on the house. It could be any one of the houses on these hills or someone outside the barricades, watching who goes in and out. Maybe a reporter who's got another cell Cervantes is using and we're going to hear the broadcast of an exclusive interview soon. Whatever the explanation, we set up a geofence to keep any of his mobile devices from working. They'll turn on, but he won't have a signal. We tell Cervantes the storm knocked out the towers, scrambled the electronics and everyone is off the airwaves."

"He has television and Internet," Magnano said from the darkness in the back seat.

"Those go down, too."

"One, how do you get this information to him?" Dix said. "Two, stopping his communications with this person you think is on the outside will also prevent us from finding whoever it is. I don't like the idea that there's a bad guy I can't identify at my back."

"Or he's got another camera we don't know about," Helmick said. He noticed that for the first time he wasn't miserable with sinus crap. This rain had washed the pollen and dust out of the air. He wondered how long the good air would last. "I think Kilgore has something right. What does Cervantes really want with the senator? He's not going to pry classified info out of him to share with some terrorist network or foreign government. Wouldn't you agree, Pam?"

"We've nothing to suggest he's that kind of threat."

"Right. This is about taking out the senator as a public figure, bringing him down. Personal revenge. Making himself feel better about his loss by taking it out on a man he holds responsible for reasons only he understands. When he's ready, Cervantes is going to release his terms to the world. Media will go crazy, the talk shows speculating whether Valles would give his life for his family. Can't you see it? Non-stop blather."

"We want this categorized as terrorism," Dix said. "We can do a lot more. We have more leeway. Why give that up?"

"Technically, since it's an attempt to influence public policy by the use of force or threats of force, it qualifies as terrorism. I want all the additional green lights we get in a terrorism case. But in our own minds, in my mind in talking with Cervantes, I don't see him that way. It won't help me deal with him."

"What happens when Cervantes realizes your story about the storm knocking out electronics is bull?" Dix was full of questions to-night. In the cold mansion they'd just left, whenever he'd run scenarios for the senator, Dix had questions about every option except shooting Cervantes and whoever was in there helping him. He'd told the senator about the HRT sniper who blew out the brainstem of a man holding a woman against his chest with a gun to her head and her son tied to his back. Both Kilgore and Valles had inched to the edge of their seats listening to that true story. Talking over each other, asking how the FBI was going to lure Cervantes into the open and how far away could a sniper be and still make that kind of shot. Helmick and Magnano had caught each other's eyes, both of them noticing neither Valles nor Kilgore had asked about the risk to Mrs. Valles or the boys.

"It gives us something incremental to bargain with," Helmick said. "Offering to give back something he's lost gets us trading. It starts the dance. Maybe insist he release the boys in exchange for restoring cell service."

"That would make my job easier," Dix said. "Only having to worry about one hostage if and when we go in. I can't see the helicopters up there." They were getting close to Santa Fe, little traffic in this weather, the road like black glass, slick and wet. "They're probably not flying."

"Then the drones aren't flying either," Helmick said, but he was thinking about the conversation with Kilgore in the kitchen. Kilgore pulling him away from the living room, saying he wanted to look for a very special Scotch, let's keep talking. It had been an excuse for them to talk alone. He wondered if Kilgore and Valles had agreed on that before the FBI arrived. It did seem like Valles had signaled Kilgore. Yes, it was Valles who brought up the owners of the house owning a distillery outside Edinburgh. It was Valles who said, "Martin, why don't you see if you can find some for our guests?" And then Kilgore saying, "Mr. Helmick, walk with me, if you would."

The heart of Kilgore's idea had some sense in it. If they could deprive Cervantes of his play on Valles, they could turn this back into a more normal hostage situation.

A *normal* hostage situation? Art Helmick, you've been doing this too long.

"Call the director, Pam. We'll need him to get the Army moving on the geofence tonight."

"The Army has that stuff?" Dix with another question.

"For suppressing social media when riots break out. Protestors and reporters can't send out photos of protestors getting shot or call anyone about it. No interviews behind the barricades. It's worked in Iraq and Afghanistan. I think there's a unit with the equipment at White Sands or Ft. Bliss. They can be here before dawn."

"Storms predicted all day tomorrow, too," Magnano said. "We've got a little more time."

Lightning crashed to their right. In the section of town where the Valles house was located, all the lights went out.

"A break for us. We can move in the dark," Dix said and got on his phone. Helmick heard him telling his team to send someone forward, plant microphones close to the house, get one on a boarded up window. Be ready with a probe if they could pull it off, there might never be a better opportunity than this. Keep an eye out for a camera placed beyond the house. Consider the vantage points that allow observation of Helmick's command post. And then, "What do you mean, you can't get closer to the house?" Dix turned to Helmick and shared what he'd just been told by one of his gun teams. "Cervantes has generators."

When they arrived the Valles house was washed in light, spotlights on the roof showing the yard and Dix's men still in place. Only a gentle rain now, the thunder quiet for a bit, Helmick heard the

147

gas-fired generators working behind garage doors. Then the squeal of a megaphone adjusting volume.

"You're back. Where's Valles?" came from the house.

Behind him, Magnano said, "How do you like that? Cell service is actually down. I've got to find a landline."

"Find one. Get us set up in the nearest house," Helmick said. Kilgore's idea was taking shape in his mind. He didn't have authority to make the call himself. "Ask the director for a time we can talk. No, tell him we need to meet in person. How soon can he be here?"

SIXTEEN

SHE COULDN'T WORK WITH the Percocet turning her brain into jelly or when the nurses let in cops and detectives and State police and probation officers and corrections officers and bailiffs and prosecutors bringing cards, candy, and flowers and hanging around long after they'd run out of things to say. She started having the hospital give the goodies to people without visitors. Good thing she and Lewis had gotten time alone with Margaret Baldonado before the floodgates opened.

At least her memory was working. She was correct in recollecting that Margaret had three children of her own, but she hadn't known about the one from a different mother who'd stayed behind when the father dumped Margaret. Margaret had moved up through state government to a good job at the State Film Office arranging receptions, pitching New Mexico to producers, helping site locators, trying to get movies shot in poor towns with amazing scenery and no economy after the monthly welfare checks had been spent.

Today under questioning from Magnano was the first time Margaret had revealed what Amy McSwaim told her back in college.

"You don't go around saying one of the most powerful people in New Mexico raped someone if you want to keep your job. Sure, you're civil service, you can only be fired for good cause. So they doctor your personnel file, turn people against you, wreck your reputation to where it's better to give up and keep your files sealed. What would I get from running my mouth except moving into an efficiency apartment with four hungry kids burning through food stamps?"

"But you told the FBI," Aragon said.

"They asked at the same time we have a new governor who's thinking of running against Valles. It made it easier."

So they talked about Amy. Margaret remembered Amy McSwaim sitting her closest friends down, the two of them and Patricia Garza, a couple days later instead of the very next day after the rape, as Aragon recalled. She also placed the rape closer to Amy's last day alive. And Amy had shown Margaret something Aragon hadn't seen: torn underwear spotted with blood. She didn't know what Amy had done with that evidence. Aragon said if she'd been a police detective at age nineteen she would have insisted on bagging the underwear and testing for semen and DNA. Margaret remembered that all Aragon wanted to do at the time was terrible things to Sam Valles's most sensitive parts.

"Will Patricia learn I talked to the FBI?" Margaret asked. "I'm more worried about her than Sam."

"We certainly wouldn't share details like that," Lewis said, in the orange plastic chair, taking notes. Margaret kept staring at the bandages on his head and then said her son had burned himself once lighting the grill with gasoline. She knew how much it hurt and she hoped his hair grew back.

"Still, she's a senator's wife," she went on. "I'm worried."

"Patricia's not talking to anyone right now," Aragon said. "Tell Rick what you remember about Amy's injuries."

Bruises on her neck, scratches on her cheek, the scraped knuckles on the back of her hand. Amy initially said she'd fallen off a mountain bike. How'd your neck get like that? How did falling off a bike make you look like you've been choked hard? Margaret remembered Aragon asking those questions.

"You already with the instincts. Amy said it had been the helmet strap snagging on a bush. You gave her a hard look and asked again."

They reconstructed the timeline. Amy had told Aragon first, she and Margaret agreed, giving bits and pieces until a couple days later she told her other close friends, sharing more of it.

"We were at her parents' house," Margaret said and Aragon mumbled, sounds right. "She'd called us over, made tea for us. I thought she was going to tell us she was pregnant."

"About that," Lewis said. "Did she ... from Valles?"

"If she was, she didn't live long enough for anyone to find out."

"She could have been," Aragon said. "But she didn't have an ounce of fat and nothing was showing. We might never know. She wasn't autopsied."

Margaret pointed to the water pitcher and tiny plastic cups on the bed table and Lewis handed her a drink. She threw the water back like a shot of whiskey. "She wasn't getting big. The opposite. The way she started running, biking, climbing rocks. Doing crazy things. She couldn't keep weight on her. Patricia and I hated her for that. You too, Denise. It wasn't fair."

"I'll be putting on the pounds now," Aragon said. "May as well let myself go and enjoy this."

"I don't believe you'll ever let yourself go." Margaret held out the tiny cup and Lewis refilled. "You were as nuts as Amy, running up the Sandias. You were the only girl I knew who lifted weights back then."

Aragon held up the grip strengthener Lewis had provided. "My left forearm is going to be massive."

"You're sitting in McSwaim's apartment, drinking tea," Lewis put in, "and she tells you she's been raped by Sam Valles? How did she know him?"

"We all met freshmen year. Student government. All of us got involved."

"Not me," Aragon said.

"You hated politics."

"Now that I've met politicians, I hate them too."

"Took me too many years to join you. I have Sam at the top of my list of 'What did I ever see in those people?' But freshmen year, he was this Hispanic hunk who talked good, had big ideas, remembered everyone. Whenever he met someone he'd right away repeat their name. 'Margaret, how nice to meet you.' 'Margaret, what a lovely name.' 'Margaret, isn't this an exciting time to be alive?' He was going to be student council president, run for city council as a student, do something about rents, the drinking age, parking off campus, get busses to the football games for free. The first Hispano president, after he was the first Hispano senator for New Mexico in fifty years. How can New Mexico always be represented by white boys? That one he only said among us. He got along real good with Greeks and geeks. He got along with everyone."

A knock on the door. A Black male nurse stuck his head in, said he had to take Aragon's temperature and would come back.

Aragon said, "Tell Rick about Sam's little business."

"You mentioned that before," Lewis said. "Said I'd get a kick out of it."

For the first time, Margaret smiled. She closed her eyes and shook her head. "I can see him, hair down to his ass. Boy, he loved his hair. In a Speedo, nothing else, delivering roses, giving a little dance in dorm rooms. 'Shake Your Booty,' that was his theme song. He carried a boom box with him."

"Or girls' night in with tequila," Aragon said. "Sam balancing the boom box on his shoulder, grooving to 'La Bamba.'"

"Stuff his little shorts with dollar bills, cop a feel…"

"He'd give you his ass and bounce it, hands on his thighs…"

"Spanking encouraged."

"This is United States Senator Sam Baca Valles?" Lewis asked.

"Before the hair went away," Margaret said. "Before Patricia married him and made him get serious."

"There must be photos," Lewis said. "I can't believe this without seeing."

"Those were the days before everybody had a camera on their phone," Aragon said. "Sam's one rule: no photos permitted."

Margaret said, "I hadn't thought of this, but I don't remember his Chippendale routine happening after Amy died. It might have stopped before."

"She laughed at him. Remember that?"

"A Valentine's Day delivery. We're in a dorm room, I don't remember whose. "Shake Your Booty" outside the door, a bare foot coming first, then a leg with muscles. You knew it was Sam. He came into the room that way, his body before his head. Calves, thighs, a little red piece of spandex, very little. His stiffy."

Margaret's eyes teared up. She was coughing and laughing to match Aragon. "He was really enjoying that special delivery," she said. "When his face came around he had this big sugary smile. 'Hiya, ladies. You can see I'm bringing more than roses.' And Amy said, 'Wake us up when it gets here.' Boy, he didn't like that. His face got dark. He lowered the roses to cover himself and got out of there."

That was what they got from Margaret before a surgeon with a string of residents in tow entered the room.

Later that night, after Lewis had left, when the room lights were dimmed and the televisions along the hallway were quiet and she was getting scared about her legs because there were no visitors to make her think of something else, Tomas Rivera came to her.

———————

He came while she was drifting on soft clouds, a fuzzy figure bending close, a gentle voice calling her awake. The hair off his forehead brushing her face, she knew its feel. His hand against her cheek, her eyes clearing, he said, "I only get to see you in the hospital anymore. We need to find something easier on you."

She licked her lips and rubbed her face. She needed to quit the Percocets. It took her two tries to get out the words, "This way you know where to find me."

He kissed her then.

"You know I can't stop you," she said. Her lips and tongue were working even if her legs weren't. She hadn't let him kiss her since she'd found out about him and the Asian woman in the yoga pants. When he came to her after surgery to rebuild the hand that took a bullet for him, she hadn't let him touch her. This felt good. "Do that again."

"First time I've ever seen you helpless," he said, their noses touching.

"Don't get used to it."

She smelled something. Something wonderful and delicious. She pushed him away and saw he was carrying her favorite red, white, and blue bag. "A Lotaburger."

"With large fries," he said. "And Limeade. I checked. You're allowed to eat this."

"I'm not hungry—these drugs they gave me to make sure I sleep."

"For breakfast, then. I know you eat cold Lotaburgers for breakfast. The complete meal, all the food groups, vegetable, grains, protein, dairy, fruit if you count the drink. See, I listen to you and remember."

"You're sweet."

"No, I'm a shit. And the only reason I got a kiss from you was because you couldn't run away."

"Turn on a light."

He fumbled for the switch on the cord by the bed. She saw the ceiling go from gray to white, the curved metal bar holding the blue curtain on steel rings, the stand with her saline bag. She shifted to see Rivera, his dark black hair coming to a widow's peak between his brown eyes.

"You don't look like a shit," she said. "Just sometimes you act like one."

"That didn't stop you from saving my life." He brushed the hair from his forehead. She loved when he did that.

He pulled the orange plastic chair close to her bed and sat, stroking the fingers at the end of her cast. "I want to give it another shot. Dropping in on you in the hospital, facing what you're facing, maybe this isn't the time to ask."

"I've been wanting us to have time to just talk. Not about cases and forensics. I don't want to give up on us," she said. "More than the training made me grab that gun. I'd do it again for you."

155

"Something you need to know … " He hesitated. "I don't want to ruin what's just happened between us, but Special Agent Pam Magnano came to see me. I was at the Valles house talking to neighbors about cooperation so we could use their houses and yards. She put me in a car like a witness at the scene. To get to the point, they're assessing you as an accomplice to Cervantes. They know about you being raped when you were a teenager and they know you think Senator Valles raped a friend of yours back in college. They see you putting Cervantes up to it, inciting him, maybe giving him more ideas than you've told them about. I'm sorry to bring bad news."

"I tell you I can't feel my legs and may never walk again? As I get older I can have complications, blood clots, infections, the impossible cost of living paralyzed on my own. Alone forever, who's going to want to be with me? Magnano's witch hunt, I'm not wasting time thinking about it."

"Denise, they've gone over your cases, talked to people, lawyers who've been on the other side. They believe you're capable of what they're thinking."

"Take the blanket off my legs."

That stopped him. He'd been building momentum, his words coming faster. When he lifted the blanket, agitation left his face.

"Tomas, there's nothing I can do about anything the FBI might be thinking." He was letting his fingertips move along her legs. She saw his hand coming toward her knee. She wanted to feel his touch.

He lifted his hand before he reached her thighs.

"Start over. Start at my feet."

Now his hand was on her instep. Sliding over the top of her ankle, along her shin. The knee again. The beginning of her thigh, the crease where her hip started.

Wait.

Something? She closed her eyes to concentrate. Yes, did she feel him? No, just wanting it so bad. That's why when the doctors tested her sensation they screened her view so she couldn't see where they were pricking her.

This is real. No, it isn't. With her eyes closed she couldn't tell where he was touching her.

"I'd get in bed with you if there was room and these tubes weren't in the way," he said.

"Hold me."

He bent over her chest, dropped one knee to the floor, and put his arms across her, his head on her shoulder.

"Can you come every day and do this?"

"No problem," he said. "They pulled me from the Valles situation. My closeness to you . . . "

"Closeness is good . . . "

" . . . they don't want me involved."

They listened to each other's breath, her feeling his weight, her chest rising, lifting his head so slightly. With her good hand she brushed his beautiful hair.

"You know what? We're not spending all our time talking about dead people and monsters. We're talking about us."

Rivera's phone rattled in his pocket. "Sorry, with everyone at the Valles barricades, I'm the duty officer." He read a text. "Body on the Navajo rez. I'll try to get back as soon as I can. We'll talk more. No dead bodies, no monsters, no hostage situation, no FBI investigations."

"We can work on closeness. I'm not liking being alone."

On his way out he kissed her feet. Did she feel anything? For sure, even if it was inside her chest.

SEVENTEEN

THE SHOT CAME AT 9:06 a.m. Dix to all his teams: "Who fired?"

The men in the arroyo had it: "Inside the house. Corner room, where we picked up the big guy."

Dix telling everyone to hold their position, only the arroyo team crawling forward, their leader asking, "Should we breach?" The chopper crew: "Ready with the helicopter, sir. We'll ladder down into the courtyard while Team Red takes the door." Dix liking it, getting an assault ready: "Team Green, you cut a hole in the garage door. I want Black taking the window to the living room. Orange, you've got the French doors in back."

Hold on. Helmick was calling him. Stand down. He was going forward.

And there he was, hands up, shirt off, wearing Bermuda shorts, sandals no socks to show he was completely unarmed and vulnerable. Walking slowly. Behind him, Magnano on the megaphone saying, "Mr. Cervantes, we need to talk. Phone service is still out. Mr. Helmick is going to give you a walkie-talkie. He's unarmed, see?"

Helmick looked in decent shape for a guy who talked for a living. Pale, though. White hair on his chest. Just a small roll above his hips.

Magnano again, "He'll put the walkie-talkie close to the front door so you don't have to expose yourself to retrieve it."

Dix's gun teams were telling him they had a clear shot. Dix told them sight in on the bottom corner where someone would have to kneel to get the walkie-talkie when they opened the door.

From inside the house, the voice they'd been hearing over its own megaphone: "Not the front door. Slide it under the garage door. Mrs. Valles will be the one reaching for it. It will be her head in your sniper's scope. If it's a bomb, she will be the one you kill."

"It's not a trick, Mr. Cervantes." Magnano had a good, calm tone in her voice, even through the filter of the megaphone. He'd heard she was a skilled negotiator even if she did come across as a mean cat lady. "What was the gunshot about?" Magnano asked. "Is someone hurt? Do they need medical attention?"

Now Helmick was on the front walk, where flagstones branched off on a diagonal to the garage. When he reached the driveway, the garage went up six inches, a garage door opener doing the work since there were no feet visible in the opening. Cervantes must have some powerful generators to be able to run everything.

Then suddenly it was quiet. The generators inside the garage had been turned off. Even the helicopters seemed silent. Helmick reached the garage, dropped to one knee, one hand came down. Dix could see the gray metal of the walkie-talkie as he slid it under the door. Then Helmick stood, both hands over his head, and backed away. He backed down the drive and Dix noticed the corner of the walkie-talkie, all he could see, disappearing into the shadows of the garage. Then the generators kicked on and the door came down.

Helmick gave his bare back to the house, dropped his hands, and walked the rest of the distance to the black panel truck where Magnano had the twin of the walkie-talkie he'd just delivered. Dix met him there.

"Cervantes came on. I introduced myself," she said. "We had a little talk. That shot. He said it was his associate testing if we could shoot through the walls."

"He give a name?" Dix asked as Helmick pulled on a shirt. "For the nervous one?"

"I asked. He ended the call."

"That was good, Art," Dix said. "The exposed walk alone was ballsy. But I know the other thing you did. You showed yourself to Cervantes as someone he could trust and didn't have to fear. You almost naked, him having you if he wanted. He's going to see that picture of you when you talk."

"Let me have that," Helmick told Magnano. She handed over the walkie-talkie. "Did you explain this is the best way for us to talk?"

"I gave him the spiel about how media might hack into his phones, how they did it in England. Broke into Princess Diana's voicemail. This way we could talk, just us, certain of no reporters listening. We know he doesn't like reporters from his son's case."

The little light on the narrow box in Helmick's hand glowed red. "Mr. Cervantes? Can you hear me? I would like to speak with you before the day gets older and we all get more tired and tense."

In a second they had an answer.

"I want my phones and Internet back."

"Good morning, Mr. Cervantes. We do, too. That was some storm last night. With your generators you've probably got more electric power than most of the city. A couple cell towers were also hit, the circuits fried. Nobody in Santa Fe has cell service. Or landlines that work. DSL, too, is down. But they're working on it. Regardless, as Pam explained, it's best we talk securely. The battery in your unit will last a very long time. These things are used by our military in places there are no recharge stations."

"Like Fallujah."

Helmick smiled at Magnano. They had gotten Cervantes talking.

"I lost a nephew in Kabul. My nephew was Army, like your boy. I know your son was in Kabul too, guarding the bridge in the center of town, before he was transferred to Iraq. I know how he fell in Fallujah. I'm not showing off, you know, how we can find out everything. It's that a lot of us share some of the same pain in losing a loved one in a country far away for things we might never see the sense of."

Nothing from Cervantes. They heard the helicopters again.

"You're very good, Mr. Helmick." Cervantes saying exactly what Dix had been thinking, noting how Helmick had even switched from his clipped manner of talking. "Where's Valles?"

Helmick kept trying to change the subject, talking about how the walkie-talkie Cervantes was holding was the same model his son's unit used in Iraq. In fact, these two actual handsets had been carried in Operation Enduring Freedom.

Cervantes wasn't biting.

"So much for that," Dix said.

Helmick had the walkie-talkie to his mouth, not giving up. "Mr. Cervantes, we need to hear Mrs. Valles's voice, to know she and the boys are unhurt." Pause. "Mr. Cervantes ... " He repeated the message three times before a woman's voice answered him.

"This is Patricia Valles. My sons and I have not been hurt. They're giving us plenty to eat, we have a place to sleep. But they are very serious about this. Please, where is my husband?"

———

Cervantes took the walkie-talkie from Patricia Valles. He was surprised again at how light it was. He remembered old Army surplus units made of steel with zinc batteries. The red light was out. It should be off. But was it? Were they still listening? Were they seeing him through a hidden camera? That other light, what did it do? Was that the camera?

He said, "It's time for showers for all of you. I don't want a bad smell coming out of your room when I open the door. One at a time. I'll take you to the bathroom and stand outside. Bobo will be keeping an eye on the FBI. Fifteen minutes each."

Then he took the walkie-talkie to the workbench in the garage and removed its guts. He found nothing that made him suspicious. Still, he put the pieces in a metal tool box and that went into an even larger, heavier metal file cabinet, then into a closet. He pushed the workbench against the door. You never know.

———

Cervantes took Clint first and told Patricia they'd stop at the boys' bedroom for clean underwear and socks. Clint didn't want to go. He clung to her shirttail, her arm, her thumb, the tip of her pinky as she pushed him out the door. That gave her a chance to scan the hall. She saw a long electrical cord and a garden hose running from the half bath in the hallway to the room at the end of the hall. A garden hose inside the house? She'd seen the cement mixer and bags of cement when she'd first arrived. Was Cervantes bricking up windows? Building a last stand for when the police came with their guns?

Patricia Valles was disappointed in her sons and hated admitting it. Clint bawling in terror about a trip to the shower. He's not going to hurt you, she told him. That's not what this is about, is it, Mr.

Cervantes? And Cervantes assuring the boy it was just a shower so they didn't start stinking in the closed room. But still, Clint sobbing, his chin shaking.

And Jimmy. Starting to bawl too. Pulling his knees to his chest and rocking. Neither of them being much support to her. Tell them 'act like a man' and what would they do? What 'man' would they think of? Dad? Their problem was they had too much of Sam in them.

She knew the Sam Baca Valles behind the makeup and padded shoulders. She'd known him with the ponytail. The Speedo dancer. Why do you do that? she'd asked. To make people happy, he'd said. Nuh-huh. To make yourself happy, Sammy. Seeing yourself in their eyes, if there wasn't a mirror in the room.

Where was he? She'd hoped it would be Sam on the walkie-talkie. Anything from him through the FBI would make this easier.

She wasn't going to comfort Jimmy. Let him pour it out so she could get some quiet when he was drained.

That was quick. The door opened and Clint returned, holding clean underwear against his chest. His hair was dry. He hadn't washed it. At least he was done crying, for now.

"The other boy," Cervantes said, the gun against his thigh. She was thankful he wasn't waving it at them anymore.

Jimmy shrank into the wall and shook his head back and forth. His chin quivered. Clint's nose ran and here he was crying again. My little men.

"Be strong for your mother," Cervantes said. "Let's go. You're keeping her from getting her own shower."

Patricia pried Jimmy's hands from his hair and lifted him to his feet. She had done this for Sam. She'd stood him on his feet and kept him there all these years. He still had that Speedo in his bottom drawer. She'd caught him posing in front of a mirror not long ago, trying to stretch out the waistband where it was cutting him.

"Jimmy," she said, "your brother's come back just fine. Look, he's not crying anymore, are you, Clint, my strong boy? You'll be fine too. Go, so Mommy can have her turn."

She pushed him out the door and a little further so she could get another look. She was completely out in the hallway now and hearing helicopters over the house, the sound coming in from skylights they didn't have in their room. She wondered again about the garden hose. Her toe was touching the green plastic casing. The hose was hot. She hadn't known they used hot water to mix cement.

"I've got him." Cervantes had Jimmy by the collar and used the gun to wave her back inside.

She looked the other way, quick, and got a glimpse of the dining room and television screens and a computer on her dining table. It was darker than it should be for daytime and she saw that the window that usually threw light down the hallway had been boarded up. But the skylight still cast a bright square on the tile floor. She was seeing men in black on ropes coming through that hole in the roof when Cervantes touched her with the barrel, a little shove in the meat of her shoulder.

"Back inside."

Clint was really better. He was back to playing with his electronic games. She wiped his nose and remembered something that made her want her trip to the shower to come quickly.

"Pitchforks and torches." Sam's great fear during the last presidential election. People were angry. There'd been shoving and fighting at some of the early polling places. The whole campaign season had been vicious. Gun sales were soaring and they had "civil war" thrown at them at a town hall meeting, Sam's last. No more after that nightmare. Now he did "telephone town halls." You can reach more people, his spokesperson explained. Or online conversations where people sent their questions in a day before. We can provide better answers if people let us know in advance what they want discussed, the flack explained.

Right. Sam was just scared of his constituents.

He had bought his own guns. She demanded he keep them unloaded in a gun locker in a closet in their bedroom. He said, lotta good that'll do when there's trouble at the front door. He stashed the guns around the house, saying they'll be close when we need them. He started using lines the gun nuts had used against him when he'd pushed for tighter controls. "When seconds count, the police are only minutes away." That was his favorite. And he'd give her a look: you can't argue with that.

She wanted to know what good those guns would do her if she didn't know where they were. So he showed her a gun in the den on the bookshelf behind a dictionary, one in the entry closet on the shelf under winter hats ("when they're at the door for real"), in the garage behind cans of WD-40.

Our boys will find them, you idiot, and kill themselves.

He added trigger locks, all with the same combination. Her name for her grandmother, *Cura.* Short for *curandera.* Clorinda Garza had grown up in Truchas and learned the plants and weeds from her own grandmother. Patricia had been able to place her photo in the Palace of Governors as part of a display on traditional Hispanic medicine. When doctors were too far away (always) or too expensive (always), people came to Clorinda with what little they could pay and she mostly refused. The boy with asthma who couldn't work with his father—Clorinda Garza made a tea so he could breathe. A girl birthing her first child, screaming in pain—Clorinda had broth for her. Fevers, infections, snake bites, skin problems.

Salves, compounds, crushed seeds mixed with honey. Miracles from the kitchen on the back of her tiny, sagging house.

She might accept a chicken, eggs, venison, elk sausage as payment. Food was a sign of love and community and family. She'd tried teaching Patricia, but her granddaughter wanted out of the little villages in the mountains where the black tar heroin was killing descendants of conquistadors. At least her grandmother showed her magic with plants instead of how to work a hypodermic needle, a family tradition among too many neighbors.

In the master bath, inside the double-door linen closet, high in a niche that had once been an air vent before the previous owner remodeled, Sam had hidden a revolver with a lock that opened when you rolled the letters to read *cura*.

"Clint." The boy didn't look up from his game. "Clint!" Now he was looking. "Which bathroom did he take you to?"

"The guest bedroom." And Clint put his eyes back on his game. "He said it was closest."

Sam had never hidden a gun there.

When it was her turn she walked ahead of Cervantes and stopped at the door to the guest bath. There was water on the floor and wet towels on the toilet seat. The boys' soiled underwear had been kicked under the pedestal sink.

"There are fresh towels in the master bath," she said.

Cervantes opened a closet. Shelves of folded clean towels. He tossed one at her.

"May I get my shampoo and conditioner, at least? I am not going to wash my hair with Irish Spring."

That worked. She led the way. Cervantes stood in the doorway while she got her shampoo. Then a hairbrush, then the hair dryer. Then a can of hair spray. Her arms were full.

"Would you get that?" She nodded at a bottle of skin cream and tried to keep her eyes off the closet door. "And my conditioner over there."

"You might as well shower here," he said and closed the door.

Now her eyes went to the closet. She needed to stand on the lowest shelf to reach. With one hand braced on the wall she felt into the shadow above the doorframe. She touched metal and rough plastic, the no-slip grip Sam had added to the revolver. She had to climb another shelf higher to get the gun.

Cervantes banged on the closed bathroom door. "You've got fifteen minutes. Get going. What are you doing in there?"

"I was crying. I'm sorry."

It was a big gun. Heavy. She could barely close her hand around the grip. The trigger lock was in place. She rolled the dials and saw her grandmother's nickname. The lock fell at her feet and she was glad for the carpet so it didn't make a sound.

When Cervantes opened the door, should she shoot him? What about Bobo? He'd hear and come running?

She hadn't pulled a trigger since her older brother forced her to take a shot at a squirrel. She'd hit it. It didn't bother her. She wasn't afraid of guns. This one felt good in her hand, heavy, solid. Its black metal, the cylinder with brass cartridges she could see when she held it out, the grip that wouldn't slip even in a sweaty hand, it all said *confidence* to her. And power.

"Twelve minutes," Cervantes yelled through the door.

Shoot him. Twice to make sure. Step over the body, hide in a room Bobo would pass when he came to investigate. Shoot that one in the back. Shoot him again. Free her sons, open the front door, hands waving. Step out into the sunlight and run for it.

"Stop crying and get washed."

She leaned into the shower and turned on water.

She would probably need both hands to fire this gun. She tried aiming with one hand. Nope. She couldn't keep it steady. The front sight kept dropping.

Was there a safety on this gun? That tab there. It snicked when she pushed down.

What if Cervantes didn't go down right away and fired back? She got the feeling he knew more about guns than her. This big gun, after she fired once, who knew where the next shot would go? Probably the ceiling or her foot. Cervantes would get her then. Her boys would be on their own, with an angry wounded man. And Bobo, charging hard from the other end of the house.

Sneak the gun back with her. In what? She was wearing pants that showed everything and a shirt already stretched over the weight she should lose. She should have asked to stop in her bedroom for clean clothes. She could hide the gun in her dirty ones after she'd changed. Wait. Why would she be taking dirty clothes back to the storage room? Try carrying it in towels, tell Cervantes she wanted some with her. But if he said no and snatched the towels away...

She put the gun back in its place in the niche high in the closet, without the trigger lock, hearing Sam lecturing her on how stupid it is to keep guns inside a safe at the other end of the house.

EIGHTEEN

The hospital had a candy striper, a nice woman with glasses on a chain and her white hair in a bun. She pushed a cart with books and magazines. At the door to Aragon's room she announced she had romances, adventures, Westerns, detective stories. Magazines on cars, cooking, and Rocky Mountain homes. Bibles and books on weight loss, pregnancy, and personal finance. Aragon asked what she had in the way of effects of dehydration and heat on the human brain. Just as she was regretting being a smartass the nice lady said, I could run to the library.

What Aragon wanted were newspaper articles on a case she read about from Carlsbad National Park. Two men hiked into the scorching desert. A week later they were found a mile from their car, one of them stabbed in the heart. The survivor said they'd lost their minds when their water ran out. His friend begged him to kill him. She'd forgotten the year and the names hadn't stuck.

The nice lady's name was Florence Peters. When she wasn't pushing a book cart down hospital corridors she volunteered at the library and would see what she could find. You're the policewoman who got those terrible men who hurt that boy. I heard from the nurses. Is this for your next case?

Aragon took a book from the cart to end the conversation and pulled the McSwaim file from under her covers when she was alone.

She'd never handled a death from dehydration and heat stroke. All her dead people had been shot, stabbed, beaten, choked, drowned, poisoned, or burned. She wanted to know if Amy's bizarre behavior, eating dirt then trying to kiss everyone, could in fact be explained by a thirst that would kill you.

Her television had been playing without sound. Using the remote, she turned up the volume for the lunch hour news. A reporter was at the Valles standoff, saying authorities had no contact with the hostage-taker, who they were now identifying as Pete Cervantes, age 67, a native of Santa Fe, a widower, the father of a soldier killed in Iraq and another son murdered at the family business. His motive remained a mystery, the reporter said. Then the screen cut to film of Pete leaving the courtroom after the sentencing of his son's murderer, grim-faced, with her at his side. She wished she could replay the tape. It looked like he'd been holding her hand.

Sure enough, the reporter noted that the woman with Cervantes was Santa Fe Police Department detective Denise Aragon, recently injured in the apprehension of the men believed to be responsible for the abduction and murder of Santa Fe teenager Chase Easterling.

Then a view from the station's news helicopter, on an angle, from far away but you could see police cars parked sideways across streets so that they formed a cordon spread over several blocks. The reporter explained they were looking at the Valles residence. He called it a "compound."

Then he passed to a network reporter in Washington, who said the whereabouts of Senator Valles remain unknown. Here came a photo of Valles on the steps of the Capitol, suit jacket over his shoulder, face turned to the sun, broad features thoughtful and strong. His office has issued only a brief statement saying the senator was praying for his family and calling upon Cervantes to end this peacefully. The reporter ended his segment by stating that Valles was believed to have returned to the United States from Europe and might be in the Santa Fe area, though the senator's office would not confirm that information.

When the screen split into three talking heads speaking from different locations around the country, experts who knew nothing but were going to talk anyway, Aragon muted the sound. If they were going to do an honest, complete profile on Cervantes, she would have told them to include something more about the death of the first son in Iraq. That had been hard on Pete. But when Fallujah was recaptured, a city his son gave his life to liberate, Pete concluded his boy had died for nothing. He always talked about the stupid politicians who had gotten his sons killed. Sam Baca Valles was at the top of his list. Valles had never opposed the Iraq war until he was running for federal office, and it was so unpopular by then that opposition meant nothing. He sure made it sound like he'd always stood against the war, calling his stance a "lonely, courageous crusade to save the nation from drowning in a quagmire." But Pete had found a photo of Valles with a New Mexico Army Reserve unit heading to Iraq, giving a thumbs-up next to soldiers holding a sign that said *Shock and Awe, How America says Hello*.

Aragon tucked the McSwaim file under the covers. This wasn't something she wanted visitors to see when they found her asleep. From down by her hip she pulled up the map of the Sandia Mountain

Wilderness that Lewis had provided and unfolded it across her chest. She wished she could bend her knees and sit up to make it easier to read, but that wasn't going to happen.

To make it workable, she folded the map into large squares to study. She started with the area around the top of the Tram: the visitor center, the restaurant and bar up there at 10,700 feet. Amy came in from the south, already fifteen or more miles behind her, and a lot of elevation gain from her start in Tijeras Canyon. She'd ask Lewis to discover the exact temperature range for different elevations that day. She had the impression it had been unusually hot.

How long had Amy been with them in the restaurant? Long enough to eat, argue about having a beer, finish her beer, and object to a second. She joked around with the gal pals come to celebrate her birthday but mostly to drink. She remembered Amy reapplying sunscreen, one of them helping with her back. And retying her shoes. That she remembered because Amy had the kind of expensive gear that made her envious. Amy was using trail shoes, something new on the market, better for running mountain paths than the superlight runners she wore when jogging city streets.

Even Amy's pack was cool. A heavy, pretty nylon with all sorts of tabs and pockets and ways to make it conform to your body. Amy wore those smart wrap-around sunglasses. Expensive.

Wait.

What happened to the sunglasses? The ladies who found Amy said her pupils were dilated. No mention of sunglasses. If she'd been running in full sun without the shades, her pupils would have been pinpricks. Even with shades, in the intense sun would they dilate like they were struggling to focus in the dark?

That cool running pack. What had happened to it? There was no reference to it in the EMT notes. These many years later, she didn't expect they'd ever get the pack to work with.

To work with. Work on what?

She felt herself dozing. They'd cut off the Percocets and the needle in her arm. Either she got signals of hope from her legs—pain—and dealt with the pangs from her injured arm, or she felt nothing from her arm and gave up on the legs for now. They were giving her only Tylenol and sleeping pills. Her arm hurt like hell with the slightest movement. It had awakened her during the night. She hadn't slept well despite her chemicals in her blood. Stay still, Denise. Let the eyelids go.

The pain in her arm woke her again. She came fully awake fast. Was that Magnano, reading the map she'd left on her chest when she dozed off?

"Planning a hike?" Magnano said.

Someone else in the room. Lewis behind Magnano, arms folded. Fewer bandages on his head today.

"I'm trying to give myself something to hope for," Aragon said. She didn't like being on her back with Magnano and her eyebrow looming over her. She felt like an animal on a butcher's block.

"This is where Amy McSwaim was found, before she died on the way to the hospital." Magnano folded the map and placed it back where it had been on the covers. "You didn't tell us."

"You didn't ask about Amy."

"I asked about your hostility toward Senator Valles. You said, old college memories. The guy was just a jerk. You didn't tell us you believe he'd raped your friend, who was dead before that summer was half over. We know Margaret Baldonado has been to see you."

"Hadn't seen her in years. All of a sudden, she was standing where you are." As she said it, Aragon understood. "You sent her. Did you have her wired?"

"Ms. Baldonado agreed to cooperate as we try to comprehend this very serious situation with your friend, Mr. Cervantes. She agreed you are vindictive, you don't let small slights go. And you were ready to assault Sam Valles when you heard what Amy Mc-Swaim was alleging."

Margaret Baldonado had three kids and another not hers, in a job she owed to politics.

"Perhaps those feelings are run-of-the-mill for you." Magnano was here to give her a speech. "We've read your file. Good police work, a lot of stepping over lines. And we know about you being raped as a teenager, your boyfriend being murdered as he tried to save you, and how that's the reason you became a cop. So bad guys never get away again, no matter what. The affection you share with Agent Tomas Rivera notwithstanding, he is our employee and he knows the rules. He told us."

"So the message is, I can't trust anybody?"

"The message is, we will eventually know everything. Keep that in mind, as well as the fact that your friend Pete Cervantes is in way over his head. How will you live with yourself if this goes bad for him or the people he's holding? When their lives are wasted? Wastes of skin, for real."

Magnano turned to Lewis. He had inched forward but now backed into a cupboard, his folded arms making his biceps look even bigger.

"Anything you want to tell us, Detective Lewis? We know you were here when Ms. Baldonado visited."

"Then you know all I have to say."

"Your daughters, I understand they're very good soccer players. Your wife's job at the Game and Fish Department, that's an exempt position, like Ms. Baldonado? Meaning she's not protected civil service but an at-will employee who can be fired for any reason at all."

"Did I just hear you threaten my wife?"

Magnano moved to the door, turned back and looked from one to the other.

"Pete Cervantes is not the only person in over his head."

"Nice lady," Aragon said when she was gone. "You should stay very far away from me, Rick. Your first instinct was right."

"She sounded a lot different. Something's changed."

Aragon pointed at the silent television screen. A still photo of Senator Sam Baca Valles above a scrolling banner reporting that he would be giving a statement in time for the evening news.

"That's what changed," Aragon said. "He's in town."

"Screw Magnano. She's not going to scare me off. Hell, I tell my wife about the threat, she'll pitch in and run errands for us," Lewis said. "Hey, I was going to tell you, I've got contact information for some of the women who found Amy McSwaim. You want to come to Albuquerque for the interviews? We can hit the Quarters for ribs. Maybe some of the great brewpubs the Duke City's sprouting. They're kicking Santa Fe's butt. C'mon. Get your stuff and let's go."

"Funny." Aragon turned off the television. She didn't want to see Sam Valles's face up there again. She might throw the bedpan.

————

Later, after visits from six detectives, twelve cousins, and a reporter who'd snuck in posing as a rookie cop, plus more cards on the wall, more flowers in the room making her sneeze, and a massage of her legs by a good-looking guy named Deke with a southern accent who'd laughed and joked and made her forget where she was, Sergeant Perez came by. In full uniform today.

"I'm going back and forth with the governor, the mayor, the chief, the FBI, this guy for Valles. Imagine a baggy-faced bulldog on its hind legs, a bent tooth snagging his lip. That's Martin Kilgore, chief of staff. Perks of my job, all this seniority I've earned, these pins on my chest for diving into a burning car, putting myself between a gun and kid, taking down a robber in a MacDonald's where he's got everyone in the cooler, and I'm the one gets to deal with the jerks." He opened the flap on his breast pocket and dug with his fingers. "I have something for you."

He handed her a sheet of paper with names and phone numbers.

"This is the EMT crew that tried to get Amy McSwaim to the hospital, their addresses and phones. I'm running out of favors in Albuquerque. Make something out of this."

She was calling, dialing with one hand, her cell on bedsheets, before he was out the door.

What the driver, Pedro Jonas, had to say: How'd you get this number? You're calling on my personal cell and I don't give that out. Okay, I'll talk. I'm waiting for my kids at the dentist. I drive for UPS now. People are glad to see me. I do deliveries, not pickups. No more bringing broken bodies down the Interstate at a hundred miles an hour. I remember this one, one of my last. You get to wondering if you'd gone faster, taken the middle lane, taken another exit, not slowed for the red light because you didn't trust other drivers to stop, you get to wondering if they'd have lived. I couldn't take that anymore. And this one, I helped take her from the SUV, I forgot what kind. Old ladies in hiking shorts and boots wringing their hands, telling us to be careful. I pushed my unit as far up that piece of shit road as I could. These women were frantic, getting in our way. The girl, it was like picking up hot coals she was that warm. But what I remember was her trying to kiss everyone. Not a thank you, you saved me kiss. A goofy, drunk girl smooch. Even the ladies. Her lips were dry, not a drop of saliva in her mouth. And she's saying strange stuff to everyone, how she loves us all, forgives us. Is sorry she hurt us. Then, look at the trees dancing. When the guys told me from the back we lost her just as I saw the sign for the hospital coming up, my second one dying on me in a day. I was done.

The paramedic, Chad Mankiller: I know, not the best name if I get sued for malpractice. But my Apache ancestors earned that name and I'm sticking with it. It gets attention, I'll tell you. I really don't remember the case. It's been a long time. You know how many dead bodies I've seen, some I can't stop seeing? Send me the notes to refresh my recollection, I'd be glad to help once I get a medical release form. I guess it would have to be from her husband or parents.

The Captain of the Fire and Rescue Crew, Roger Parra: I know about you. I'm sorry you got banged up nailing bad guys. You're at St. Vincent in Santa Fe, right? I'm finishing a class here at the Law Enforcement Academy. I'm off the street, so to speak, teaching cops and paramedics and firemen. A lot less stress. It's a blessing. Give me your room number. I'll be right over. I've thought about that case over the years. With what we know now, I worry that we got that one wrong.

The nurses kept her busy in the meantime and she kept telling them to hurry up with the humiliating things they were doing to her. She wanted to be ready when Parra arrived. "I worry that we got that one wrong." Him and Perez seeing something in Amy's death nobody else saw. A nurse gave her a sponge bath, then four of them turned her gently to change the sheets under her. Neat how they made the bed with her in it. Temperature check. Blood pressure check. She knew they were pricking her toe with a needle without seeing it. She had seen through their ruse of distracting her, like shining a light in her eyes. As though there was anything wrong with her eyes. They were right in being deceptive. If she had seen them pricking a toe she'd never be sure she wasn't fooling herself when she said she felt something.

At first, she thought Parra was someone with the hospital staff. He stood inside the door watching the nurses at work. He stayed when they left and introduced himself. With his name, she'd thought he'd be Hispanic. But he was dark-skinned, Pakistani maybe, some Asian ethnicity. Small of build, fine features, the hands of a child, smooth skin and a cowlick that made him look boyish. All the things he'd seen in his work, none of it had left a mark on him. She envied the smile in his eyes.

"Are they exercising you?" His first words after his name.

"I squeeze this thing in my good hand."

"They should be making you use your legs," he said. "Providing locomotion until you can move them yourself."

Was Parra a quack? Everyone knows you don't move if you've suffered a spinal injury, right? She'd never say a word to Lewis, but he probably shouldn't have carried her in his arms. Maybe he'd pinched something, folding her against his chest. Maybe she'd be walking right now.

"Use it or lose it," Parra said. His little hands had palms lighter than his skin and he waved them as he talked. "Good, simple advice. I've seen men who've fallen off buildings and thought they'd never lift their head off a pillow. If the spinal column has not been impinged or severed, there's always hope. By moving the muscles we're telling the nervous system it is needed. As with weight lifting and dementia. We are learning that putting demands on the body stimulates the brain and keeps it healthy. These men who've fallen, the ones who were forced to move, they came back. The ones who practiced lying in a coffin, they were ready years before their time. The body is a marvelous creation and we should never give up on it. It will never cease to amaze us as long as we maintain that sense of wonder and awe in our hearts."

Now she understood why he looked so young. He loved his work.

"Educate my doctors," she said.

"I most certainly will. You have a very good body, if I may say so. You have prepared it for a challenge such as you now face."

"Sit down, Mr. Parra. Let's talk. Read this first."

From under her covers she withdrew the notes from the EMT team that had transported Amy McSwaim off the mountain.

Parra chuckled as he read and she wondered about him. Maybe he liked his work too much.

"Like hieroglyphics. We no longer use this system of abbreviation. But I remember it. And I remember this case without my notes, though they help sharpen the details."

"You said you thought maybe you had missed something, looking back with what you know now."

"Every year, so many new advances, knowledge persistently marching forward. This is not the only case that would perhaps have benefitted in retrospect from the current state of knowledge. The eyes," he said, and she felt something go through her with his next words. "Extremely dilated. We had been trained to interpret dilated pupils as consistently associated with heat stroke, a condition that can be fatal, and heat exhaustion, which is rarely fatal but can be. But the studies behind that presumption were thin. More and more papers recognized pinpoint pupils in patients suffering from heat stroke. You think about the physio-mechanism of heat stroke, that makes sense. To me, more sense than dilated pupils. Those papers, the more rigorous studies, were not widely disseminated until after Ms. McSwaim's death."

He slowed the pace of his words. "As a police officer, certainly you are aware of an unfortunately common explanation for dilated pupils."

"I know where you're going. Amy didn't use drugs. She was a health nut. Beer, yes, maybe a little wine at parties, that was it."

"Her behavior when we loaded her onto the gurney was quite odd. As though she wanted to have intimate romance with everyone around her. And then she was angry at herself, saying she was sorry over and over. We had to clear her mouth of dirt before intubation. The 911 call from the distressed hiker ladies said she'd been eating dirt. I wonder if there was not a psychotic event that preceded the onset of her physical maladies. Unless we admit the possibility of some form of drug abuse. Would she have ingested stimulants to enhance her physical performance? That is one of the things I've wondered about. At the time, I did not have the opportunity to investigate that possibility."

Amy had been pushing herself harder and harder. How she did some of the things in the time she pulled them off, the speed of her long-distance mountain runs, how fast she could pedal up to Sandia Crest on the twisty, steep road, Aragon had always been impressed. Amy never would have told anyone if she'd been doping.

"Her case shares similarities with soccer players and football players who, using stimulants"—Parra's two-tone hands were waving again now that he was done reading—"collapsed and died in extreme heat and high humidity. I handled one such unfortunate athlete's death. He was hoping to make the cut, as you say, for a college football team. The vials for his stimulants were found in his locker. An autopsy was conducted and stimulants in large concentration were detected in his blood, urine, and liver. That explained why an extraordinarily healthy young man was killed by exertions he normally found pleasing."

"There wasn't an autopsy for Amy."

"Everyone was so confident, yes. We were certain why and how she died. Heat stroke and dehydration brought on by a foolish disregard for the harsh terrain and environment of New Mexico wilderness," Parra said. "As a younger man, I was generally far more certain about things than I am now. Frequently in error, never in doubt, that was my frame of mind. Now I see how truly in error I may have been in my unshakable self-confidence. You need always to ask the next question and never stop questioning yourself."

"If you question yourself too much," Aragon said, "you're paralyzed. Sometimes you just have to make that jump and take what comes when you hit the ground."

"As you did. Your role is to jump. Then it is my turn to step in and pick up the pieces. May I?" He touched her legs where sheets had slid off. "Do not give up on these fine tools. I do not feel death here. I feel life eager to return."

"What are you, a mystic, too?"

"There is more to the world than we put in our books of science. So many things I've seen that cannot be explained by what we pretend to know. If it is acceptable to you, I'd like to pray for healing. May I?" But with his eyes already closed and his lips moving, he wasn't waiting for an answer.

If she'd been able, she would have pulled away. What was this? She caught some words. At least it was a Christian prayer, not Hindu or whatever religion they had wherever he was from. Her last experience with Christianity was listening to her mother yell at the Jesus on the cross over the bed. The family had abandoned the church after she was raped. Her mother insisted she'd never left Jesus. She still had a relationship. I'm angry with him, she said. I tell him every day.

When she was about six, her parents had let her see a *penitente* ceremony in the mountains up above Chimayo. You parked off a dirt road, then walked a mile on a rough, rocky path to the stone church, centuries old, a secret place kept up by families who'd come to these mountains hundreds of years ago. She recognized some of the Catholic ceremony, the lit candles inside the cool darkness showing the hand-carved *santos* among the shadows. What happened outside in the church yard, a patch cleared of trees and boulders, terrified her: a shirtless man cried out to God, shouting the words of Jesus about being forsaken and forgiveness, flecked with blood, real thorns pushed on his head, whipped by his friends with leather strips studded with granite shards. She ran away before they could nail him to a cross.

Several officers had tried getting her to come to the house church run by a State Police captain turned fiery evangelist. She went once to shut them up. All the weeping by grown men, the statie shouting to the ceiling, a woman falling backward, hands raised above her head, to be caught and eased to the floor by two "deacons" she knew were prison guards. She couldn't wait to get out of there.

The city's long-time sergeant in charge of child abuse was another pray-er. He had photos on his desk of the children in his cases. You'd see him in the middle of the day, head bowed, palms turned up to the acoustic tile ceiling with pencils stuck there. He'd work his way through the photos, praying for the children in his cases.

None of those men were nuts, not even the shaking, shouting statie. She'd worked cases with them all. She'd trusted them with her life. They were clear thinkers, smart, tough, no-nonsense people.

Why was she trying to pull away from Parra?

Hell, she'd let her friend the Buddhist priestess talk her into a guided meditation inside a quiet room in the temple on the south side of town. That hadn't hurt. In fact, she'd learned a few things about herself. It didn't come out the way her gentle friend had hoped. She emerged more fired up about policing than she'd gone in. She knew the job was what fed her, defined her, gave her a reason to live. By the end of that week, she'd shot and killed the Silva brothers.

She let Parra go on with his mumbled praying. Another very smart guy. She'd respected everything about him until the praying started. Now she realized that was more about herself than him.

He was looking at her, his hand off her leg.

"Have I made you uncomfortable? I apologize. I was presumptuous."

"Nobody's prayed for me like that. You surprised me. You're a doctor, well, almost. I didn't see mumbo-jumbo coming after all the science you were giving me."

His hand hovered above her leg. She imagined—it was imagination, right?—that she'd felt warmth on the surface of her skin.

"I attended a two-week training at Johns Hopkins in Baltimore," Parra said. "One of the finest, most advanced medical facilities in the world. In the wing where the doctors keep offices there's an atrium and a huge brass statue of Jesus Christ. The foot is polished smooth and bright. Surgeons with more skill and knowledge than I, great men and women of science, touch that foot before they enter the surgical theater. They have touched it so often, it glows."

He was glowing.

"Pray some more," she said. "What do I have to lose?"

He lowered his hand to her leg and soft, patient words she could barely hear, some she could not make out, came from his lips. There! Warmth. No, she wasn't feeling anything, no instant miracle. No deep, booming voice from above. No take up your mat, rise and walk, my child.

But after a while she heard, *It's going to be okay.* It wasn't Parra speaking. What the hell? Wrong question. She closed her eyes and went with it.

She wished Parra had stayed longer. Minutes after he was gone the face of Senator Sam Baca Valles filled the television screen. She upped the volume. She knew his voice and hated it. It was now saying he had full confidence the FBI would find a peaceful resolution. He spoke to the camera, but he was addressing Pete Cervantes. She could hear his voice from the corridor. All the televisions on the floor had this on.

"You have been injured, your heart broken. Your family has suffered. How can you find solace in causing another family to feel pain and terror? I know of you, though we've never met. You are a good man. You've led a responsible, honorable life. Please release my family unharmed. I will hear you out, away from the guns and the fear."

What about Cervantes's terms? The senator's life for his family's?

What are you going to do, Sam?

Then Valles asked everyone gathered around him and in the viewing audience to join him in a prayer. For peace, understanding, compassion, a lifting of the darkness. He prayed for Cervantes, for his broken heart, for God to still the rage inside him and not to throw away a lifetime of respect he had earned.

A lot of God stuff today.

Finished with his prayer, Valles looked straight into the camera. "If I could give my life for my family, exchange my security for theirs, I would do so without a second's hesitation."

Well, you can, asshole. Walk up to the house with your hands over your head.

Aragon searched for something to throw. The bedpan had been removed. Good thing. Only the juice glass, real glass not the filmy plastic pink drinks with medicine, was in reach. It shattered on the wall, not close to the television. She'd never been good throwing lefty.

A nurse came, the one on day shift. She looked at the shards of glass, the wet stain on the wall, Valles's face on the screen. She returned with paper towels and a dustpan and cleaned up. The screen was now dark and Aragon had pulled a pillow over her eyes.

The nurse's station was too far away for Aragon to hear what went on. She would need to be right there to hear the nurse speaking into a telephone in a soft voice.

"Agent Magnano. You told me to call if my patient, Denise Aragon, said anything about Senator Valles. She didn't *say* anything, but I thought you should know…"

NINETEEN

LORNA PIERSON SLEPT WITH her face turned away, a bar of sunlight sneaking under the curtain and slicing her in two at the hips. Danny let his eyes travel her fine long body, saying to himself, handling calls from wingnuts got me this. How else did you land in a multi-million dollar house, all the booze you wanted, and a woman who knew what she was doing telling him how lucky *she* was, my own nineteen-year-old Energizer Bunny, never runs down. Always ready to go, I'm the one who needs a break.

Lorna's lipstick and a film of Grenadine on glasses by the bed. They'd sipped the sweet red liquor between soaking the bedsheets with sweat. Lorna took him around the guesthouse, trying out other surfaces. All good except the Astroturf putting green in the corner of the living room. Let's play Tiger Woods, Lorna had said. And a whole bunch of bad jokes involving putters and driving irons. He had to quit on the Astroturf before his shins and knees were worn to the bone.

There was a whirlpool bath in the bathroom. He opened faucets to fill the tub and made himself coffee in the galley kitchen. Lorna, taking the whole bed, rolled onto her back, an arm across her eyes, her nipples pointing straight up at the ceiling. He walked past, gathering clothes to wear, and closed the bathroom door behind him.

Some kind of bubble bath selection in a rack over the tub. He went with "Southwest Sage" and it smelled good. He sank into the foam and pushed the button for the whirlpool, feeling the raw skin on his knees where the jets hit. There was a depression in the side of the tub for your head. Lying there he saw he was facing a television screen. On the rack with the suds and salts was a black remote control.

A local station came on, broadcasting from Santa Fe the latest on the Valles hostage standoff. A family photo of Senator Valles and his wife and sons in the upper left, shots of police activity filling the rest of the screen. Now a reporter with a microphone to her lips. She looked like a high school girl who spent a lot of time with a curling iron. Then the name at the bottom, *Erica Gabaldon reporting*. He knew her. She was a cousin from Tierra Amarilla. He used to watch Erica and the other big kids hanging out at *matanzas* away from the adults and wanted to be part of their circle. She'd made it big early in life and gotten out. Now her relatives watched her every night, so many across the state and in southern Colorado they boosted the station's ratings. She was under an inch of makeup, hair that didn't move in the wind, tight dress, talking to someone with a windbreaker that said *FBI*. The FBI guy was saying they still had no clue as to the motivation behind this act of terrorism. "Nor," he said, "has Mr. Cervantes stated any demands. Negotiations have not been initiated because Mr. Cervantes has not told anyone what he wants."

The man saying it, Danny was sure he'd seen him last night arriving with the other FBI people. It was the thick glasses. He had a hard time seeing FBI agents wearing glasses like that.

"Danny?"

There was Lorna, naked, her bush darker than her hair. At eye level with suds up to his chin, with the bright lights here in the bathroom, he saw a couple white hairs in there he hadn't seen in the candlelight.

"You're watching TV." And the remote control was in her hand, the screen black. "You don't need that. There's nothing in the world better than this." She found room for a foot on the other side of his body. She stood above him while the whirlpool pushed bubbles around her calves. That hungry look in her eyes always surprised him, how fast it came on. She surprised him again when she dropped the remote into the bathwater before she put her knees on his shoulders.

Back in the bedroom, after he'd survived not drowning, he looked for the remote for the television on the dresser. He'd seen it last night by the mirror. Now it was gone. He pressed *power* on the set and nothing happened. He started to look behind the screen to see if the cord was plugged in and felt her teeth on his butt. Lorna pulled him backward to the bed, her fingers using his hip bones like handles. Those long muscles of hers, he'd learned he couldn't fight her off.

They broke the slats on the bed. The mattress crashed through the bed frame and Lorna said, "Nine point ohhhhhhh on the Richter."

They showered and dressed together. Walked to the main house together, after she'd followed him to the edge of the terrace to look at sky and mountains and the helicopters in the distance above Santa Fe.

"Come, help me in the house." She tugged his hand. In the kitchen she bumped hips, pinched his ass where she'd bit him. "Ask the senator and Marty if they want anything to eat."

Senator Valles and Martin Kilgore stood in front of the house by the driveway, talking. The view here was to the south, the Sandia Mountains, smudges of more mountains beyond that, the Manzanos and the Magdalenas with desert in between. They shut up when he came close and didn't start talking again until he was reentering the front door.

"Sandwiches. Whatever," he told Lorna.

"Whatever isn't helpful."

"That's what they said." He noticed the television that had been in the kitchen by the breakfast nook was gone.

Washing dishes, she made sure the front of her shirt got wet and made sure he noticed.

Only when he went to the bathroom off the hallway that went back to the bedrooms where Senator Valles and Kilgore were staying was he alone. Shaving kits were open by the twin sinks, the kind that are bowls mounted above the counter. Dirty towels and men's underwear clogged the floor. It looked like his bathroom without rust and peeling paint. A phone was in here. He tried it. No dial tone. But the television worked. It was on an extension arm so you could position it while you shaved or sat on the john. He turned on the fan and opened the faucet and locked the door and put the volume on low. He scanned channels until he found a news network. It was a shot from the sky looking down on Santa Fe, a reporter speaking over propeller wash telling listeners that was Valles's house down there, where no cars or anything moved. Then, "Earlier today, Senator Valles gave his first public statement on the crisis. Here it is again for our viewers."

The square-headed man with the strong chin eating sandwiches outside at a table under an umbrella with the World's Ugliest Man, fifty feet away, there he was on the screen. Somber. In a dark jacket and tie, not the loose clothes he was wearing now. Kilgore behind him, waving other people out of the shot. Then it was only Senator Valles on the screen. Danny listened to the statement and heard nothing about Cervantes's demands. What he heard was Valles lying.

How can you have *no idea what Cervantes wants*? I told you on the plane.

"Danny, are you in there?" Lorna knocking at the door. "C'mon, I want to brush up on my golf game. I found shin guards and knee-pads in the kids' room. These people's grandson must be a catcher."

Danny turned off the television and flushed the toilet though he hadn't used it. He left the fan on. When he opened the door Lorna looked past him, right at the television.

"You suit up, sweetie. I'll be right there."

She pushed past him. As she closed the door he saw her reaching around to touch the back of the screen and he wondered why; the power switch was on the front.

He was trying to figure out the straps on the shin guards when he understood: to see if it was warm.

Now Lewis looked like he only had a very bad sunburn. The bandages were off his head. His ears were peeling. They'd cut all his hair, front and back, as short as hers so he could apply salve to the burned skin.

He rubbed his scalp when he stepped in the room.

"We make quite a pair," he said. "Except I don't have to wear a wig to court." He jerked a thumb behind him. "There's a big meeting in the corridor. They're talking about you."

"I told them I'm not going to practice lying in a coffin." Parra's line had spoken to her. "I want them to start moving my legs. They can bicycle my legs while I'm on my back. Or turn me over, let me try pushups."

"One-handed."

190

"I've always dealt with injury by pushing back stronger. They say I might cause permanent injury if I move too much too soon. I told them how much worse can it get? If I have to be like this for the rest of my life, it's going to be a very short life."

"I don't like hearing that," Lewis said. "You could be the female Ironside, solving crimes from a wheelchair. You could still shoot at the range, but lock the wheels on your chair when you practice shotguns. You'd still have a career."

"A job and no life."

"Like what you have now."

"You drop by to lift my spirits?"

Lewis took the orange chair. Again it creaked under his weight.

"I talked to those ladies who found Amy McSwaim. I figured an in-person after all this time was better than you calling them cold. When you're back at work and we're on our next case, we should try fake bandages and injuries to get in front doors and start people talking. Now I see how it works for con artists and serial killers."

Aragon worked the grip strengthener in her good hand. "Tell me."

"I talked with two of them. One has died and one moved out of state. They're in the same retirement community down in Albuquerque, the fat life."

"Full life. *La Vida Llena*. I know it."

"They had this hiking club called the Lost Girls. Like the Lost Boys in Peter Pan. You never grow up, you never grow old. Four of them were out that day. They parked at Tunnel Springs and took the easy grade up. Longer, with switchbacks, not as rough and tricky as going straight up the drainage."

"I know the route. I've wiped out a couple times taking the shortcut to skip the boring switchbacks."

"They say they were heading for the overlook opposite North Sandia Peak for a view of the aspen forest. They got there, had lunch, and retraced their route coming down."

"Except for that little switchback in the drainage, it's the only route," Aragon said. "I've been studying the maps."

"They heard Amy McSwaim before they saw her. At first they believed it was a cat, way up there, lost in the wilderness. Maybe it wandered from the village down below. Maybe it was hurt. They found her off the trail, on her stomach, shrieking and eating dirt. She was wild-eyed and scared the crap out of them. But they saw she was in serious trouble. She was on fire to the touch. They poured water over her head and made her drink after they got some of the dirt and gravel off her tongue. Her eyes were bugging out, huge and beautiful and scary all at once. She kept getting more crazy. Trying to make out with them, then crying, sobbing, saying she was sorry for all she'd done, then angry and punching trees and rocks. Then giggling about the trees dancing. And get this, she was cursing somebody named Sam. They couldn't understand it all. They thought he was a boyfriend who dumped her."

"They had no idea."

"It took all of them to lift her and forever to get back to the car. One had a cell phone and started calling as soon as there was a signal. They'd lose it when the trail curved around a hill. They got enough information to know an ambulance would try to meet them on the road out to the highway."

Aragon interrupted to tell him about talking to members of the EMT crew.

Lewis picked it back up. "The Lost Girls read in the paper the next day that she'd died. That's how they learned who her parents were. One of them, it was the one who's passed, said she would give them McSwaim's backpack. They'd forgotten to give it to the ambulance crew. The two women I spoke with don't know if their deceased friend ever contacted the family."

"It wasn't an ambulance," Aragon said. "One of those Fire and Rescue trucks."

"I know. But they remember it as an ambulance."

"I wonder what else they got wrong talking to you."

"We can figure out where they found McSwaim. The Lost Girls gave me a few landmarks. Where's that map I got you?"

Aragon pulled it from under her covers. Lewis spread it over her legs, tapped a spot, and turned it so Aragon could see.

"That's about two miles from the parking lot," he said. "She'd come around ten miles since you saw her."

Aragon studied the map. "The ladies didn't see her on the way up yet they passed the spot where she collapsed. Amy might have been quiet, or she might have gotten there after them. Amy said she was going to do loops to add miles. There's a network of trails that would have led her there another way. They go off on the east side of the mountain and connect back to the main trail here." She showed Lewis. "She could have rejoined the main trail below where the ladies stopped and turned around. Or she could have been wandering off-trail, crazy out of her head, and gotten close enough to the main trail they heard her."

They estimated distances on the loop trails and calculated the mileage totals she might have covered. Aragon told Lewis about Parra's suspicion that stimulant abuse could explain Amy's condition, and her opinion that Amy using performance-enhancing drugs was out of the question. But studying the map, appreciating the distances and terrain, she grew to accept it as a possibility.

She said, "When we talked about this before, we hadn't considered that Amy may have been abusing performance enhancing drugs. With stimulants in her system, maybe Amy was misreading signals from an exhausted body."

"Did you know her parents?"

"I met them when they helped her move into the dorm and at the funeral, the last time I saw them. I doubt they'd know if Amy was using drugs. She didn't tell us. Why would she let them know?"

"I was thinking about the backpack," Lewis said. "You should call. It might be the only physical evidence we'll ever have."

"Evidence? As in we're working a real case and not just helping a gimp kill time?"

"I'm not going to dignify that," Lewis said. "The backpack is evidence. Of what, we'll find out. We're not the only ones to run the Lost Girls down and ask about McSwaim. About ten, twelve years ago someone named Patsy was asking."

"Patricia?"

"She told them her name was Patsy. I showed them a photo, pulled it up on my phone, there's dozens on the Internet. Patricia Garza wanted to know if they had the pack McSwaim was using. She said it was hers and would like it back."

———

Patricia Garza told herself she had to think of her boys. If she ever got back to the master bath and the gun was still high up in the linen closet, okay, how did it go then? She shoots Cervantes, but she still has to get Clint and Jimmy out of their prison while worrying about this Bobo character. So Cervantes goes down. Then she has to dig through his pockets to find the key to open the storage room and keep an eye to the left and right, no telling which way Bobo would come at her.

So she gets the key. She also gets Cervantes's gun. The gun he waved around was a semi-automatic, more complicated with more bullets than Sam's revolvers. She now has two guns for the shootout with Bobo. Six bullets in the revolver in the linen closet. Or was it five? Subtract what it would take to put Cervantes on the floor. Unless Bobo were right in front of her, a dead certain shot, she'd need all those bullets in Cervantes's gun and hope she got lucky. Could she even make a semi-automatic work?

Put that gun in my hand, I'll figure it out.

How would it feel to actually shoot someone, to be putting a real gun on them, pulling the trigger, seeing the blood, the smells? And shooting again while they were staggering, gasping, groaning? She had a hard time imagining it.

Maybe it would be better just to run. Grab the boys. Hope they moved when she told them "go." Lead them, no, push them to the front door. Then out into the sun and keep moving. Bobo might try to shoot them in the back. But the cops would have snipers ready, right? It didn't matter. If they make it out of the house, don't worry about Bobo. Run like crazy.

"Listen. Clint. Jimmy." The boys looked up from their games. "If Mommy tells you to run fast, as fast as you can, to the front door, will you do it? Race to see who gets there first. Don't look back. Just go. Okay?" They nodded and their eyes went back to electronic screens.

She had to get back to the linen closet. They'd all had their showers. That opportunity wouldn't come around again very soon. And when Cervantes took them for bathroom breaks he took them to another bathroom, the one closer, just down the hall.

Lie to Cervantes that she needed pills her doctor prescribed. He says, what are they? I'll bring them.

Say, I'm having my period. I need some female things. He says, I was married once. Just tell me where to look.

What if she said, these boys are not washing their hair. There's dirt on their necks. I want to sit them down in the tub in the master bath and get it done right. He had boys. He'd understand.

Then she'd have them with her. After shooting Cervantes—*listen to you*—they run for the French doors in the bedroom, forget the front door. Get outside before Bobo got close.

How would it feel to shoot Cervantes?

Sam said revolvers were easy to use. Heavy, but that made it easier to shoot. Why would a heavier gun be easier? It wouldn't jump out of your hand. He said the .357 bullets would knock a man off his feet. Hit him in the arm, it would spin him around. Hit him in the chest, the bullets would go in small. Out the back, they'd blow a hole you could put your foot in.

She could see it happening this way: Cervantes takes the three of them to the master bath. She makes the boys get into the tub. She wants Cervantes to hear water running while she gets the gun from the closet. She dries them, dresses them. Shhhhh. Now remember what I told you. The boys are behind her, behaving, quiet, this is a game. The lock for that bathroom is on the inside so she doesn't have to wait for Cervantes. She opens the door. "We're done." He's outside, keeping guard, thinking he's got it under control. She steps into the hallway, the gun under a towel. She says, they're afraid. They won't come. He's exasperated. She can see he doesn't like her sons. He reaches past her for the door handle. He's telling them, get out here with your mother.

She shoots through the towel. What is she feeling? Can she hold it together? The gun will be really, really loud. He's thrown backward, there's lots of blood. It's a mess.

She says, "Guys, let's go. The double doors. Don't look. Run!"

Maybe Cervantes is moving, dragging himself after them, bringing up his gun, aiming at their small backs as they fiddle to open the tricky lock on the French doors. So she shoots him again and again. His body bounces a little off the floor.

Shoot him until the gun is empty. It would feel so good.

TWENTY

"WE'RE TAILING LEWIS ON the theory he's acting for Aragon," Pam Magnano said, in the command center with Helmick. She'd been out all day and had been instructed to return and report. Her replacement on the negotiation team was a man out of Quantico who had worked hostage situations in Afghanistan. He'd taken over the duties of keeping notes and dialing up any information Helmick spun around in his captain's chair and demanded. Another man was there, almost part of the furniture, hidden in a corner where the lights didn't reach. He didn't rise when she entered. Helmick didn't introduce him. He sat behind her and she wanted to turn around and get a good hard look. She was pretty sure that was the director of the Federal Bureau of Investigation staring at the back of her head.

She'd been surprised she was enjoying the investigative work so much. It got her out of the truck, into the field where she was making her own decisions, making things happen. Negotiations work was waiting for calls from the person behind locked doors. And then it was all talking, a chess game, a shrink session, a religious confession, brand new friends over make-believe beers. Now she was digging, running down leads, following people, learning stuff, plotting the next moves she would take when she was ready. Like the old days, before Helmick had pulled her out of the Newark office.

Work hostage release, see the world, he'd told her. He'd been right. She'd traveled the country with him, overseas to London several times, once to Palermo, Sicily, a man holding American tourists inside a church full of alabaster statues and mosaics. Helmick had told her to do the talking since the man on the other end of the phone was Italian and she spoke her father's language. But Helmick had it wrong. Like when he'd recruited her, taking her to Italian restaurants in lower Manhattan when the best Italian was the corner place by her aunt's house in Clinton, New Jersey. The guy in the baroque church with knuckle joints of dead saints set in gold and jewels spoke Sicilian. He may as well have been speaking Arabic.

Another reason she was glad Helmick had put her on investigative detail: She imagined the next call with Cervantes, Helmick holding the walkie-talkie so the director could hear every word. Helmick would be worried about the director's response to everything little thing he said, every inflection in his voice, filing it away for the after-action accounting.

Better to be three cars behind Lewis on the interstate knowing why he'd gone to Albuquerque and why he'd met old ladies in the retirement home. She'd waited for him to leave, then went in and asked them what they'd talked about. "First a Santa Fe detective, now a lady G-man," one of the woman said and called her friend over from a bridge game in the fellowship hall.

She told Helmick what she'd learned, and, of course, the director listening in his corner. "Lewis asked about finding a woman named Amy McSwaim. She's the one Aragon believes Senator Valles raped.

That's the source of her deep hatred. McSwaim died from dehydration and heat stroke. Lewis wanted details of her condition when these woman found her while hiking the north end of the Sandia Mountains."

"I suspected Lewis was more involved than he let on," Helmick said. The director probably wasn't going to say anything until this situation was over and the work was done right or not. Either he'd say, "We're proud of the excellent performance of our personnel who ended this crisis peacefully." Or he'd say, "We're investigating whether the agents in charge committed errors, either in judgment or deviating from standard protocols, resulting in this tragic loss of life."

"I had our people in Albuquerque obtain the EMT notes," Magnano said. "There's a coroner report but no autopsy. A brief one-page police report put this down as accidental death."

"But Aragon thinks it isn't?" Helmick looked past her at the director instead of meeting her eyes. "Has Aragon also been harboring the delusion that Senator Valles is responsible for this woman's death? That's her motivation for assisting or inspiring Cervantes?"

"The records make this an unremarkable death. A young woman exceeding the limits of her endurance and succumbing to harsh environmental conditions. Out of caution I sent them to Quantico. Aragon and Lewis work homicides all the time and might have detected something hinky. I've never done a homicide."

"I'm getting you help," Helmick said. "All the people you need." She heard shuffling behind her. A cough. Helmick saw something and nodded. "Your findings will be reported only to me. The sensitivity of this situation requires we keep our small circle very small. You were working on Aragon's phone records?"

Decisions had been made before she got here. She didn't need to know. She said, "We pulled up her phone records. We see calls between them going back to the date of the son's murder. Contacts increasing in frequency to about the date of the killer's sentencing. Then intermittent contacts, every couple weeks, sometimes none for a month. And two since Cervantes took the Valles family hostage."

"They've been in contact while he's holding hostages?" Helmick and her replacement were staring at her. "He's not talking to us but he's talking to her?"

"A two-second call from Aragon at the start of this. Later a longer call from Cervantes to her. We've traced his number to a pre-paid cell. It was the same number used to call the Valles senate office. The pattern could be suspicious. She calls his regular cell and her number appears on his phone. They don't talk. Later he calls back on a pre-paid cell."

"You're a police detective. You get a call from a man holding a family hostage. One, you'd report it. Or two, you'd talk as long as you could, pull out information, get a reading on his state of mind. She didn't do that. What would they say in a few seconds?"

She'd had the same questions. "Something prearranged," she said. "A signal they both understood."

"Get a warrant for a phone intercept," Helmick said. Her replacement made a note of the instruction. A veteran of Afghanistan, dealing with Taliban, tribal leaders, seeing more death and destruction than any of them in a full career, now playing secretary. "I'll have the US attorney start the application."

"The application is ready, along with my statement of probable cause," Magnano said.

Helmick lifted his thick glasses off his face and rubbed the bridge of his nose. He had red marks there, pits where the pads carried the weight of those heavy frames. He said, "Let's get that tap up pronto so that next time I speak with Cervantes I can shake the tree. I'll tell him his friend is in the hospital. Build her up. Such a brave warrior, selfless, all she's done for the people of Santa Fe and never thinking of herself. Did you know she may never walk again? That might get him on the phone to her with us listening."

"You truly believe Detective Aragon is complicit in this crime?"

That came from behind her. The director speaking. She turned to face him, a small man in a blue suit barely denting the cushions on the bench built into the side of the truck.

"We need to identify only one overt act," Magnano said. "We'll have her on conspiracy. If Cervantes kills anyone, we'll have her on felony murder."

The director steepled hands against his chin. She was seeing him as a judge on the bench, a small man, a tiny head poking out of a black robe. He'd had that job before the president gave him something else to do.

"From what Art tells me, I fear this is not going to end well. The way Mr. Cervantes reiterates his one demand, he has no fallback position. The possibility of felony murder you mentioned, you're only considering Mr. Cervantes hurting his hostages. Keep this in mind, and this may be the more likely scenario: Aragon faces felony murder charges when one of our snipers kills Mr. Cervantes. That's a homicide resulting from the chain events set in motion by the commission of a felony. She'll bear personal responsibility for the violence necessary to resolve this situation."

"You know what to do," Helmick said to Magnano. "Happy hunting."

———

Sergeant Perez showed Aragon on the Forest Service map all the places where a runner could find water in the Sandia Mountains.

Aragon wasn't interested in springs and streams Amy might have crossed on her way to the Tram. She'd looked fine when she arrived. She'd tanked up, two pints of beer inside her, and refilled her water. Strange, that business of Patricia Garza calling the Lost Girls to ask about Amy's pack. She needed to speak with Margaret Baldonado again. Memories were dim. Together, old friends thinking back on old times, they might be able to dredge up things they'd forgotten. But she couldn't trust Margaret. The only way the "remember when" would work would be if they were honest and easy with each other. She didn't want to say anything around Margaret knowing she could be wearing a wire for Magnano again.

"North of the Tram," Perez was saying, getting to the territory that interested Aragon, "when you pass the parking lot and little snack bar at the crest, there's no water anywhere along the ridge. That final stretch, where your friend was found, is the driest. It gets the hot western sun in the afternoon. There's long sections without shade. Black rock that soaks up the heat. You leave the ridge, take some of these other trails, the only place I know is this lousy seep that cattle trample into stinking mud pies. Here." He tapped the map. "There's not supposed to be cattle in the wilderness, but they're up there. You have to get on your belly for a sip of shitty water. No way you could refill your water bottle."

"If there'd been an investigation," Aragon said, "we might know if anyone saw her. We could have run down the people who paid to park at the crest and checked the sign-in logs at trailheads. We could have broadcast requests for the public's help."

"I've been thinking about what Parra told you, that maybe your friend took some kind of stimulant. All this crazy stuff she was doing. Did you ever think maybe she wanted to die and pushing limits was her way to getting close?"

"She could have simply jumped off the mountain," Aragon said. "There's places, right where the Lost Girls turned around, you can fall five hundred feet and still have air under you. Dying like she did, it wasn't a sure thing if that had been her plan. And what a way to go out. There's easier ways."

"Maybe she wanted it to look like an accident. Spare her parents the added grief of their daughter killing herself. Be remembered as an adventurer, not a suicide."

Aragon had just finished her first session of physical therapy when Perez arrived. The therapist had started by lifting her legs, then settling them on the bed. She'd felt that in the small of her back and told him it hurt. "My sworn duty as your personal physical terrorist," he said, pausing to make sure she was catching his joke, probably one he used in the beginning with every patient, "is to make you hurt." She'd tried helping, telling her legs to move, and got no response. He went to the end of the bed, held her feet in his hands, and moved her legs like she was pedaling a bicycle. She could have sworn when they were done the soles of her feet felt warm where he'd been pushing.

"Or another possibility," Perez said. "What if she ate something she found in the woods? She's fine when you see her. Hours later she's ranting, running a fever, crazy eyes. What grows on that mountain that could do that?"

"That gets us more questions and no more answers."

"I'll take the EMT notes to somebody who knows about poisons. You keep doing whatever you're doing."

"I'm not doing anything but lying here."

"You're doing something. Did you know that when you talk about McSwaim's case, you move your foot?"

She looked along her body and told her feet to move. Nothing happened.

"When your mind is on the job," Perez said. "That's when I saw it move."

She hit the buzzer for the nurse, who was there immediately.

"Get the physical therapist back here," Aragon said. "We have work to do."

She didn't get another therapy session right away. Too soon, according to her nervous doctors. But she got another massage from Deke, the funny, good-looking Southerner. Watching his blond hair sweeping across his broad, smiling face gave her something to think about besides Amy dying on a mountain. Deke complimented her muscle tone. He didn't say, "You have a nice body." He said things like, "These are good quads. You do squats?" He'd been a second string safety on the University of Alabama team and tried to stay in shape, especially with hand strength. Maybe they could work out together someday.

She wished Rivera would say things like that. She wished she could see them in a gym together. He could use some upper-body work.

When the Crimson Tide left, she called Rivera. He was in Shiprock interviewing witnesses. Another sad reservation killing: a husband wakes up in an arroyo with the bloody body of his wife next to him. There's a screwdriver in her chest. He remembers them drinking tall boys and Everclear, nothing else.

Rivera said he'd be on the rez a couple days. How was she coming along? She told him about Perez seeing her foot move. Silence. Was Tomas crying? It took another second before he came back with, "We're going for long walks when you're better, Denise."

And long talks that might get them back on track.

Her next call was to Amy McSwaim's parents.

205

She got Amy's mother, Carol. Of course, Mrs. McSwaim remembered her, the only friend who ever understood Amy's love for pushing herself physically. And you have such beautiful black hair. Amy envied you.

Aragon ran a hand over the stubble on her scalp.

"I envied Amy's stamina," Aragon said. "That girl could run all day."

Carol McSwaim had seen the news on television about her being injured. Listen, Aragon said, why I'm calling, this is related to something up here in Santa Fe. We've talked to the women who found Amy and they say they delivered Amy's pack to you.

"Why are you asking questions about Amy?"

"It's a matter I can't talk about in detail right now. We're not sure if Amy's death is even related."

"It's that Valles, isn't it?"

Aragon had to take a moment. She didn't think Amy had said anything outside her small circle of friends. Mrs. McSwaim broke the silence.

"I've been watching it on television," she said. "I have a heart of sympathy for his family. But something happened between him and Amy that hurt her terribly. He brought her back from college for spring break. We didn't see her when she got home, but the next morning she had bruises and scratches on her face and hands. She was wearing a turtleneck but I saw what she was hiding. Black and blue on her throat. She said she got hurt playing rugby and couldn't give me an answer why she wouldn't see a doctor. She wouldn't tell me any more but began refusing rides with him. I had to bring her home when she couldn't get rides with other friends."

Amy had initially told her girlfriends the bruises and scratches came from falling off her bike. That was about the same day she'd been telling her mother about getting hurt playing rugby.

"I can't comment on that, Mrs. McSwaim, or what we're working on. Do you have Amy's backpack?"

"I couldn't bring myself to throw it away. We gave away her clothes, but that pack. That was the last thing she had with her. It's just the way we got it. That water thing is still in there, too."

"The water thing?"

"Patricia Garza wanted it. She said it was hers, but I knew Amy had talked about buying one of those … Camelbaks you call them. That was right before her last run. Patricia, well you know her, she's definitely not a runner. Patricia wanted a memento for herself, something to remember Amy, was all I could see. If she'd been honest I might have given it to her. That's a strange thing to want to remember someone with, don't you think?"

"This was Patricia Garza?"

"Patricia Valles now. I didn't know until later she was involved with Sam."

"My partner, Rick Lewis, will be down to get the pack, if you'll let us have it. In addition to what we're working on up here, it might tell us some more about why Amy died."

"I know why she died," Mrs. McSwaim said. "Sam Valles killed her. What happened between them, it took the light out of Amy's eyes. All this extreme stuff she did, she was making herself feel pain to kill the hurt inside her. It always took more and more. You could say she overdosed."

Why did Mrs. McSwaim use that word? Aragon wondered for the rest of the day. "Overdosed." Had Amy told her mother something she'd hidden from friends?

TWENTY-ONE

"You wanted to know if we heard anything interesting. This qualifies."

Magnano took the call in her car in the parking lot of Aragon's apartment complex. She'd been knocking on doors and learned Aragon was never home except to sleep. Nobody knew her until Magnano mentioned her nearly shaved head. A couple neighbors thought she was lesbian. The woman on the top floor told Magnano that Aragon was definitely straight; Aragon had made that clear the time she'd asked, a couple years back, if Aragon wanted to go dancing at Rouge Cat. Aragon had said she knew the place, she'd had call-outs to deal with women fighting in the nightclub's parking lot, and it wasn't her kind of fun.

The call on Magnano's phone was from one of the four-hour shifts working the wiretap on Aragon's line. Such quaint images—"wiretap" and "line," like they were inserting something three dimensional, something you could touch and hold, into a thread of copper carrying words between people. Now it was "intercept." You could do it from anywhere. Thank you, NSA.

Magnano told them to send an audio clip and she had it in her inbox before she hung up. She listened in her parked car: Aragon was speaking with the mother of Amy McSwaim, continuing her delusional pursuit of Senator Valles. But Mrs. McSwaim rattled her. In the tape from the wire that Margaret Baldonado had worn, she'd heard Aragon and her old friend recalling the colors of McSwaim's bruises. She had wanted to believe Baldonado was playing along to keep Aragon talking. But here was the mother describing the same bruises. It came through like she'd seen them yesterday.

Even if Valles had assaulted McSwaim, that was a very long time ago. The complainant was dead. There never would be, never could be, a prosecution. More important was Aragon on her vendetta, manipulating the emotionally unstable Cervantes. Whatever had happed back in Aragon's college days, it didn't justify what was happening now.

Another call. The monitoring team again.

"Mrs. McSwaim just called Aragon back. It was a short conversation. She said that when Lewis came by for the backpack, they might have a few photographs for him. There'd been a birthday party for a grandmother. Amy McSwaim was there. You could see bruises around her eyes when she removed her sunglasses for the group picture. Grandmom insisted Amy never play rugby again, never had any idea it might have been something else, Mrs. McSwaim said. They didn't want her upset."

Now photos to back up memories.

In the apartment complex's management office, Magnano asked about Aragon's rent—whether she paid on time, if she paid in cash, any complaints about her conduct, the way she kept her place, the company she brought round. The woman behind the desk said she wanted a whole building of Denise Aragons. Why in the world would the FBI be asking about her?

Another call. The same number on her screen, the intercept team reporting. Aragon had just called the US Forest Service district ranger asking for any reports about McSwaim being taken off the mountain. After that, Aragon called the University of New Mexico student newspaper for the article that had run about McSwaim's death and everything on Sam Baca Valles, especially articles about him running for city council as the sophomore who might make history.

"The call that really might interest you," the intercept monitor said, "is the one with someone at the New Mexico Office of Medical Investigator. She asked for anyone familiar with the effects of stimulant abuse, the kind of things athletes might use to enhance performance. And also someone with expertise in toxic plants that grow in the Sandias. They'll pass the request along and see what they can do."

At the restaurant where Aragon and Cervantes had their conversation about "taking out" Senator Valles, Magnano detoured into the women's restroom when the report from the intercept monitors came. Aragon had contacted the US Weather Service about the precise range of temperatures and relative humidity for the day of McSwaim's fatal mountain run, both at the crest and on the lower slopes. Then Aragon had received a call from an attorney. Under their minimization instructions that came with the warrant, they backed out of the call. But they thought Magnano should know Aragon might be lawyering up.

Returning to the restaurant proper, Magnano had the manager pull up credit card receipts and found a charge in Cervantes's name. A numerical code corresponded with the name of the server. Cervantes had put a hundred dollar tip on his card; Aragon had talked about them holding up the staff who'd wanted to close. That was nice of Cervantes. It also made it more likely the server would remember them.

He was there working a double shift. He was a recent arrival from Jalisco but had a face from County Cork. He started pulling out papers showing he was here legally before they sat down. He had red hair and freckles and an Irish name and spoke with a clipped Mexican accent. Not a trace of brogue. Liam McMurphy explained without asking that his family had sailed to Mexico instead of New York when they'd heard Irishmen were being conscripted off the New York docks into Lincoln's army. His family had been Mexican that many generations.

Sí, he remembered the tip and the odd pair who kept him late. *La chicana* was a linebacker shrunken down to five foot two, sleeves pushed up her arms, a super-short haircut that made her big eyes pop out. *Muy linda* inside the muscle. He thought the man might be her father but changed his mind. They didn't talk about the usual things he heard from people over enchiladas and chile. They talked *cosas pesado*—heavy stuff. It seemed like the man's son had been murdered. You hear that word when you're refilling glasses— "murder"—it sticks with you.

"Something else stuck with me," McMurphy said, his red hair and freckles not going at all with his accent. "They were talking about that senator from here, the one whose family is in trouble *ahora*. The man was cursing, really angry. Cursing the senator person. You want to get away from the table when people are like that, because they're going to say to you, 'What are you looking at?' As I'm getting around the table to go back to the kitchen the woman said, 'Someone should take him out.'"

"The woman said this?"

"*Seguro*. I hear 'murder,' then I hear 'take him out,' and I get a hundred dollar tip. I remember pretty good."

Magnano pulled up a photo of Cervantes on her phone. "That's him," McMurphy said. When she showed him one of Aragon, taken from the newspaper, her in uniform, he said, "That lady's a cop?" Magnano made him answer directly whether that was the woman with Cervantes who said someone should take out Senator Valles. He answered affirmatively, and she had Aragon on a federal felony for lying to the FBI.

———

Rivera called ahead to say he was back in Santa Fe and would smuggle in Lotaburgers and beer. Aragon told him Lewis and Perez were with her. In that case, I'll bring a couple six packs, he said. We can have a party. Something to cheer you up.

He came to her room with a roll-on suitcase. Clever. The nurses would never suspect.

"Large fries for all, and a Lotaburger apiece. One extra for our wounded Amazon."

Then came the beer, from a soft-pack cooler, and cold, the bottles sweating.

Lewis said, "I'll tell the nurses we're discussing sensitive law enforcement matters and can't be disturbed." He closed the door behind him as beer tabs were pulled.

Rivera folded back the wrapper on a burger and brought it close to her mouth. With his other hand he lifted her head so she could take a bite.

Cheeks full, she said, "All is forgiven."

Next came the touch of cold aluminum on her lips and a sip of beer.

Lewis was back and went straight for a red, white, and blue bag. Perez was dropping fries in his mouth.

"Gimme," Aragon said, and waved fingers for her own bag of fries.

The men pulled chairs around her bed and rested their burgers in wrappers on top of her covers. The nurses were going to wonder about those ketchup stains.

"How's your case on the rez?" Aragon asked Rivera.

He took a long chug of beer, wiped his mouth on the back of his hand. "Closed. Another right after. A kid shot his friends when they took his truck. That same day, a four-year-old paid the price for no milk in the fridge for a stepdad's Cocoa Puffs. Did you know the Navajo reservation has a per capita murder rate four times the national average, more total murders than Boston or Seattle?"

"But not a police force to match," Perez said. "I don't envy those guys out there, all those wide open spaces, no support for a hundred miles."

"The gangs haven't helped," Rivera said. "It's turned into a scary place. Nothing like what Hillerman wrote about. The charm is gone. The only mystery is how long before the next body drops."

"Speaking of charm," Aragon said. "I got a call from Marcy Thornton." She waited for the groans and the 'what the hells' to end. "She offered her services said she'd be honored to represent me."

"Why would that piece of shit think you need the sleaziest lawyer in Santa Fe?" Lewis asked. They'd crossed swords with Thornton on the Geronimo and Montclaire cases, and Thornton had barely escaped getting convicted herself. "Why would she think you want anything to do with her?"

"I thought her law license was suspended," Rivera said.

"She's back in the saddle. She said my case would be a grand re-entrance."

"Your case?" The three men said it together.

"She got a visit from FBI Special Agent Pam Magnano, asking about every instance where Thornton suspected I'd crossed the line in nailing one of her clients. Thornton told her they'd need to block out a week and she didn't have that kind of time to give the FBI for free. Then she called me."

The first empty cans went into the trash can by the door. Lewis passed out the next round. Rivera let Aragon have another sip.

"We're waiting," Rivera said. "What did you tell her?"

"That she had her head pretty far up her own ass thinking I would ever want her on my side."

"Magnano's casting her net very wide," Perez said. "She's been talking to your fellow officers. She wanted your personnel file and asked if you'd disclosed what happened to you as a teenager."

"Who'd she ask?" Aragon said.

"The chief, HR."

"She probably dropped it with the cops she was interrogating," Aragon said. "Now everyone will know."

"She went into the locker room..." Perez trailed off. "This is going to piss you off. She was asking do you like boys or girls or both."

"Buzzkill," Lewis said. "This was fun while it lasted."

"I am sick of lying here while Magnano digs through my life," Aragon said. "This is the best I've felt and now she's ruined it. Give me another taste of that beer."

When Rivera came close with the can she wrapped her good hand around his and didn't let him take the can away until it was nearly empty.

"Give me my phone." Aragon pointed to her bedstand. Lewis tossed it and she caught the phone out of the air with her left hand.

"Nice," he said.

She did a quick Internet search, then dialed. The men ate their burgers, drank their beer, and watched.

"Hello," Aragon said into her phone. "This is Pam Magnano. I'm sorry to call after hours. I hope you get this message. I would like to schedule an appointment. I am very much in need of your services. Please call me to confirm you got this message. I must get in as soon as possible."

"What was that about?" Lewis asked.

"Impersonating an FBI agent," Rivera said. "What are you doing?"

"Here." She handed the phone to Lewis. "Your turn. Pretend you're agent Magnano's assistant. She's too busy to make the appointment herself. Call the next on the list."

"What am I calling to schedule?" Lewis asked. Then he saw the screen and started laughing. He passed the phone across the bed to Perez. With a chuckle he passed it to Rivera.

Rivera read the screen and made the first call. He affected a lisp.

"Good evening. I hope yours is going as well as my spectacular night. Unfortunately, my boss, Pam *Mag-nano*, isn't doing so well. She needs your help, really needs your help. Tomorrow when you open, right away, pretty please, would you call her to get her in so you can, well, get in her? This is very much an emergency. Here's her number. Okey-dokey. Bye now."

When Perez was done it was Lewis's turn. He ended with, "It's out of control. She's afraid to sit down or bend over. Please hurry! Call her first thing tomorrow."

"Give me that," Rivera said and went deeper into the list, calling businesses as far away as Albuquerque and Las Cruces and asking everyone to call Magnano's number back as soon as they opened.

In the basement of the FBI offices off St. Michael's Drive, a few miles from Aragon's hospital room, Agent Magnano dropped into the monitoring station to review their log and ensure they were accurately noting their minimization efforts. She was very curious about the call from the defense attorney named Marcy Thornton. It came just after she had left Thornton's office. No doubt Aragon now knew the FBI was talking to even her worst adversaries.

The log looked complete and accurate. She found no gaps in the record of Aragon's calls. The team had minimized several conversations with physicians, with appropriate notes that the listeners had stopped listening to avoid infringing on doctor-patient confidentiality. But they'd listened to calls by Aragon collecting information about McSwaim's death: to the *Albuquerque Journal* morgue, the funeral home that handled the burial and processing of the body, a call with Lewis discussing retrieving a backpack from McSwaim's parents.

"Agent Magnano, you might want to hear these yourself."

One of the intercept monitors held out a set of headphones she settled over her ears. She recognized Aragon's voice. And Lewis. Two other calls from two men, one with a heavy Mexican accent that reminded her of the host on a Univision variety show, one with a smooth, effeminate voice. Later the same voice made a call without any affectation. It sounded like Tomas Rivera, but she'd only spoken with him once and could not be certain. They were calling to make appointments for her, dropping her name, leaving messages on answering machines of businesses closed for the night. The names of the businesses didn't mean anything. Easy Waters, the Colonnade?

The agent had moved to a computer screen. Another looked over his shoulder. Why were they laughing?

She swung her chair around to see what they were seeing. Each of the businesses that Aragon and pals had called to make an appointment in her name, asking for return calls tomorrow to set the date and time, was for a business specializing in colonic irrigation.

The intercept monitors were watching her face, waiting for her reaction.

She ran a finger along her single eyebrow. She had to say something. Before she did, one of the agents pressed the earphones tighter to his head.

"Now they're making appointments to get you a brow wax. They just called a place named Hair Be Gone."

"Cute," Magnano said. "And terrific. Aragon has no idea that we're listening to everything she says. She's showing us all her moves in going against Senator Valles, and the side comments, when she runs her mouth, it will give the prosecutors all they need to show motive. Just hit *play* for the jury and sit back. We've got her on tape lying to us. We've got her egging on Cervantes, the coded call between them while he has the senator's family, something she didn't report. If Aragon ever walks again, it will be round and round a prison exercise track. I have no intention of letting her know I know who's responsible for this stunt. I want her on the phone as much as possible."

"Hey, Pam," the man with headphones shouted across the room, "they're back to colonic irrigation. They just left a message at a place called Inside Out. You want the number?"

TWENTY-TWO

THERE. CERVANTES SAW IT again. One of the snipers behind the volcanic rocks stepped behind a tree. In the same motion he reached into a cargo pocket and pulled out a cell phone. The phone went to his ear and his mouth moved.

And still his own cell phones weren't working.

He needed to call television stations and *The Santa Fe New Mexican* and tell them why he was doing this and what he wanted from Valles. He was starting to think the FBI was keeping his terms from hitting the news.

Cervantes pushed his chair from the dining table with the monitors and reached for his bullhorn. He was about to open the front door and blast Helmick when he thought again of the men behind the rocks. And in the arroyo, on the hill, on the neighbors' roofs. They probably had a dozen rifle sights fixed on the front door. They could put crosshairs between his eyes. They wouldn't even need a clean shot. That door, thick as it was, wouldn't stop the bullets from a high-powered rifle.

He'd risk the walkie-talkie. He got it from its metal box inside the closet off the garage and put it back together. He should do more than talk this time. They'd cut him off from the world. They'd been playing him with. Maybe nobody out there, beyond the circle of cops and FBI surrounding the house, knew this was happening.

Had anyone even told Valles what it would take to free his family?

He went to the locked door with Patricia and her brats. Neither of these boys would ever step up the way his oldest son had rushed to serve his country after 9/11. Or the way his last son had fought to the death to protect his wife. Neither deserved the life of privilege they were enjoying. Going into this, he'd been worried he wouldn't be able to take the terror in the kids' eyes. Now he didn't care.

Inside the storage room they were lying on their mats. The place was trashed. Crumbs, empty wrappers scattered everywhere, ends of red licorice bit off and spit out. And though he'd let them shower, it smelled in here. The camp toilet in the corner, it needed to be emptied. Let the boys do it when this next part was over.

"Get up," he told Patricia. "You, too." He nodded at the brats. "C'mon. Move."

To the closest boy he said, "I want you to know how to use this," and held out the walkie-talkie.

"Show *me*," Patricia said, pulling her son back and reaching to take it.

"No, him. He'll need to know when you're gone." That froze her. "Look, you press this metal pin all the way in to talk. You let it out when you're done so you can hear what the person on the other end is saying to you. Two people can't talk at the same time. The red light has to be on for it to work. See, it's on. Here, try it. Push the button and say your name."

"I'm not going anywhere." Patricia, recovered, took the walkie-talkie from her son.

"I want him to do it," Cervantes said.

"I want them hearing the boys. To know they're okay. That's good, right?"

"I'll tell them."

"You won't be able to."

He saw she had her finger on the pin. It was pushed in. Right now Helmick would be hearing this. Good. Let her hold it, thinking the FBI listening would help.

"Give that back to him or I'll kill you in front of your boys, right here. You want that? You want them carrying that in their heads all their lives?"

He saw the pin pop out when she handed it to her son. But the FBI had heard that much already.

"Now you do it," Cervantes said to the boy, Jimmy or Clint, he didn't care if he got the name right. "Press that pin and say your name. Then let it out and listen."

The boy needed both hands. "This is Clint Valles."

"You have to let the pin out." Patricia was shaking. "So you hear them answering."

Clint did as he was told and the speaker in the walkie-talkie crackled.

"*This is FBI Special Agent Art Helmick. Are you okay?*" Helmick's voice was tinny but clear.

Cervantes grabbed Patricia. "Let's go." To the boy with the walkie-talkie, "You tell them what's going on. Bobo and I are very angry at your mother. Bobo wants to see her in the hallway."

He pushed Patricia before him and locked the door. She was swiveling her head, scanning the hallway the way she did whenever she got out. Her eyes grew big, with something in them besides fear.

"There's no Bobo," she said.

"Bobo's busy." He aimed the gun and fired. Again. And again. Once more to make sure. Man, it was loud.

Art Helmick wondered why one of the boys was talking to him. He identified himself and asked about their welfare. The boy was back on saying *they took my mother* when he heard the gunshots.

"What's going on," Helmick said into the walkie-talkie, raising his voice. "Who's shooting? Who's hurt?"

"They shot my mom." There was another voice in the background. Another child. Sobbing. Shrieks. What sounded like banging on a door. "Help! They shot my mom."

Radios were a jumble of excited voices, all the fire teams talking to each other. Dix shouted over the chaos, giving orders, demanding information. Helmick walked outside, the boy on the other end not releasing the talk button, not letting him get in a word. He needed more information but the boy kept repeating the same words. *They shot my mom.*

Everybody had heard the gunshots. It was agreed there had been four. Three quick ones, pause, then a fourth. The drones over the house dropped lower. People were crouched behind cars, long guns leveled across trunks and hoods. Two men ran across an open space and dove into a ditch on the side of the driveway. They'd gotten fifteen yards closer to the front door.

Finally, a break in the boy repeating himself. Helmick could talk and said, "Take a breath. Are you alone? Tell me exactly what has happened. Remember to push the button in to talk, let it out to hear me."

He learned that Mr. Cervantes had taken his mother outside. Bobo was angry with her. They shot her on the other side of the door. There were men shouting, then it got quiet. He and his brother were locked in the room. Is their mom okay?

"What room?" Maybe they could locate where the hostages were inside the house. Entry through a wall or ceiling might be possible.

The boy named Clint described the room. It was down the hall from the guest room. His mom used to keep food in here. And mops and the vacuum cleaner and suitcases. But Mr. Cervantes had taken everything out and put in mattresses.

"Can he see into the room?"

"I don't think so," Clint said. "He opens the door to talk to us. Sometimes he takes us to the bathroom. But there's a smelly toilet with a bag in here."

"Any windows?"

Clint was calming down but the child in the background was wailing. "The only way out is the door and he keeps it locked."

"Who is Bobo?"

"The other man. He's mean. I don't know what my mom did to make him angry. She's always with us and she didn't do anything… Wait, Mr. Cervantes took her to her bathroom. Maybe Bobo was there. I don't know. Who are you?"

Helmick repeated his name and explained his job. He told the boy there were police—keep it simple, no need to explain what the Hostage Rescue Team was—surrounding the house. The police would get them out of the house. They would be okay.

"What about my mom?"

Helmick watched another sniper team setting their rifles on rocks.

"We're going to do everything we can to get you out of there," Helmick said. "Can you tell me where Mr. Cervantes and Bobo are? Do you hear them in the house? Can you hear anything?"

The garage door was going up and stopped eight inches above the ground without any feet or legs in sight. Helmick stopped talking at the now-familiar screech of Cervantes's bullhorn adjusting volume.

"Turn my phones, Internet, and television back on, or one of the brats is next. Tell Valles his foot-dragging and your games cost him his wife. His boys don't have a mother anymore. His family is getting smaller the longer he waits."

Then the door was down and Clint Valles was saying, "What was that? Is my mom dead?" Helmick looked at the walkie-talkie. His talk button had been pressed. The boy had heard Cervantes.

"We don't know, Clint. Listen to me—how did you get the walkie-talkie?"

Now two children crying. Someone in the room with them. A scream. What sounded like a face being slapped. "Shut up." That was a man's voice.

"What's going on?" Helmick shouted. "Talk to me."

"Sure thing." He recognized Cervantes's voice, the Hispanic accent. "What would you like to know?"

Helmick took a breath and told himself, change gears.

"Mr. Cervantes, we want to know that Mrs. Valles is unhurt. Would you put her on?"

"I've seen people out there talking on phones. Your guys in the rocks, maybe one of their wives was calling and they had to answer."

"Mrs. Valles. We must know if you've harmed her."

The boys squalling. Another slap. An open hand against a face? There was force in that sound.

223

"Have you hit the boys?"

"Turn all my stuff on and get Valles here."

Helmick had been at this point before. When the violence began you couldn't start giving. It was time to get.

"I can't do that. I must first know that no one has been harmed."

What was that? A body hitting a wall? A door slamming. It was quieter. The boys' cries were muffled.

"I'm putting this walkie-talkie to bed." An echo trailing Cervantes's voice in a big, open space with hard surfaces. Where was he? Helmick checked the diagram they'd drawn of the house. Most likely the hallway. Walking which way? The room where they'd identified the other suspect, or toward the garage? Then the sounds of something heavy being moved. *Ztipp, ztipp.* What the hell? He recognized that sound, carpenters working in his house putting down a new subfloor. A nail gun.

"Mr. Cervantes!"

"*Adios*, Helmick."

"Today we have fun with gravity," said Deke, wheeling in something that looked like a cage on wheels. A new man was with him, extremely tall and gray in the face, something wrong with his pallor. He had huge hands that he slipped under her, and Aragon felt his strength as he and Deke lifted her off the bed. Deke's toe nudged the cage thing closer and the man raised her over its edge. There was a saddle, handholds; the sides were cushioned. Deke engaged a lock on the wheels and she was lowered into a seat with holes for legs to drop through. They strapped her in, a belt around her waist, another crossing her chest.

This was the first her feet had been lower than her head since she'd dived through the opening in the meth lab's roof. She looked down and saw them dangling close to the floor. Deke turned a wheel, lowering the saddle, and the floor came closer. Now her feet were touching linoleum. She told them to move, shuffle, please, just a little.

Deke said, "Give it time."

She hadn't realized she'd been talking out loud.

The gray man was Vernon. His palms were pale pink and very warm when he touched her. She felt his heat through her thin robe and wondered what was wrong with him and why a hospital would employ someone who looked so sick himself.

She saw herself in the mirror she couldn't see from the bed. Her arm in a cast raised to shoulder level and resting on the cushioned edge of the contraption. The gown had gotten loose, the string around her neck almost untied. Her color made Vernon look healthy.

Deke cinched the gown up on her shoulders and retied the string. "All dressed up and ready to hit the town," he said. "See the sights. Meet your neighbors. Strut your stuff."

"Easy for you to say." She tried to push her feet against the floor, telling her abs to do the work her legs wouldn't. She could squeeze her butt. That was good, right?

By working a handle she could adjust herself so her legs slipped cleanly through the holes and didn't chafe.

Chafe? That was a feeling. She'd take it.

It was really bright in the hallway with sun pouring through the window at the end. She asked Deke and Vernon to take her there. On the way she couldn't help peeking into rooms at shrunken people, people with tubes going in and out of them, some never going for a ride like this ever again. It made her feel grateful.

The window showed her a parking lot and lots of sky. Sun bounced off windshields and she thought how hot it would be inside the cars and the cases she'd had of children cooked on vinyl while their parents camped on barstools.

She said, "Let's see what's at the other end."

They wheeled her around, her feet sliding along the linoleum, her knees bent a little, down the hall past the nurse's station. This view was better. She could see the mountains, starting out brown and dry and then turning green higher up, pine forests covering the slopes, then a lighter green for the aspen groves up high, then gray like Vernon here, where the trees ended and bare limestone scraped the sky.

She'd had a case in those mountains, the one that brought Rivera into her life. The girl who'd tried to feed herself to ravens so she could become one of them.

She couldn't look at anything and not think of death.

"Is there a children's ward in this building? I could use some cheering up."

"How do the legs feel?" Deke asked. "Blood should be going into them. It might feel like your legs have gone to sleep. If you feel needles, give us a big smile. Try curling your toes."

"Nothing's happening."

"Okay. We look for kids."

Actually, her legs felt heavy. C'mon, feet. C'mon, toes. She kept her eyes down as they rolled through swinging doors, Vernon going first to hold them open and Deke pushing her under Vernon's arm. The feet bounced as they crossed a rubber seam in the floor where a newer wing connected another wing of the hospital. That was exciting, seeing her feet move, though she'd had nothing to do with it.

She smelled food. There was a sign for the cafeteria. They had green chile stew today. Her eyes stayed on that sign as she went by. Deke caught it and stopped.

"Our treat if you're up to it."

"I want that." She pointed at the sign and felt herself sink in the saddle. She hadn't realized she'd been holding herself up with one arm, scared about her feet getting caught under her.

Again Vernon held the door and Deke pushed her into a cheerful space, bright colors on the walls, tables yellow and red. More smiles in here than she'd seen in days.

"I'll take milk with the stew. The largest bowl they have," and they parked her at the edge of the tables, a television there she could watch while they got trays and stood in line.

Not everybody in here was smiling. A man and woman one table over were holding each other, her head against his chest, his hand on her hair. Aragon looked away and found herself facing the television.

Live coverage of the Valles hostage situation. A panel discussion with a window in the corner showing activity close to the scene. She could barely hear what they were saying, something about the FBI's next move. Then a photograph of Patricia Valles filled the window on the screen. Her round face, black hair pushed back from her forehead, a string of pearls around her neck, sleepy eyelids that made you think she was keeping something from the camera. Her nose had gotten bigger as she got older. How had that happened?

Now the man on the end of the panel of windbags, a guy with a thick neck and square head was talking. Just below his face words printed on the screen said *Former FBI Hostage Rescue Team*, the people with the sniper rifles and flash-bangs. He was saying, "Things just changed, the planet shifted, with one life lost. This has gone from a hostage standoff to a rescue operation very quickly. Now the FBI has no choice but to move assault and rescue to the front in their thinking. On one hand, with only two lives at stake, it's easier. The logistics are simplified. Chances are the boys are together in one room. If that room can be secured, HRT won't need to control any other area of the house. But the price of guessing wrong, hitting the incorrect room, could be two young lives."

With one life lost? She looked for the brake release. She wanted to get closer to the television. The moderator was saying, "We could get into Osama bin Laden's compound. Why can't we get into a single-story house in Santa Fe?"

The former HRT man: "We weren't interested in preserving life inside Bin Laden's compound. The SEALs went in shooting at anything that moved. The only thing they had to bring out was a photograph of a dead body. They can't risk hitting the boys. Now that Cervantes has shown he's willing to kill, they have to consider the possibility of him taking the boys with him if he's cornered. Or killing one of the boys to show his ... determination? Wrong word, his ruthlessness. He'd hold one life in reserve as a bargaining chip."

The brake release was on the side with her broken arm. She was staying here.

The moderator turned to the cameras: "Still no word from Senator Valles on the likelihood his wife, Patricia Valles, has been killed. The FBI has released no further information after shots were heard from inside the Valles house. Peter Cervantes and possibly one other person have kept their motives hidden. We still do not know what Mr. Cervantes and his cohort want."

"This is very good." Deke was next to her now, putting a tray with a plastic bowl of green chile stew and Saltines and a glass of milk on the table.

"Good?" Aragon looked again to the television. A view of an Air-force base, rows of dark helicopters, a woman walking under the blades saying these were the kinds of helicopters that dropped Navy SEALs inside the wall of Bin Laden's compound, nearly soundless, the likely means of getting rescuers onto the roof of the Valles house and into the courtyard at the center of the building.

"Good?" Aragon repeated. "Patricia Valles may be dead. A man I know, someone I thought I liked, has turned into a murderer."

"Very good, yes."

She wanted to smack Deke. Why the hell was he smiling? That was sick. And Vernon was also nuts, was showing white teeth under creepy lips.

"What's wrong with you people?" A quick glance at the television, photos of Patricia and Sam Valles, their two sons, the Washington Monument in the background. She'd never been close to Patricia. She'd always had her guard up around her. But they'd shared good times, stumbled into adulthood together. And now she might be dead, her boys without a mother.

"Cryin' out loud, what's wrong with *you*?" Deke said and she turned to tell him to get away from her. His head was tilted down, his gaze on her feet. "How's it feel to be standing on your own?"

————

Danny Luna watched the news, in the bathroom down the hallway where Senator Valles and Kilgore had bedrooms. Mrs. Valles dead? How horrible. She'd been so nice at the reception for the interns, giving each of them *I Love DC* ball caps. She'd repeated everyone's name after she was introduced, filing it away to impress them later. She was famous for that, remembering names, always standing next to Senator Valles when he waded into crowds at home, the first to reach out to shake a hand and say, "Esperanza Saavedra, how are you?" And then Senator Valles would say, "Esperanza, so good to see you. How's the family in Chama?" And Mrs. Valles whispering, "The Esperanzas are from Chamisa." Senator Valles recovering quickly and talking about the acequia system he was getting money to fix.

Danny had met the Valles boys, but they'd never talked. At the reception they'd peeled off from their parents and hung around the food table. One intern had the job of picking up after them.

Now they didn't have a mother. Senator Valles didn't have a wife.

What was this about nobody knowing why this Pete Cervantes was doing such evil things? Why was Senator Valles hanging around the house here outside Santa Fe by two championship Jack Nicklaus Signature Golf Courses instead of being on the front lines, manning up, offering his life to save his family?

What was left of his family.

Valles and Kilgore had been in the living room not long ago talking about "the next move." What was there to talk about? The next move should be Senator Valles putting one foot in front of the other and walking up to his front door. Let the whole country see what kind of man he was.

Senator Valles hadn't made any move except to lie to the cameras.

Danny left the bathroom and passed through the kitchen. Lorna had her back to him, hands in the sink, water running. She didn't hear him open the door and head to the guesthouse.

Outside, he estimated the distance to Santa Fe, cross-country, miles of rolling hills and arroyos slicing the landscape. A lot of walking. He could do it. He never wore out, that's what Lorna said.

———

Kilgore stuck his head in the kitchen and ordered Lorna to get them something to eat. She called out, Danny, give me a hand. Danny didn't answer. She thought he might be downstairs sneaking a bottle of wine to drink later instead of the syrupy Grenadine that made their teeth and lips red. But he wasn't down there. She went to the guesthouse. Danny? The clothes he'd dropped on the bedspread were gone. So was that silly backpack.

Back in the main house, she told Kilgore that Danny had left.

"You had one job," Kilgore said. Senator Valles right there, the television with the sound on low saying something about Mrs. Valles being shot. She wanted to hear that. It couldn't be true. But Kilgore stepped between her and the television. "To keep his dick inside you so you'd know where he was. Where the hell could he have got to? Take the car and check the roads."

She got keys from the guesthouse, the top drawer of the dresser under the window. Way out there in the distance, at the top of one of those hills that folded the land, she saw a little figure marching away, sunlight bouncing off something bright on its back. That little kids' backpack of his, it was coated in stiff shiny plastic.

On her way to the garage she stopped in the living room. Kilgore and Valles were watching television, a bowl of chips between them on the table.

"I think I know where Danny went," she said. "Pretty sure he's headed to the clubhouse. He's been wanting to use the pool. We'll hang out down there for a while, make him feel he's not a prisoner."

"Then put him in bed and see he doesn't go anywhere. Use your impressive skills to keep him occupied," Kilgore said and made his ugly lips into a circle.

"Yes, sir. You can count on me."

The keys she had were to the homeowners' Grand Cherokee. She'd been using it to get groceries and stuff Senator Valles wanted for his hair. Those eight cylinders firing up made her feel confident. The gate at the end of the drive swung open, something in the mechanism reading something in the car. It closed behind her. Soon she was a couple miles from the development, looking for a road that would take her to the hill where she'd seen the little marching figure.

Good thing this was a Jeep. She saw him far away, across open country, and she headed off the blacktop, bucking and rocking over broken desert. Dust rose into the sky behind her. He had to see her approaching. He'd be thinking it was the landowner, a rancher or tribal police, coming after him for trespassing.

She topped the hill and he was gone. But there were footprints, clear as could be, breaking the dry crust of the soil. They disappeared into a clutch of alligator juniper. She drove slowly now, sure he was watching her from inside those trees.

She saw the colors of his cheap backpack peeking through, sunlight exploding off the shiny plastic surface. She braked and stepped out to show herself.

"Hey, cowboy," she said when he came out of the trees. "I'm seeing us riding into the sunset together."

He swung his backpack over his shoulder. His clothes were soaked with sweat and damn if his fly wasn't open again.

"You're not taking me back?"

"I was thinking Vegas. We get a hotel room and don't come out for a month."

"We'll be sore."

"We'll be happy."

He was coming around to the passenger side, reaching for the door, when he said, "I have to make a stop first. Do you know how to get to the senator's house in Santa Fe?"

TWENTY-THREE

"I WANT TO TALK to Pete," Aragon said, working at controlling her excitement at standing on her own. She needed to focus on Cervantes killing Patricia Valles and how crazy this was getting. There were two boys that needed help. Pete Cervantes needed help. "Maybe he'll listen to me. We shared so much about his sons. I can remind him, help him step back. I don't see him as the kind of person who'd think, I killed one, what's two more?"

"You didn't see him as someone who'd hurt anyone," Lewis said over his cell phone, driving into the hospital to see her.

"I misread everything. I really fucked up."

"You call him, you're fucking up again. Take your idea to Helmick. You don't talk to Cervantes without the FBI listening in on every word."

"I don't have any magic words to say. We just connected, Pete and me. Maybe some of that is still there."

Her regular nurse was in the room, tidying up, frowning at the beer bottles in the trash can, holding up a Lotaburger wrapper like a bloody glove. Aragon didn't want her hearing any more of this. She changed subjects.

"Hey, I stood up today."

"You saved that news for last?"

Her nurse rolled a beer bottle from under the bed, came up with it on a pinkie, and shook her head. She was moving out the door, the wastebasket hugged against her chest, heavy with empties.

"I need to get out of here," she said.

"It'll come. You stand, then you walk, then you run. You skipped over the crawling first part. Be happy. Be patient."

"Today. Right now. There's someone we need to see."

———————

The nurse with the trash from Aragon's room put the wastebasket by her feet under the desk in the nurses station and called the number on the business card. She ducked below the pegboard with room keys when the call was answered by FBI Special Agent Pam Magnano.

"She's talking about calling that man who's holding the hostages. She wants to meet the FBI first."

Magnano said, "Now that someone's died, she wants to call it off."

———————

How Agent Magnano read it: Denise Aragon pops off to a very disturbed man, a man broken in spirit, a man who's always handled every situation, overcome every obstacle, figured everything out and still followed the rules, now feeling helpless. He wants to make one last mark on the world, some way of paying back the forces that hurt him and his family.

Back up: Denise Aragon intentionally provokes a very disturbed man. She'd been with him enough to know how fragile he was and the rage burning below the surface. She's hated Sam Valles for years but could never touch him. He kept moving farther from her reach. Little she could do to a US senator anyway, across the continent, most of the time inside the Beltway, jetting around the globe on the taxpayers' dime.

Along comes this man with nothing to lose, pain and anger seeping out of every pore. A few crafted words to steer him in the right direction, words she tossed off casually but they were barbed. *Somebody take Senator Valles out.* Aragon also let slip calling Valles a waste of skin. You think "corpse" when you hear those words. Subtle. Slick. Another barb pricking Cervantes to act.

Maybe she learned about the query from Mrs. Valles to hire Cervantes and Sons for a remodel. That's opportunity. It would never get better. She educated Cervantes on criminal investigations in connection with his son's case. Maybe she tutored him in hostage situations. Cervantes sure seemed to have a good idea how the game would be played.

Aragon and her partner just happened to be in the vicinity of the Valles house at the same time Cervantes was delivering his threat to the office on Capitol Hill. She was making herself available in case he needed her. Cervantes put on a show to immunize her, placing a laser sight on her face but never having any reason to shoot. Lewis reported how she'd lingered behind, strangely unconcerned. It now had spun out of control. The plan had been to embarrass Valles, show him to be a coward, destroy his career by revealing him as a man who'd rather sacrifice his family's lives than risk his own. But the FBI was playing cards Cervantes didn't anticipate. Cutting off communication with the outside world—maybe that had been far too clever. So clever it had cost Patricia Valles her life.

Now Aragon was scrambling to save herself, maybe come out of this a hero. Two superstar cop plays in one week. But she'd have to play it so Cervantes never talked.

Magnano called Helmick and said to expect a visit from Aragon. He didn't believe it. She was paralyzed.

"Not so much," Magnano said. "You might have good reason to turn on Cervantes's communications when she gets there. What's going on in the house?"

"No more on the walkie-talkie. And thank God, no more shots. We can't confirm anyone's been killed. We're operating on the assumption we have a fatality. Mr. Peter Cervantes is now a murderer and will be treated as one. Dix is ready to go in the second we get the word. The director will make that decision."

"He's still there?"

"He was never here."

"Yes, sir. He was never here. I don't know who we were talking about." So many things she didn't understand, because she was no longer in the black truck with Helmick where decisions were made. "What's this about us having no idea what Cervantes wants? The news keeps repeating it."

"Publicizing his throw-down to Valles would give Cervantes everything he wants. We don't start negotiations by meeting his opening offer."

"Instead we wait for a body to drop."

They didn't have conversations like this when she was at his elbow. She liked it, the space between, a chance to say what she was really thinking because she was an agent in the field and not his secretary.

"We've shifted the ground under him," Helmick said, and she heard his voice losing patience. "Taking away his communications gave us something to discuss that avoided any movement on his primary goal. We have him talking about a subject of our choosing."

"I signed up to protect lives, not political careers. Especially the career of someone who maybe never should have been elected."

"Magnano, what's going on?"

"I want to be there when Aragon arrives. Call me."

Aragon would take the hit for conspiring with Cervantes. She deserved it. But in listening to her telephone calls—put aside the stunt she'd pulled and the dozens of calls from waxing boutiques and colonic irrigators—she was inside the head of this detective, a good detective, working a closed case. From a hospital bed, even. She was facing the possibility of never walking again and what had she been doing? Tracking down evidence, reports, witnesses. Studying forensics.

That gag, she had to admit it was pretty good. Maybe she'd pull something like it on Helmick someday. Or pay Aragon back.

The more she listened to Aragon, the more Magnano realized that her hatred of Valles might be righteous. She was seeing the outlines of a crime in what had been forgotten as an unfortunate mistake by a reckless athlete. The corroboration from three witnesses of Amy McSwaim's injuries, concurrent with her claim that Valles had raped her. Questions about McSwaim's physical condition that might be inconsistent with accidental death. Questions made more troubling because they should have been asked fifteen years ago. Instead, McSwaim's death had been filed away without the slightest skepticism.

And the curious detail that Patricia Valles, formerly Garza, had sought to get her hands on McSwaim's equipment. Magnano had seen pictures of the woman in her college days. She wasn't in much better shape then. The same soft arms and hips wider than her shoulders. Patricia Valles hadn't been seeking the athletic gear for her own use.

237

Another call from the intercept monitors. A toxicologist at the Office of Medical Investigator getting back to Aragon. What did he say? He said swing by so they could talk, he had some ideas. Aragon said she liked the sound of that, swing by. He apologized, said he'd forgotten what had happened to her. He couldn't imagine her immobilized in a hospital bed instead of leaping tall buildings. Aragon replied she was doing a marathon tomorrow, didn't he know?

Apparently Aragon's feeling a lot better. She said she'd even stood up and expected to be walking very soon.

Good. It would be easier on taxpayers not having to cover expensive medical care for decades in federal prison.

But, damn. She wished the toxicologist had told Aragon over the phone what he was thinking.

———

Lewis had taken to wearing a light blue bill cap with a flap out the back covering his blistered neck. After standing in line at Whole Foods hearing children behind him asking about the "boiled man," he decided he'd had enough. He never took it off outside his house. He kept the hat on in her room.

"Amy McSwaim's backpack," he said and lifted a black plastic trash bag onto the bed. Aragon was in a wheelchair in a corner reading documents she'd received in response to her calls. "I knew you wouldn't be in that bed for the rest of your life. The nurse told me on the way down the hall. You really did stand up."

"For all of sixty seconds," Aragon said. "I'm telling everyone I'm doing a marathon tomorrow."

"I'll be at the finish line cheering."

"Let's see what you've got."

"Her parents kept this, the only thing left from McSwaim's last day. Her clothes and shoes were discarded at the hospital. They're still angry about that. This pack, they say they've never looked inside. It's been in this bag on the top shelf in their bedroom. They see it every time they get dressed."

It wasn't exactly a backpack. It was a Camelbak water reservoir, tough deep blue nylon material on the outside, lightly padded shoulder straps and a flimsy waist belt. It had a long vertical zipper to get the water bag inside. A set of keys, a tube of sun screen, lip balm, a few unused Band-Aids, and fruit leathers hardened with age were in the mesh pockets on the outside.

Aragon saw right away there was weight to the thing, more than explained by items in the pockets. It held its shape when Lewis lifted it from the plastic bag.

"It's not empty," Aragon said.

"There's a half liter of water in here," Lewis said.

"But Amy died of dehydration."

"It stinks." Lewis pulled out the water bag with the long hose and mouthpiece for sipping. "Take a whiff." He held the open top under her nose.

"It smells like … " Aragon thought a moment. "Home brew." What prisoners cooked up from kitchen scraps to get drunk.

"Fifteen years and the sugars in the drink rotted, maybe turned into alcohol."

"Amy used sports drinks, powders loaded with carbs and protein. She was way ahead of everybody." Aragon took another whiff, hoping she could identify the smell. It was just rot. "It doesn't make sense she had this much water left. Can you reach that phone?" Aragon pointed to her cell on the bedstand. "Look up Chuck Whitman. He's the toxicologist at OMI I asked to put on his thinking cap."

She put it on speaker so Lewis could hear. Whitman said he'd had more ideas on her questions. There were several substances that could produce symptoms easily confused with heat stroke and dehydration. He couldn't talk right now but could come by later.

Aragon said, "No, it's fine. We'll meet you at your office."

"We've all been pulling for you," he said. "We can't imagine Denise Aragon not moving mountains. How's the marathon training coming?"

"I'll be setting new records for how long I take to finish. Months. Listen, we have some liquid that Amy McSwaim was drinking. Yeah, after all this time. If you can do that chromatograph thing, print out those pretty graphs that tell what's in it, we might have an answer or two."

Whitman said, "For you, we'll make lab time. We can run the Cuisinart while you wait."

"Cuisinart?"

"What we call the machine that makes those chromatograph things and prints out those pretty graphs."

Aragon told Lewis she wasn't going to wait for the doctors to let her out of jail. He settled her into a wheelchair and pushed her down the hall. A nurse at the nearby station saw them and shouted, "Wait!" But he pushed Aragon fast inside the elevator as soon as the doors opened.

That nurse picked up a phone. After a moment she said, "Agent Magnano, she's left. Her partner, the large detective who was burned, he's pushing her in a wheelchair. I don't know where they're going."

On the other end of the line Magnano said, "We do. I wish I could be there."

Lewis made the drive to OMI's offices in Albuquerque, on the campus of the University of New Mexico, in fifty-two minutes. Aragon told Whitman they were almost there and he was waiting for them outside. He came to the car to get the Camelbak so Aragon need not use her wheelchair. Give me ten minutes, he said. I'm set up and ready. She took the opportunity to sleep, surprised at how tired she was. He returned with written results and the Camelbak, now sealed in a larger clear plastic bag and a little lighter after liquid had been extracted to test.

Then they made another stop. Lewis did the return trip to Santa Fe in about the same time, never dropping below ninety except on the ramps. He pulled into the huge lot of the Joseph Montoya State Office building and parked in the space reserved for *Prospective Film Projects, Visitors Only*. He went in and was out soon with Margaret Baldonado.

"Oh my God," she said to Aragon. "Look at you. You're out of the hospital."

Aragon sat in the back with her legs straight out across the seat, her shoulders against the door behind the passenger seat.

"We need to talk," Aragon said. "Without the FBI listening. Get in, Margaret."

Margaret swallowed and nodded, her painted face dropping. Lewis drove around to find shade. He found a sick elm a couple blocks away. He kept the AC on while Aragon dropped something over the seat into Margaret's lap.

"This is Amy's pack, from that day. Her parents have had it all this time."

Margaret said, "Why did you take me out of work?"

"Because you and Magnano would have been ready for us if we'd called ahead. Unless you're running around with her wire all the time. I do expect you're going to run to her when we're done here. I'm not going to tell you not to talk to the FBI. But I don't like you coming into my hospital room playing the long-lost friend when you're on a secret assignment. This way, maybe we can have an honest discussion and roll back the years with a little more trust between us."

"I'm sorry for that, Denise." Margaret lifted the pack. The part with the weight of the rancid water in the reservoir stayed on her thighs. "I remember this. Patricia gave it to Amy, all wrapped up. A birthday gift."

"I wanted to see if you remembered," Aragon said.

"Now that I see it."

"I'd forgotten the details. You've helped me get it right. Amy didn't have the Camelbak when she arrived at the tram. Do you remember how it went?"

"Amy came out of the woods. She had that belt of little yellow plastic bottles she squeezed into her mouth to drink. They were really awkward. She was always complaining about them falling off."

"Right, that's what she was wearing when she showed up. They were empty and she needed refills. And, yeah, I think she'd lost some of the bottles."

"We were at our table, a couple beers in. Patricia had brought her gift up on the Tram. Maybe she'd told us what it was, I don't remember exactly. But I was impressed she was so thoughtful. She'd never shown any interest in Amy's crazy endurance stuff. She always said Amy was plain nuts. She didn't go to any of the races, never went along on even the easy bike rides. Lo and behold, she's found what Amy said she'd been wanting since it came on the market, so much better because it had this." Margaret flicked the clear plastic drinking tube. "She could drink more, without stopping."

"Something else," Aragon said. "Think."

"Something else?"

Aragon and Lewis waited, the only sound the AC fan blowing cold air.

"Did Patricia bring another gift?" Aragon asked.

"Wait." Margaret tugged a lock of hair, twisted it. "She did. Patricia had a can, a plastic jar of some kind of super-duper sports powder. She got up from the table and said she'd fill the bladder in the pack for Amy. Another first for Patricia, helping instead of mocking Amy behind her back."

"And all this just came to you."

"It doesn't mean anything," Margaret said.

"Why did you wear a wire for the FBI?"

Lewis angled the rear-view mirror so Margaret in the passenger seat could see Aragon's eyes.

"You can take me back now," Margaret said.

"The jobs you've had in government," Aragon said. "The political appointments, positions you weren't qualified for. It was Sam and Patricia pulling strings, I get that. You have kids, you needed the work. That doesn't explain coming to my hospital room, old pals reconnecting. I can't make you tell me your motivation. But I can tell you what I suspect."

"You don't know me. It's been more than ten years."

"I know your type. You're looking ahead. When this is over, you can go to Sam, tell him you did all you could to help. You were ready to sell out a friend. You're looking at your next step up into some better government job. Maybe a spot in Washington, DC on a senator's staff. You've stayed in touch with him all this time, Patricia knowing you were one of the people Amy told about Sam raping her. I wonder how many times you've reminded her."

"We don't know he raped her." Margaret tried to turn in her seat but her bulk made it difficult. She had to pull herself forward, hands on the dash, gain a little air under her, before she could turn to face Aragon. "It was just Amy saying."

"You saw the bruises and scratches. You think she made that up?"

"Patricia said Amy was jealous. She and Sam had been getting close. Amy couldn't have him. She tried hurting him after humiliating him. The time she laughed at him when he was doing his birthday greetings routine."

"The future senator in a Speedo not impressing anyone." Lewis took the Camelbak and handed it over the seat to Aragon. Margaret looked glad to be rid of it. "What you were just holding," Aragon said, "is what killed Amy. And you just gave me something I didn't know. That Patricia and Sam were an item before Amy was killed."

"Killed?" The heavy makeup didn't hide the blood leaving Margaret's face.

"The crime lab analyzed the liquid left after all these years. Sugars turned to alcohol and two other things. Atropine and scopolamine. High concentrations."

"Amy was doping herself, is what you're saying, so she could do extreme things?"

"It wasn't Amy who put those chemicals in her drink. It was Patricia, when she mixed her super-duper sports drink as a birthday favor for her girlfriend. It's why Patricia tried to get the Camelbak from the women who found Amy and later her parents."

"Amy died of heat stroke, dehydration."

"Not quite. Her dilated pupils don't match up with natural causes. The experts thought so back then, but not so much anymore. They do match up with atropine and scopolamine in her bloodstream. And I think I know how Patricia did it."

Margaret was working at a fake fingernail, now prying it loose with her teeth.

"I know you're running to Magnano next," Aragon said. "Tell her to send someone over to the museum at the Palace of the Governors. Patricia once made a big deal about getting her grandmother recognized as a *curandera*. She learned about poisons from her. The chemicals that killed Amy, they came from moonflowers probably growing in her backyard."

"What does it matter? Patricia's dead."

————

Lorna Pierson wanted to touch Danny Luna, her beautiful boy. Those lovely lips, that olive skin, so soft and warm, energy making his body hum.

He didn't know enough to be afraid. She was carrying that for the both of them. What he wanted to do, she told him he had to do it right. A head shot. She'd heard Martin Kilgore talk like that about the senator's enemies.

Danny had been determined to hike all the way into Santa Fe and hope he had it figured out by the time he got there. He was so innocent, he thought just walking up to any policeman would be enough.

Look where things were now, the police, the FBI, everybody pretending they didn't know what this Cervantes wanted. If Valles or Kilgore found out about the kid with the cartoon backpack bugging policemen with a story about Senator Valles hiding the truth to save his own ass and let his family die, they'd sweep Danny off the street and put him somewhere without a guard as nice as her.

Danny could disappear. Northern New Mexico—she'd heard the stories. Somebody gassing up on their way to spill on talk radio everything they knew about a governor's connections to organized crime in the southern part of the state, the Dixie Mafia or the Mexican Mafia or some other flavor of Mafia. They were lucky they only had their jaw smashed so they couldn't talk until the election was over. The man checking his mail in the morning and not making it back to his door, a bullet between his shoulder blades, nobody finding him until the propane delivery men saw dogs fighting and chewing on something in front of a double-wide. That man had handled road contracts and had been talking to the Attorney General.

Some of those people going over the bridge at the Taos Gorge had help. Taking a leap wasn't their idea. They'd been unfortunate enough to find out that a county manager owned a piece of a casino boat. Or even bigger stakes, that the start-up company getting tens of millions of state investment dollars was nothing but a pretty front office with pictures stolen from the Internet for its brochure.

So she told Danny it had to be a head shot. And then they'd drive out of New Mexico very, very fast.

"Lorna." Danny bounced on his seat. He was excited and it got to her, like jumping your dead battery off a running engine, Danny's charge going straight into her bones. "Should we hand out something? I see the senator's press person doing that before he makes a statement. He puts it down in writing so the reporters get it right."

"We don't have time," she said. They were now pushing through traffic into the city from the south. She could tell where to go by the helicopters in the sky. And she'd been to the senator's house plenty of times. It didn't stay unused when he was in Washington; Danny hadn't been her first assignment. Kilgore said he'd never tell her how to do her job, just don't do it on the senator's bed.

She'd been with other campaigns before Kilgore discovered her. A political junkie, chasing rising stars, offering the kind of bright face and nice body all the male politicos wanted in their HQ. She'd met Kilgore on those other campaigns. He'd hooked her up with jobs through the winners he backed. One day he called to say he'd hitched himself the next United State Senator for New Mexico. He asked if she'd be willing to do something to really, really help Sam. Back then it was always "Sam." There was this man on their team they didn't trust, Kilgore explained. He was part of Valles's top team, a fundraiser who also dealt with the unions and enviros. They thought he was cozy with the other team. Could she get close to him, get under his defenses?

"Under the covers, you mean?" She wanted to show Kilgore she wasn't dumb.

Kilgore told her, when he's drained and you're lying back feeling close, talk a little how you don't like Sam, he's not the man you thought he was. But you're stuck. You've got no future if he doesn't win. You feel like a whore—Kilgore had actually said that. You wish there was something you could do to help out the person who really deserved to win, who unfortunately is not Sam. Be creative but believable. Use your head after you give him head. Kilgore had said that, too.

Danny had rebelled right away. It had taken her all these years.

So, her hand across the console onto his thigh, *Danny, listen, this is what we do.*

They'd sat in the Grand Cherokee on the top of that hill, off the road, trespassing on someone's land while they worked it out. Now they were past the busy, wide, straight streets onto roads that curved with the slope of hills where big houses hung off concrete cliffs. The helicopters were close. Cars that didn't look like they belonged with the expensive houses were in the street. All the houses had driveways and garages. The people who lived here did not park at the curb.

Then the backs of people to whom the cars probably belonged, the curious, come from other parts of the city. Looking up the street, a police barricade ahead, Lorna saw the roofs of the patrol cars and lights flashing without sirens. She didn't see what they needed and backed around in a driveway to try another approach.

Danny saw it first. "There. The satellite antenna."

It was a television news van, sawhorses with the station's letters cordoning off an area serving as an outdoor broadcasting booth. A man in sweatpants had a camera on his shoulder and was panning the helicopters. He brought the lens down. Now he was panning the crowds by the barricades. Now he was swinging the lens their way.

Lorna killed the engine and gave Danny's leg a squeeze. "This is different for me. It feels good. Thank you."

She met him on the other side of the Jeep to make sure his fly was zipped. She combed his dark thick hair, loving doing that. She straightened his collar. She'd told him to put on the white business shirt he'd worn flying from DC. It was wrinkled but better than an *I Love DC* tee. The darn shirt was untucked. She fixed that and forced her hands not to linger inside his pants when she shoved the tails as deep as they could go.

Then it was her turn. She brushed her hair in the side mirror and pinched her cheeks to give them color. She opened her top buttons and revealed a pretty gold pendant against her breastbone.

"Sparkle and shine," she said. Words she'd heard Sam Valles mumble to himself before going on camera.

There was another man with the cameraman, hair rising straight off his forehead and standing still in the breeze, a lot of product in there.

"Let's try the cameraman first." That one had already seen her in his lens. He was looking again their way through the eyepiece, the camera on his shoulder. She tugged Danny's hand to follow. On the way she popped one more button to show the stitching of a black brassiere.

She thought about what they looked like, her and Danny. He couldn't be her kid, she didn't look that old. Why were they together?

The cameraman would be wondering. They were at the sawhorses now. The reporter had noticed them but stayed by the truck. He was putting on a tie, inspecting himself in a mirror someone inside was holding out the window.

Lorna leaned across the barrier, her shirt falling away. "We have something for the media," she said. "We're members of Senator Valles's staff. You want to hear this."

Lorna gave her name and told Danny to do the same. Danny had a business card issued to interns. Lorna didn't have any identification as an employee of a US senator. She wasn't sure who actually paid her. But she did have a pass to get into the Hart Senate Building. She showed that.

Lorna went first, the more senior staffer, the one who'd caught and kept the cameraman's eye. She explained her job guarding Danny Luna, keeping him isolated and away from the media, computers, and telephones. He carried a secret Senator Valles did not want known. A secret that would destroy the senator.

So why was she coming forward? The cameraman was a tough sell. Her conscience had rebelled, she said. She had to speak up and help Danny get his important information out, so the public would know Sam Baca Valles was not the man they thought they'd voted for. He was a man who would sacrifice his wife to protect his career.

That got the cameraman taking his eyes off her and staring hard at Danny.

Danny explained his job for the senator, the calls he had from Pete Cervantes, exactly what Cervantes wanted, how the senator had lied on television, how he'd been kept a kind of prisoner. *What kind of prisoner?* The cameraman interrupting with a question. Kept way out in the country in a big house against his will, Danny explained and looked to Lorna.

"I was instructed to screw his eyes out," she said. "Make his knees weak, okay? Orders directly from Martin Kilgore, chief of staff for Senator Valles. Throw sex at the kid so he wouldn't want to leave. The senator knew what I was doing. He said 'good work.'"

The cameraman waved for the reporter with the tall, stiff hair to come over and talked with him quietly, nodding at Danny and Lorna. Just as she thought they had it, the reporter shook his head and walked back to his truck.

"No dice," the cameraman explained.

"This is a great story," Lorna said.

"You're not the first crackpots with fake IDs to bother us today."

The cameraman left them at the sawhorses and was back with the reporter by the truck.

"We'll keep driving around until we find a television crew that will put us on camera," Lorna said.

From the truck, the person who had been holding the mirror for the reporter stepped down.

"I know her," Danny said and waved. "It's my cousin."

The woman, black hair, mocha skin, high forehead, big brown eyes, waved back. In a second she was with them.

"This is Erica Gabaldon," Danny said and introduced Lorna.

"You're working for Senator Valles, aren't you?" Gabaldon asked. "I heard you were in DC. It's been a long time. I remember you at the *matanzas*, so shy, always off by yourself. I wondered why you didn't come over."

"I was scared of you, to be honest. And the older girls."

Gabaldon looked between Danny and Lorna. "Are you still scared of older girls?"

"He's got a real story," Lorna said. "It's huge. I work for Senator Valles, too. You have to hear this."

It wasn't long before Erica Gabaldon told the cameraman, "Let's have them stand with the police behind them."

"Side by side," the cameraman said. "I focus on Lorna first. After she tells the story about keeping Danny under wraps, people will be falling out of their La-Z-Boys to hear what comes next."

"Lorna, Danny, always look into the camera when you talk. I'd button up a little," she said to Lorna. "Don't touch each other like that. Not on camera. Step a bit apart."

"Looking good," the cameraman said, his face behind the eyepiece. "Identify yourself, state your age and home address, and then Erica will begin the interview."

"I want to get right into what Senator Valles is hiding. That work for you, cuz?" Gabaldon asked Danny.

"Works for me," he said, and Lorna Pierson glowed.

———

With Margaret's information and the lab results on the contents of Amy's Camelbak, Aragon asked Lewis to drive her to see Helmick. On the way she called Perez and shared the evidence that Patricia Valles had poisoned Amy McSwaim to prevent her from reporting her rape by Senator Valles. Perez said it would be great stuff if Patricia were alive to be prosecuted.

"Hats on rocks," Aragon said.

Perez came back with, "Cowboys and Indians?"

"I keep saying, and I will continue to believe, that Pete Cervantes wouldn't physically hurt anyone, let alone kill the mother of two boys."

"So far … "

"Hold on. I've spent more time face to face with him than anyone. That counts for something. I also don't believe there's anyone helping him. His brothers, they've been contacted, right? Tell me they're not as shocked as anyone else."

They were approaching the eastern hills where helicopters filled the sky like mosquitoes. The first police barricades were up ahead, past a television news van with its satellite uplink antenna poking through the roof.

"What friends could he pull into this?" asked Aragon, stretched out in the back seat with Lewis at the wheel listening. "He wasn't political. He's not part of a secret militia with wackos eager to join an armed uprising. He's doing this with hats on rocks."

"Tricking your enemy, making them think there's more of you when you're actually alone?"

"Nobody's seen his backup. Nobody's talked to them."

"He's named Bobo. Why are you laughing?"

"Everybody that is a pain in the ass is Bobo to Pete Cervantes. When he can't remember someone's name, they're Bobo. He calls waiters and busboys Bobo to get their attention."

"The FBI, they've seen Bobo. They've detected him using infrared."

"I'll bet Pete has rigged something. He's a smart guy. He ate up everything I shared with him about police procedures, how the courts worked. How they didn't. I'm sure he went from that to studying hostage situations and the tools the FBI has. Hats on rocks, I'm telling you."

Lewis said without taking his eyes from the road, "His guns are real enough. The laser sight on your cheek. I saw that."

"The kids didn't actually see him shoot Patricia. He could have fired blanks, set it up so the FBI heard the sound while the kids were on the walkie-talkie. Look, Pete doesn't make his point that someone like Valles is a worthless piece of shit by killing a woman and her children. It would make Valles a martyr. He'd get the country's sympathy. The problem now is that Pete has been too convincing. He's got the FBI looking at him as a murderer, a very dangerous, heavily armed man. They'll bring more firepower to bear. I think, though, I have a way to get everybody out of the house without anyone getting shot for real."

Perez said, "They're not going to believe someone they're investigating as Cervantes's accomplice."

"Then they're stupid and this will end ugly. They'll come out of this on the side of a rapist and a murderer. Hey, Rick, that's Erica Gabaldon from KSFM. She's a straight shooter. I want to find out why we haven't heard anything about Pete Cervantes's demands."

"You sure you should be talking to reporters?"

"Get me in my chair with wheels. That boy. He's Jerry Luna's son."

"And Jerry Luna is?"

"The *patroñ* who owns every vote north of Espanola. The Lunas are related to everybody north of Socorro. That kid and I are distant cousins. Who's the babe holding his hand?"

TWENTY-FOUR

THEY HAD REACHED THE point in these dances with lunatics when Art Helmick would look at himself and Ty Dix and ask, is this really us?

He wasn't any more a natural for this than Dix. Three kids, a wife he'd been married to his entire adult life. The two of them in a bridge club, her idea but he'd grown to enjoy the calm, harmless nights with unexciting people playing an unexciting game. Iced tea, no alcohol. Snacks, Rice Krispies squares, small talk about families. And the dinner group they'd kept together with the same circle of friends for two decades, tracking the progress of their lives by children marrying, having their own kids, hairlines receding, cheeks sagging, trifocals when the contacts stopped working, most of them reading the cards wrong now and then and everyone laughing about it.

Who am I to be making these kinds of decisions?

Do we risk entering the house only to find Cervantes holed up in the same room as the boys? Do we risk another death by continuing to withhold communications? Are we willing to accept three innocent deaths instead of turning over a US senator because of the national security information in his head? Cervantes wasn't a political terror-ist. But who the hell was Bobo? What did he want out of this?

And Kilgore's idea: "We find an agent who looks like Valles. Sure, he'll have to be a little out of shape but we have enough of those. A desk jockey. Some makeup, dye his hair. Make it good enough to look like Valles from a distance. He steps into the open, hands up, maybe a gun taped on his back just inside his collar. Maybe a der-ringer up his sleeve. He gets close enough, Cervantes at the door, stepping back to let his prize enter. Our man takes him there. We move in fast and follow the most direct route to the boys' room. At the same time, we block Bobo from leaving his post. Game over."

"What if," Helmick said, thinking of his workshop, the bridge games. Hell, flannel pajamas on cold mornings with a cat on his lap. Wishing for all that instead of this in front of him. "What if Cervantes uses that sniper rifle to shoot our actor before he gets to the door? He's got the person he thinks is Senator Valles offering his life for his fam-ily. Suppose he accepts the offer from twenty yards away? That's a very easy shot. Body armor won't stop a Lapua magnum round."

"How about this?" Dix pointing like he was holding a pistol in each hand. "We add something to the water going into the house through city pipes. We drug Cervantes and Bobo. No resistance when we take the door."

"How would you know the bad guys went to sleep?"

"You'd know if you were talking to him. You'd hear it in his speech."

"And as the room started spinning he'd realize what had hap-pened. He and Bobo hurry to the boy's room before they nod off and we pick up bodies later."

Dix's hands opened and closed around a coffee mug. "We use silencers to take out Cervantes so Mr. Bobo doesn't hear anything."

255

"They have cameras."

"I'm going back to my dose-the-water idea. Knock them out with tranquilizer dissolved in their drinking water. We can tap the main to the house where they won't see."

"But Cervantes is seeing everything." Helmick went to the window. A hill blocked the Valles house from view. "Maybe we use that fact. Give him a show. Use his surveillance to our advantage. It would be nice if your guys found the cameras he has looking at us."

Someone was pounding on the outside door. Now it was open. With sunlight backlighting his silhouette, the agent just in from Afghanistan pointed at the television.

"You might want to turn that on. There's a chubby kid and a woman who say they work for Valles. They're talking about Cervantes calling the senator's office, offering to trade the family for the senator's life, and how Valles and his chief of staff have bottled up that information, let the wife die to save the senator's ass. I've got reporters at the cordon wanting comment from the FBI. What do I tell them?"

"Forget the reporters. Call Kilgore. Tell them Valles is in the game and get his ass down here. We don't have time to get a stunt man ready."

When the agent was gone, Helmick told Dix, "The director instructed me that if we got to this point, give Valles his one and only play. You and I are the tacklers. This doesn't go beyond us."

"I've got to get someone to take my place with my teams. Let me line that up. Then I'm following your call. I don't like this."

"Remember this was Kilgore's idea. The senator is willing to step out there for his little show. The director says it can work for us. Scenario one: Valles comes out of this a true hero. He runs for the White House. Meanwhile, we flesh out Aragon's case against him and hold it as an ace up our sleeve. It doesn't have to be good enough for a conviction, just good enough to destroy him if need be. He's elected, we own him. Or else we decide the other team is better for us and play our ace during the election.

"Scenario two?"

"Cervantes kills him. The governor of this dusty state appoints his replacement from her party, which happens to be the same as the director's and his current boss's. They're then one vote closer to a filibuster-proof majority in the Senate. Like Kilgore said, there are many other interests to go on the scales, some of which Kilgore and Valles don't seem to see."

Dix shook his head and left, already on the horn appointing his replacement. Helmick got back to wondering how it was exactly he had ended up in a job like this.

———

Kilgore finished the call with Helmick's man and said to Senator Valles, "This will be a billion dollars of earned media. It will play and play and play. The bobbleheads won't have anything else to talk about. No, a golf shirt isn't right. It shows your nipples. Business shirt, with a white tee underneath so they can't see you sweating when you raise your hands."

Valles pulled the pinkish golf shirt over his head. "Tell me again, they're going to stop me before I get too far?" He opened a package of clean white tees and shook one out. "Do I struggle, try to break free and run to my house?"

"You won't be able to resist." Kilgore played it through in his head, the way the cameras and the tens of millions watching would see it. "The FBI guys will overpower you. Throw out an arm, a hand straining toward the house. Look back as they carry you away."

"What do I say?"

"Let me think." Would the camera crews pick up sound? There would be helicopters overhead. You definitely want the aerial angle, the lone figure separating from the crowd and police cars. It would be dramatic, seeing him close the distance to the house where the gunman held his family. So exposed. So vulnerable. So selfless and brave. "Shout, and make it loud, 'No, let me go. Please. My family.' Got that? Shout 'my family' a lot."

"How about I add, 'My life means nothing'?" Valles now had a crisp shirt on a hangar, light blue with white collar and cuffs.

"Not that one. You look like a banker or a lawyer. All white. Not button-down. Don't roll up the sleeves. No tie. You want to look dignified but not formal."

"Shouldn't I look like I've been sleeping in my clothes, unable to rest while my family suffers?"

"You want to look like a US senator, a man in control of himself if not the situation into which he has been thrust. Remember, the video is going to play a million times down the road."

Valles slid his arms into the shirt and looked at his pants and shoes. "The president dresses like this when he speaks in the Rose Garden. Hair?" Valles checked himself in a mirror. "Mussed, wind-blown. Or the Capitol steps helmet hair?"

"Chaos swirls around you, thunder rolls, lightning flashes, the winds howl. Everyone else is biting their nails. But you are self-possessed. The calm in the storm. A vision of confidence and determination. Exactly the kind of man we should have as commander in chief. Make it the helmet hair. Ready? Let's do this."

———

Aragon watched the way the woman with legs and breasts kept touching Danny Luna. He introduced her as Lorna Pierson and said they worked together for Senator Valles. She got the "together" part fine, but couldn't figure out what work it was that Lorna Pierson might be doing on Capitol Hill. They didn't act like coworkers. Even when she wasn't touching him, she stood close, her eyes on nothing but the man-boy six inches shorter.

Little Danny, the chubby, awkward kid she'd last seen when his father and uncles pulled the pig from the hot coals at the annual Taos County *matanza,* the smell of burned flesh turning everyone into ravenous Neanderthals. Back then Danny couldn't get close to any of the girls. His clothes a tangle, not fitting right, a boy still more a child than a young man. He was a sweet kid. He tried to give a hand and help pull the pig up from the pit, but you could see he wasn't adding much. Still, he jumped right in and got searing hot grease over his chest when the carcass rolled and he leaned forward to keep it from falling into the fire.

Today, with this babe in tow, little Danny had become a man.

Again he'd stepped up. He was burning down a US senator because it was the right thing to do.

"What he's telling you, and this is off the record," Aragon, looking up from her wheelchair, told Erica Gabaldon, "is true. I heard the demands myself. Valles for his family. I reported it to my superiors, drafted a report. And told the FBI personally."

"Valles won't comment," Gabaldon said, and they watched Lorna Pierson leading Danny by the hand to a Grand Cherokee. On the far side of the SUV she pulled him into her and kissed him on the lips. Go Danny.

"Call Sergeant Perez at SFPD. Go on background and ask him. Rick Lewis will confirm, too, as long as you keep his name out of this."

"Three sources, wow," Gabaldon said. "Any documents? We'll get out a Freedom of Information request to the FBI and Santa Fe Police."

Danny and Lorna were leaving in the Grand Cherokee. Nope, they were necking. Now they were rolling.

"Valles has been MIA except for his scripted five-minute statement and the phony prayer he led for the cameras," Gabaldon said with a smile as they watched Lorna and Danny. "He'll have a lot more to say when we run with this."

Lewis had walked to the closest barricade to try to get through. Helmick wasn't returning their calls. They wanted to tell him everything about Amy McSwaim and Aragon's hunch about Cervantes faking everyone out. The FBI and its sniper teams needed to know about hats on rocks.

"I've got my news director on the line," Gabaldon said. "Would you tell him what you told me? Off the record, same deal. You'll be our well-informed source confirming what Danny said."

Lewis was coming back this way. The look on his face told her he'd had no luck in talking his way past the barricades. She got out her phone and called the very last person she wanted to talk to.

Magnano answered immediately. "You've been busy for a quadriplegic."

"I wasn't that bad."

"I know what you've been up to. Do you really think you can make a case against Patricia Valles? The poison she used, I'm betting there's no record of her ever purchasing atropine and scopolamine. There's another source she could have used, one that wouldn't leave any inconvenient records. But you've already thought of it. It's still nothing you can prove."

Lewis was now at her side and shook his head. No way they were getting past the barricade. Aragon mouthed, "Magnano."

Aragon said, "You've been following our steps."

"You're good at what you do." Something very different in Magnano's tone. "Flat on your back, you don't stop. Maybe you did provoke Cervantes. But you've got a solid murder case. There's more to consider than your loose tongue. A lot more."

"So you think Amy McSwaim was murdered?" Aragon asked. There was commotion among the camera crews. Men were coming out of news vans, checking their satellite antennas, hefting cameras onto their shoulders. Reporters were doing sound checks. Something was up.

"Poisoned," Magnano answered. "Patricia Valles put it in McSwaim's water, in a sports drink. She tried to get the evidence back after McSwaim was dead. That didn't help her."

"Put *what* in Amy's water? You tell me."

Down the hill, sunlight flashed off a limousine, black and shiny. It rolled past, all the television cameras following its progress. The barricade that had blocked Lewis was pulled aside, police sentries stood out of the way. The limo moved up the hill toward Helmick and the FBI command post.

"Senator Valles has made his appearance."

"I liked Brazilian Boutique," Magnano said, "but I'll pass on a couple hours at Colonnade. I'll leave my cell on."

"We have a lot to talk about, but later." Aragon hung up and saw a chance to get past the barricade. The sawhorses had been moved aside, police officers turned away, their gaze following Valles's limo.

"Let's roll," Aragon said. "I've been wanting to say that."

Lewis pushed her like he was leaning into a tackling dummy. His powerful legs built up speed and they were a blur passing startled police sentries. They ignored angry shouts and kept moving, now seeing the limo stopped outside the black FBI command truck. A racing engine to their right made them turn their heads. Lewis braked, digging his heels into the pavement, just as a black Suburban cut them off.

It was Magnano.

She leaned out of the driver's door. "You don't want to go up there. They'll just haul you off. Go the back way, down the hill to the house with the low stucco wall and flower pots. I'll meet you there. I'm going to brief Helmick on what you've turned up. Better it comes from me."

She closed the door and was off, pulling up behind the limo and racing to where Valles and Kilgore were talking with Helmick and Dix.

"You notice something different about her?" Aragon asked.

"She had two eyebrows." Lewis turned her chair and let it roll ahead of him, the gentle incline doing his work. A block downhill they found the spot Magnano had mentioned and waited.

"We'll give her fifteen minutes," Aragon said. "Then we go on background and tell our reporter friend that Patricia Valles is under investigation for the murder of a woman raped by Sam Baca Valles."

———————

"Not now, Magnano." Helmick would not face her. Valles stood a step behind Kilgore, listening, not taking a lead in the conversation.

"Sir, I have information you need to know."

"We have enough to manage here. Write it up, Magnano. Excuse us."

He brushed her back, Dix at his shoulder, Kilgore motioning for Valles to go forward toward the no man's land in front of his house.

Magnano gave them a minute, then followed, keeping a distance and keeping quiet.

From behind she saw the shape of a Kevlar vest under Valles's white shirt, and a microphone transmitter clipped to the back of his waistband.

"It's your show," Helmick said.

Kilgore pointed out how he wanted Valles to proceed. "You start from here. Plead with Cervantes. Tell him he's got what he wants. Tell him you'll lay down your life for your family if that's what it takes. Speak clearly. You'll have to shout."

"What if he shoots me?" Valles didn't seem so sure about this.

Dix said, "There are a dozen snipers, more, focused on every square inch of that house. If they see a rifle barrel, they send a bullet up the muzzle and twenty through the sights. They'll holler for you to lay flat. You're not going far, so relax."

"As long as the cameras are getting this."

"Oh, they're getting it," Kilgore said. "We're going to leave you here. When you get Helmick's signal that everything's in place, start walking. Keep your hands up. It looks good, Sam. Dramatic."

Magnano was now alone with Valles, the other men a distance away and motioning for her to get out of there. She said under her breath, "Good luck here with whatever you're doing. We'll be talking later. About Amy McSwaim."

She caught up with them downhill behind a tree. She couldn't understand what they were doing so far out of position. Why wasn't Dix supervising his gun crews? Why wasn't Helmick in the command truck commanding? Instead they were looking smaller than they both were, in shirts with *FBI* on the back, something new for them. Kilgore was with them, a phone in each hand, saying, "Senator Valles is calling the lunatic's bluff. Yes, he is offering his life for his family. He is revealing the kind of man he truly is." And, "Agent Helmick, can one of the stations get on top of your truck so they can catch all of the senator's walk into the jaws of death?"

"He's a rapist, Art," Magnano said. Kilgore flinched and talked into his other phone but kept an eye on her. "And his wife's a murderer.

Aragon nailed it. If Mrs. Valles isn't dead, they're charging her with killing the girl Valles raped to shut her up."

Kilgore jammed his phones in his pocket and pushed his face in front of hers. Such an attractive man, a tooth clawing over his lip, bulges above his eye sockets, veins on his nose.

"Your name?"

Breath that reeked of gum disease. She ignored him and noticed that Dix was listening closely.

"Aragon worked it up from her hospital bed. Remember, I've been listening to her calls. Patricia Valles, then Patricia Garza, slipped atropine and scopolamine into a sports drink Amy McSwaim was carrying on a long, extreme run in the summer heat, end-to-end in the Sandia Mountains above Albuquerque. The chemicals mimicked the symptoms of heat stroke and dehydration. They pushed her already-stressed system over the edge. The chemicals were extracted from moonflowers. Beautiful and deadly. It grows everywhere around here, in places where nothing else will. Patricia knew what she was doing. She learned about the flower and its toxic seeds from her grandmother, a native healer, a *curandera*."

"Slanderous fantasy," Kilgore said. "Aragon's been spreading them for years, going back to a grudge against the senator from college days. She has nothing but unsupported accusations."

"She has McSwaim's water sack, called a Camelbak, with some of the poisoned water still in it. She also has two witnesses and both can testify to McSwaim's injuries after she was with Valles. One can testify to Patricia Valles providing the Camelbak and filling it with a sports drink she provided. Oh, and a couple witnesses who can testify that after McSwaim's death Patricia Valles attempted to retrieve the Camelbak. All to keep a rape victim from ruining the career of a young politician on his way up."

"The senator," Kilgore said. They had forgotten Valles.

He was twenty yards from where he'd started, hands still up. Shouting, "Here I am. Let my family go." But looking over at them instead of ahead at the house.

"Valles must have known about McSwaim being murdered," Magnano said.

"It's time," Kilgore said.

"Time for what?" she asked.

"Keep talking, Magnano." Dix was ignoring Valles, who was looking their way with every step. Cameras rolled. The news choppers overhead were kicking up dust and rustling leaves. "How far along is the investigation?"

"Take him out!" Kilgore shouted, leaving Magnano puzzled. Take the senator out? Those words had started this madness.

"Aragon has forensics on the water and its toxicity," she went on. "She has the captain of the EMT crew, who's now convinced he misread McSwaim's symptoms based on what he's learned since. Plus witnesses who can explain the reason for Valles's animosity to McSwaim."

"Which was?"

"She laughed at his little pecker. In college he did a one-man Chippendales act delivering birthday greetings for bachelorette parties. Back then he had a ponytail he could tuck in his underwear."

"You've lost your mind." Kilgore shoved her and Dix nearly lifted him off the ground by his collar.

Behind them, Valles had stopped walking. His face was pleading. He turned his palms up, shrugged his shoulders.

"What's going on with Valles?" Magnano asked.

"We're supposed to run out there," Helmick said, "tackle him and drag him away. Let him put on a little show of what a brave man he is. Where's Aragon?"

"She tried to get through the barricade. She was coming to tell you Cervantes has been pulling your leg. There is no Bobo. That's a name he uses, like Tom, Dick, and Harry, for people whose name he can't remember, slow waiters, idiots in traffic."

"You've got to go." Kilgore was thrashing in Dix's grip. "Get him out of there. Now!"

Dix laid Kilgore on the ground with a palm in his chest. Valles saw it. His feet shuffled, so little it was hard to tell which direction, forward or to the side, angling away from the house. Then suddenly his hands were down and he was running for the shelter of trees and rocks.

Magnano lost sight of Valles but could tell where he was by the flow of reporters and cameras. There he was, climbing a wall and dropping down the other side, a wave of reporters and cameramen cresting on the same wall, rising and falling, and a single figure in white in front of them growing smaller.

When her eyes returned to the area in front of her, it was no longer empty. A single person was approaching the Valles house. Rolling herself forward in a wheelchair.

It was hard with one arm. The chair kept veering to her right. She eased up and let the downhill slope do the work. She made it to the sidewalk leading to the front door and there it got tricky. If she didn't keep both wheels on the strip of concrete, she'd tip over and land on her side. Forward a couple inches at a time, checking her wheels, backing, then rolling forward again. She got to the front door. The doorbell was too high.

She might be able to stand for sixty seconds but she couldn't get herself out of the chair. She should have thought of this.

She looked behind her. There was a wall of television cameras back there, and FBI people in their shirts, Lewis standing away from the crowd. She waved to him. Waved again. *Come here.* His hands went up. *What?* She pointed at the doorbell and he was running toward her.

Was Cervantes seeing this?

"Pair of geniuses," she said when Lewis reached her. "Push the doorbell, would you?"

She waved Lewis away when she heard chimes inside the house. "It's better I do this alone." As she was turning her chair to squarely face the door, it cracked open.

"Denise."

The voice she knew. The voice behind the laser sight. The voice of the heartbroken man across from her all those nights in restaurants wanting to close.

"What happened to you?" Cervantes asked.

"I'll tell you when this is over. That can be right now. Pete, you won. Did you see Sam Valles turning chicken in front of the world? Running away to save his own ass and abandoning his family. He's through, unless you hurt them and make people sorry for him." Now for the question she wanted most to ask. "You didn't shoot Patricia, did you?"

She saw the tip of a toe behind a door.

"Keep your head and body behind that wall, Pete. Don't show yourself until we wrap this up."

"I didn't shoot her. I wanted my cell phone and television back. They said the storm knocked service out across the city. They lied."

"You were right about that," Aragon said, feeling hundreds of eyes on the back of her neck. She wished the helicopters would go higher and cut the noise. She wanted a quiet talk with Pete. The racket put her on edge. Probably Pete, too.

267

"Can you hear me okay?"

"Clear enough. The kids are fine," Cervantes said. "Wastes of skin like their old man. The mother's got some spit in her."

"She wanted the ride to the top. That's over. We're going to charge her with murder."

She waited for a response. The toe of the shoe pulled back. The door almost closed. She knew a dozen snipers had their crosshairs trained on the door jamb waiting for the first sign of a body. They might be able to penetrate the door and maybe the wooden frame, certainly with a .50 caliber round. But she didn't see them taking a shot not knowing what they'd be hitting. There was a chance the hostage-taker had a hostage with him as a shield.

"Where is the family?" she asked when more seconds passed.

"I've got the brats in a storeroom. The mother's locked in a bathroom. The boys think she's dead."

"And your pal, Bobo?" The broken arm was really hurting. It was swelling inside the cast. She raised it as high as she could, a white L sticking out from her shoulder. People behind her would be wondering what she was doing. "You could have come up with a better name. Bobo, sheesh."

Cervantes laughed behind the door. "Hey, it worked. But not on you, huh? What do you mean you're going to charge her with murder?"

"She had a bright young star, a guy going places, all the winning ingredients. But Sam Valles is a fraud. Everything you and I said about him when we were having fun, it's true. He raped a college girl. I knew her. So did Patricia. Patricia killed her to keep her from talking."

"That woman killed someone?"

"Poisoned her. She died horribly, in terrible pain. And slowly."

"She's capable of that?"

"Before Valles did his skedaddle for the cameras, I was going to tell you the case against his wife would take him down. The underlying rape would be front and center, even if we couldn't prove the rape itself. We'd have the cover-up as the motive. And everyone with the question hanging in their minds despite the denials: Did Sam Baca Valles know? Was he part of the plot to kill the young woman? When Patricia learns he ran out on his family, she might be inclined to shed some light on that question."

Man, the arm was killing her.

"Pete, we need to get going on this. As you can see, I'm not in peak condition. In fact, I'm hurting like hell."

Something landed in the flower bed. It came from behind the door. A semi-auto with a laser sight lay at the base of a rosebush needing water.

Cervantes said, "I'll send out the boys first."

Gunshots. Not snipers. From inside the house. The heavy door shook, swung open, and Pete Cervantes staggered forward. The front of his shirt was torn open, huge exit wounds showing white ribs. His eyes rolled to the sky. He fell and she was looking at Patricia Valles in her underwear holding a big revolver. The gun aimed at where Pete had been standing was now pointed straight at her.

Her ears rang for hours. Even now, everything quiet, Patricia still heard the high-pitched ringing inside her skull. Cervantes had fired those four shots in the hallway, all hard surfaces, a low ceiling at that point. The gunshots were explosions. Covering her ears did nothing.

Cervantes had put orange plastic plugs in his ears before shooting.

He'd come into the room ready, this whole show staged for the benefit of the boys and the people listening on the walkie-talkie he'd showed her kids how to work.

Cervantes had pushed her, stunned, to the master bath and yanked the door shut. While she stared at herself in the mirror, pale, her hair a mess, terrified at being separated from her children, he drove nails into the wall outside. When she was confident he'd gone, she opened the door. A sheet of plywood filled the frame and kept her from getting out.

She spent the first hour on the floor of the bathroom with her back against the edge of the tub, knees pulled to her chest, arms and hands locked around her shins. Finally she forced herself to stand, to throw cold water on her face, to think.

The gun was here with her, up high in the back of the linen closet. She got it down. Holding it made her feel better. This time, when Cervantes opened the door, she'd shoot him in the face. Bobo? She'd deal with that. She was not going to pass up another chance to fight for herself and her boys.

But Cervantes did not return. Hours passed. She had water, but she was hungry. She put toothpaste on a finger and tried that. Not until she was starving was she going to make a meal of Crest.

The vitamin C-zinc lozenges, there was some nutrition in those. Think.

The air vents were out of reach and only big enough for a cat.

The light above the shower came through glass bricks. She couldn't break them with anything in the bathroom. The hardest objects were nail polish bottles that bounced off the glass when she tried throwing them. She could shoot them out but that would tell Cervantes she had a gun.

She scratched at the grout around the glass bricks with a nail file. A waste of time.

Think.

What was on the other side of the walls?

The wall with the towel racks: Sam's study on the other side. But that was solid adobe bricks at least eighteen inches thick.

The back of the shower: outside, great, but it was tile over probably some kind of waterproof wallboard over more adobe brick.

Behind the sink: the utility room. In fact, this had once been part of the utility room. They'd framed and plumbed soon after they bought the house. When Cervantes added radiant heating to the floor, he'd cut the plumbing out of the wall. She remembered doing laundry and being able to look into the bathroom.

This was not an old adobe brick wall.

She pulled out everything from under the sink and saw a panel penetrated by the plumbing. The pipes came out on the other side close to the utility sink and the washer. She tapped. The panel was just plywood held on by screws. It wasn't very big. She wasn't sure her hips would fit through. But she had nail files that would fit the screws.

The first screw was tightened so hard she couldn't get it to turn. The next screw was looser and the nail file worked. She was able to undo all but the first screw she'd tried. The panel loosened when she pried a nail file into a gap, then got her fingers in there. The single tight screw split the wood when she pulled and she found herself looking at laundry hampers and dirty clothes on the floor, with the hot water heater to her right and the washer to her left.

She put her head through, then her shoulders. Her hips caught and she backed up.

The pants came off. Then the panties. Somewhere she had Vaseline. Here it was, in the medicine cabinet. She covered the points of her hip bones, her flanks, the outline of her thighs. Then for good measure the edges of the opening, all around.

She put the gun ahead of her and squeezed through. The wooden frame left long scratches down both sides of her body, from rib cage to thighs. She reached back for the panties she'd left behind and pulled them on.

Where was Cervantes? Where was Bobo?

In the hallway she touched the garden hose that had puzzled her. It was warm. Where did it go? What was this about?

There was sunlight at the end of the hallway. The front door must be open. She heard voices and recognized Cervantes's. That put him between her and the room where he'd locked Clint and Jimmy.

In her bare feet she padded toward the voices. Maybe she'd catch Bobo with Cervantes. Shoot them both at the same time and it could be over just like that. Come around the corner firing. Shoot anything standing. And shoot it again.

As she got closer, her heart took off. Her eyesight started changing, too. Darkness at the edges. Light pulsed. Her chest tightened and breathing was difficult. She'd have to do this quick before she fell apart.

A deep breath. She was there at the entry. Cervantes would be six, eight feet away when she came around. That didn't sound like another man he was talking to.

Another deep breath. She squeezed her eyes tight, then opened them wide and came around the corner shooting.

The gun jumped when it went off, and it hurt, but she was holding with two hands and pulled the trigger again. She saw a man's back at the edge of a door barely open, the door swinging wide, the man falling forward, bright light pouring into her eyes, someone there in the glare.

Now sounds behind her. Things breaking. Footsteps coming her way fast. Heavy footsteps. Someone heavy. Someone very large.

Bobo.

She fired as she spun around to face him, the gun slamming into her hands, feeling the kick up her arms. She fired again and saw flashes and a terrible pain ripped through her chest and her cheek burned and the floor was coming up fast. Her head bounced when it hit.

The floor was cold. Her feet were cold. She heard herself breathing, a sucking sound that scared her, and a man's voice saying, "Shit."

————————

Aragon jerked her chair hard and threw herself off the sidewalk onto the dirt yard. She landed on her cast and screamed as gunfire erupted in the hallway just inside the house. Bullets kicked up earth and splintered the door. Men yelling. A woman moaning, and when it was quiet someone said "Shit."

Men in black tactical gear with automatic weapons and shaded helmets came out of the door and were yelling and signaling to the police up the hill. One bent to check on Cervantes and stood up shaking his head. Two men helped her up while another righted her wheelchair. Back on the sidewalk she could see into the hallway. Patricia Valles lay face-down on the tile, her legs stretched behind her, a .357 magnum not far from her hand.

Helmick and Dix. And Lewis and Perez. And Magnano and lots of other people were now here. One of the men in black raised his visor and said, to everyone and no one in particular, "She was shooting at us. She was backlit. We couldn't identify her. A couple of our vests took hits and we returned fire. Only when she was down did we realize who it was."

Another man came from inside and said, "We led the boys out through the garage so they wouldn't see."

"The other, guy? Bobo?" Dix now taking charge. "Did you clear the house?"

"There is no other guy. It's an inflatable Santa Claus sitting in a kid's swimming pool and pumped full of hot water. He had a hose running from the kitchen."

"That's what we were picking up on infrared? The large heat signature?" Dix turned to Aragon. "You alright?" He pointed at her cast. A piece was missing. "You were hit."

"I'm fine." Her arm hurt like it had been broken again. But she wasn't thinking of herself.

They had Pete on his back, open eyes staring at the sun, big chunks of his chest and the front of his shirt gone.

"He was coming out," Aragon said. "It was over."

Someone was pushing her away from the house. She looked up and it was Magnano.

"Let's talk," Magnano said. "We'll leave the boys out of this for now."

Magnano had to roll her for several blocks until they found a place without cops and reporters. At the edge of the chaos, an old man was watering his flowers as if it were a normal day. Magnano stopped down the street in a patch of shade under a Russian olive.

"You'll find out soon enough," she said. "We've had an intercept order on your phone. I understand why you hate Valles. You should have told us up front. It would have eliminated a lot of suspicion. It still doesn't excuse what you said to Cervantes about Valles."

Aragon opened her mouth. Magnano held up a hand and continued talking.

"Did you lie to the FBI? I have a witness, the waiter who overheard you saying someone should take out Valles. How convincing would that be to a jury in the face of your denial? Certainly not beyond a reasonable doubt. And there's your explanation that Cervantes just took it the wrong way. You deserve severe discipline from your employer, but not a federal prosecution."

"May I speak?"

"Your turn."

"I would have been surprised if you hadn't tapped my phone."

"You knew we were listening?" Damn if Magnano's separated eyebrows didn't ride halfway up her forehead.

"I was hoping," Aragon said. "You got to see the truth for yourself. If I'd come to you cold, while you had me in your sights, and tried to sell a murder case of Patricia Valles silencing her husband's victim, you would have closed a door in my face. But bringing you with me, step by step, you convinced yourself. That was better than any case presentation I could have made."

"The prank about the waxing appointments, and the other thing. You knew I'd be listening."

"A friendly 'fuck you' because you were really starting to piss me off. The eyebrows look great, by the way. Very pretty."

"What are we, girlfriends now?"

"Not close. But we do understand each other."

"And trust each other about as far as we can spit."

"Good enough for me. Now take me back. I want to see they don't leave Pete in the sun."

EPILOGUE

THE CLIMB BEFORE THE trail leveled out was as tough to run as she'd remembered. An early morning start in Tijeras Canyon, jogging the switchbacks, constantly gaining elevation, crossing the soda dam water fall, finally breaking tree line with the sun still low in the east. Cool air, tiny yellow and white flowers, an open meadow on top of the Sandia Mountains, and all hers. Not another human face for the next ten miles.

Then her cell going off inside her pack, a volley of calls from beauty salons and wig stores saying they were getting back to her about an appointment for extensions, real-hair wigs, perms, dyes, and sets. Payback from Magnano, who knew she'd be running today. Aragon had told her over ribs and beer last week. She'd return the favor somehow. She had all day to think of something.

It had taken a year for Aragon to recover the full use of her legs. "Recover" meant coming back stronger than ever. Not having to take time off from training to go to work, she'd emerged from her cast and braces a more powerful version than the woman who dove through a roof hatch to avoid being shot. She'd caught up to Lewis on squats if not chest presses. She would never come close to his upper-body strength, but her short thick legs, and the fact that Lewis hated squats, had her moving the same weight as her much larger partner.

She'd taken up mountain running with the best equipment and shoes she could find. Passing hikers on their way up Santa Fe Baldy and doubling back, seeing the look on their faces after she'd already touched the top and was coming down as they were breathing hard going up, she had to admit it gave her a rush. From contemplating life on her back to flying over mountain tops on her own power. Life was great.

She was making today's run in Amy's memory. The same route, trying to match her time but not throwing in the extra ten-plus miles Amy had snagged. Later she would pass the spot. She had a fair idea where the Lost Girls had found Amy eating dirt and raving about dancing trees. In her pack she had a white plastic cross with a picture of Amy under glass. She would plant it far off the trail where it would never be removed by Forest Service maintenance crews or bothered by the Sandia Pueblo patrols. Since Amy's death this part of the mountain had reverted back to the tribe. They didn't allow hunting or guns. She doubted they permitted memorials to dead white women.

Or dead, broken-hearted Hispanic fathers. Her pack carried a second cross, this one for Pete Cervantes.

Now she was at the jagged edge of the mountain, a spot where the trees thinned, looking out on Albuquerque and the brown, dusty flats along the Rio Grande a mile below her. It would be forty degrees hotter down there. The heat was rising to meet her. But she was ready, as Amy had been ready. Fit and strong enough for any challenge except poison slipped into the sports drink a friend had promised would make the run easier.

At the start of the day, when it was dark and she was lacing up her shoes and loading her pack, she'd seen moonflowers still blooming after their nighttime show. Long, fluted, beautiful white flowers. The yucca was New Mexico's state flower. It should be this flower. Death and beauty combined in a bloom that grew only in the harshest, most barren soil and showed its true self only in darkness.

Tomorrow she'd put on gloves and yank out every moonflower by its roots anywhere it grew near her apartment.

Ahead, blazing sunlight. The trail broke from the trees. There were the ski lifts, the platform and cables as thick as her arm for the tram that came up from the city below. Now it was really hot. She felt it through the soles of her trail runners. Sunlight bounced off rocks into her eyes.

The mountain tumbled into pieces on the west side. Fractured spires, sharp cliff edges, slides disappearing into scrub. A bear and its cubs moved down there. Nothing unusual. People riding the tram saw mountain lions sometimes.

Perez and Lewis were waiting for her in the new restaurant, empty beer mugs at their elbows. The old bar and dining room that had stood for a generation, where Amy McSwaim had been toasted by her friends and murderer, was gone. The incredible view hadn't changed. When fires were raging in Arizona, two hundred fifty miles away, they said you could see the wall of flames from up here before the wind brought the smoke this way. Today mountains a hundred miles west stood in air so clear she could make out road cuts.

Against her better judgment, she joined them for a beer, enjoying the cool air inside and wondering where Tomas was. He'd promised he'd be here. She would be disappointed not to see him. But there he was, coming in from the tram just arriving, in running gear, carrying a pack with a drinking tube.

"I thought you could use company," he said and leaned in to kiss her. She smelled the sunscreen on his cheeks. She needed to replenish hers. You could burn very fast at this altitude.

"Only if you can keep up."

"I've been training while you've been recuperating, and hitting the weights. I ran a 10K last weekend."

"And didn't tell me?"

"I didn't know if I could make it. It was easier than I realized."

"This is different."

"Everything with you is different."

She kissed him again and tugged the waistband of his running shorts.

"You've lost weight."

"And you've gained. All muscle."

"Let's stop with the mutual admiration and get going. We have almost a dozen miles ahead of us."

"More than miles," he said. "I want to think we might have years ahead of us."

She didn't know what to say to that. Or when Perez and Lewis rose from the table, also in running shoes and shorts. Perez was in cut-off sweatpants and a University of New Mexico Lobos sweatshirt with the arms ripped off. No hydration pack for him. He was going old school with the plastic soda bottle on the table filled with plain water. His skinny legs and pot belly looked hilarious. He knew it and patted his gut.

"Tell you what," she said. "You guys finish, dinner at Cocina Azul is on me."

She didn't wait for an answer and started for the door, jogging by tables and not turning to see if they were following. She picked up speed on the short paved walkway that ended where the nature trail took off to the crest. A mile later she was climbing with an open meadow on her left and looked back. There was Rivera in the lead running smoothly. Then Lewis, his body loaded with muscles more used to dead weights, moving slowly but steady and strong, a trident of sweat on his chest. Last came Perez, the first-generation mountain runner. He wasn't last because it was the best he could do. He was just enjoying himself. He tossed a handful of nuts in his mouth, chugged from his water bottle, and waved.

She waved back and decided to let her friends catch up. She'd run with them to the end. No matter how long it might take, it was better than running alone.

ACKNOWLEDGMENTS

So much goes into each Denise Aragon story. A big thank you to the people of New Mexico. Denise belongs to you.

Tim Manly, chief of the Brinnon, Washington, fire department and a career paramedic with over three decades of emergency medical experience, schooled me on not only how an EMT crew responds to calls of distress, but also what they carry away inside from every tragic case.

Elizabeth Ann Scarborough, who served as a combat nurse in Vietnam and has gone on to write over forty novels, including her Nebula Award-winning *The Healer's War*, provided more insight into trauma treatment and was my first reader for this book. As well as providing friendship and encouragement, Annie moved the manuscript forward with her early edits.

Thanks as always and forever to my agent, Elizabeth Kracht of Kimberley Cameron & Associates, and all my editors at Midnight Ink on this and every one of the Denise Aragon installments. It was a pleasure to again work with Sandy Sullivan on this book.

I can never acknowledge enough or be sufficiently grateful for the support and encouragement of my wife, Kara. Thanks, darling, for your love, patience, and wisdom.

© Deja View Photography

ABOUT THE AUTHOR

James R. Scarantino (Port Townsend, WA) is a prosecutor, defense attorney, investigative reporter, and award-winning author. He lived in New Mexico for thirty years before trading high desert for Pacific Northwest rain. His novel *Cooney County* was named best mystery/crime novel in the SouthWest Writers Workshop International Writing Competition. His previous Denise Aragon novels are *The Drum Within* and *Compromised*.